THE RIPPLE EFFECT

JOHN CRAWLEY

Archway Publishing books may be ordered through booksellers or by contacting:

Archway Publishing
1663 Liberty Drive
Bloomington, IN 47403
www.archwaypublishing.com
844-669-3957

Cover design concept: Meredith Crawley
Cover art execution Archway Design Team

ISBN: 978-1-6657-4673-1 (sc)
ISBN: 978-1-6657-4672-4 (e)

Library of Congress Control Number: 2023913055

Print information available on the last page.

Archway Publishing rev. date: 07/14/2023

Other novels and books by John Crawley

Among the Aspen
Baby Change Everything
The House Next Door
Under the Radar
The Uncivil War
Between Sunday's Columns
The Man on the Grassy Knoll
Beyond a Shadow of a Doubt (a novella)
Stuff
Dream Chaser (a serial e-novel)
The Myth Makers
Fishing Lessons
Letters from Paris
The Perfect Food
The End
Lincoln, Texas USA (Short Stories including a print
version of Dream Chaser)
Wrong Number (including the novella The Gift.)
Of Poets and Old Men (a collection of poetry)
One Elephant Too Many

Dedicated to David van Oz

Who, a long time ago, taught me to fight for truth.

A note from the author

The day after I turned the manuscript of this book over to my editor, another mass shooting occurred in America: at a mall in Allen, Texas – a suburb of Dallas. At this point eight are dead including a three year old.

My hope is this book will help light a fire under America and her political leaders to get this problem solved.

On another note, my daughter, who lives in Europe was about to board a plane to come visit my wife and me, when the airlines handed her and her partner an advisory notice that The United States was considered an "at risk" nation in which to travel. Think about that for a moment. Your country and mine is thought to be so wild and so accommodating of guns and gun violence visitors are warned travel could be unsafe.

God help us.

1

Father Mise

Major historical milestones are populated with the questions, "where were you when"…people ask each other, "where were you and what were you doing when…when John Kennedy was assassinated? … when Martin Luther King was shot?... or how about Robert Kennedy?"… "What were you doing when you first saw the planes crash into the twin towers on 9-11? Where were you when you first heard about Columbine? About Sandy Hook? About Uvalde? Where were you when you heard about Lincoln Mall?"

Remember? Father Richard Mise sure does.

It was the 13th of November.

Shots rang out shortly prior to noon. Lincoln Township Mall. Twenty people dead. They had come to the mall to buy presents. To try on new shoes. To catch a pre-holiday sale. To have lunch with friends. Some were on a school outing, about to top off their lunch with ice cream. They were there for hundreds of reasons, and in an instant their lives were ended.

And Father Mise was squarely in the middle of the carnage.

Yes, it was the 13th of November, a pleasantly cool day, just before noon.

If it weren't fall, if it was in the heat of the summer, the waves of invisible radiation would be shimmering up from the blacktop roads, which stretched for miles around Grand Lake crisscrossing into and out of the oil fields and cattle ranches that make up the region– a region some call the last vestige of the Old Confederacy. The pine trees would be bent, not so much in a bow of respect, but from their desperate attempt to survive yet another year of drought in northeast Texas. The riverbanks would appear higher – taller – as the creeks and rivers recede lower and lower – the flow of the streams they cradled having lessened to a trickle. The lake itself would be showing her edges, like a woman wearing an evening gown pulled down on her shoulders. Rarely would a bird venture out from its protected shade and fly across the sweltering sky. Everybody – everything – would be moving in slow motion. Even time would seem to stand still in the oppressive heat of the summer. A lone cloud drifting over the sun in midday was cause for celebration and joy.

But in October – late October – just at the beginning of November – it finally rained. Not much. But enough to renew life and spirits in Lincoln, Texas.

Lincoln, Texas sits on the sandy loam of the eastern shore of Grand Lake. A great body of water created out of the dammed Sabine River, across the lake from its big sister, Kilgore and below Longview.

The town is perched on a rise above the valley into which the lake grew in the late 1950's after the Corps of Engineers impounded the river. To its northeast is an extension of what remains of the northern arm of the Piney Woods of East Texas. Just north of Lincoln lies a band of red clay out of which has been mined a rich seam of grey-black lignite coal that fuels power plants, which dot the shores of the giant lake, sending their electrical waves to population centers as far away as Dallas to the west and Houston to the south.

To the southwest, are rolling sandy grasslands below which, were once home to the bountiful East Texas Woodbine oil pool; from whose deposits millions of barrels of crude and hundreds of millions of dollars were pumped to the surface making the region and some of its more fortunate inhabitants quite wealthy; while others continued to subsist as they always have, by the scrub of the parched land.

In the middle of the county, sits a small, humble town – Lincoln– that at one time was proud of its rich reserves of petroleum and coal, but today was waging a battle to keep its young people from leaving for new, more exciting- more profitable jobs. Trying to keep the schools at the top of the lists in the state. It's a town, starting to ebb downward. But just.

The slide was just starting.

That morning, November 13th, Father Mise pulled his small Chevy sedan up to the self-service island of Eddie McAlister's Shell station. It was about the only one in town that had full-service mechanical bays. The station offered everything from car washes to complete engine overhauls. Eddie had won a contract from the Township of Lincoln to fuel and service the patrol cars while they were on duty. Something he did between the hours of seven in the morning until seven at night, when he turned the lights off and went home.

Parked next to Father Mise's sedan was patrol car No. 7. It was driven by Darrell Hampton, a parishioner in St. Elizabeth's church, where Mise was the pastor. The two spoke.

"Morning Father," said Darrell as he walked around his black and white patrol car letting his hand softly stroke the smooth surface.

"Moring, Darrell. Getting any more rest?"

Hampton had been taking care of his sick daughter and wife for what seemed to him to be over a month. The morning was slowly getting near the lunch hour and he was getting hungry.

He yawned.

He would love to park the patrol car somewhere on a shady back road grab a sandwich out of the paper sack on the passenger front seat, then catch forty winks; the kid had been awake all night crying with the croup. Phyllis had been sick with the same respiratory illness the week before and missed her teaching job for five straight days; something she had never done. Even the principal Mr. McMichaels came to the house to check on her. But the bug was going about and they had as many as fifteen to twenty percent absentees from school over a ten-day period. Teachers and students even administrators were ill with it. Darrell had told her to rest. He would get up with the kid and walk her and hold her until she fell back to sleep. No sooner than he had her in the crib, she began to wail again. "It almost makes me want to give up religion and start drinking. Again."

Mise smiled. "Keep the faith, Darrell. God will grant you the strength to endure. I assure you it will pass."

"Everybody seems to be coming down with this crud," offered McAlister as he approached the policeman and the priest in their conversation wiping his hands on a red cloth. "Wife says we're good to go. Say about seven? Say, you might tell your chief that the city is late paying its bill again. Just saying…"

"I'll let him know. See you this evening. And bring some beer, would ya? You got it." Darrell turned back to Father Mise. "You want to join us, padre? Some nice fishing at dusk on the big lake?"

Mise shook his head. "I'm a fisher of men not of fish. But if you catch some, I'll fry 'em up for a fish fry. Fridays were made for that."

"I hear that." Said Officer Hampton. With that he got into his patrol car and rolled away.

"He's good one. Darrel is." said McAlister, as the service station manager and the Catholic priest watched the patrol car turn onto U.S. 59 then turn again onto the road leading to Grand Lake.

Eddie had known the policeman ever since the third grade. They had played on the only Lincoln football team to get into the state playoffs. That year, the team lost only two games in the regular season. One to Carthage and the other to Gilmer – both of whom won state championships that very year. Carthage was becoming something of a state powerhouse on the gridiron and Gilmer was no slouch, either. So a twelve and two record with the only two losses to those schools was something to be proud of. That is, until they faced Rockdale in the state semi-finals and lost 31-13. That game is still not talked about much inside the city limits of Lincoln. It was over fifteen years past and was still a raw topic for many. Bob Armstead, who owned Angry

Bob's the best barbeque spot in East Texas, was Lincoln's quarterback that year. He had been intercepted six times in the Rockdale game and many people believe his first restaurant in Lincoln failed because a lot of the old timers wouldn't support him. They were still angry with him. Hence the name of the barbeque joint. "Scabs in this part of the country are slow to heal," Bob once told a food critic from a Dallas newspaper.

Mise finished filling his car and placed the nozzle back into the holder on the pump. "You guys have fun tonight out on the lake," he said to McAlister.

"We won't be long. I bet you Darrell falls asleep in the first hour."

"He has had it rough with a sick wife and child. But have fun just the same."

"Thanks, Father. You take care."

Richard Mise pulled away from the service station and drove toward the mall, which was no more than five minutes away. He needed new shoes and a present for his sister who was about to celebrate yet another birthday.

It was less than a half hour from the chaos, which lay ahead.

Heading in the opposite direction, Officer Darrell Hampton drove the black and white Dodge Charger east on Carroll Street, which led to the old lake road- County 14: it was referred to as 17th Street in the town. From there he found a blacktop lane he knew was fairly isolated and had several dead-end turn offs. He chose one, turned the cruiser around, stopped it under a pine tree that had seen better days. He rolled down the window in hopes to catch a fleeting breeze. He closed his eyes and in no time was sound asleep.

There was little to no crime in Lincoln. Shoplifting by high school kids and drunk teenagers racing along neighborhood streets in their parents' cars were about the most serious crimes he dealt with– that and an occasional drug bust along the highway, but usually that was done in assistance with the DEA or the Texas Rangers. Other than that, life was easy in Lincoln for a cop. Almost as easy as catching a nap on a side road along the edge of the county's electric grid right-of-way.

Darrell woke himself up once snoring, but was soon back asleep as the morning grew warmer. A tractor slowly made its way back and forth across the utility easement, mowing the thin grass. It made more dust than it did clippings.

2

Matthew Stevens

His mother had already left for her job at the beauty salon. It was the smallish white, ship-lapped building, which stood off U.S. 59 – just in front of their low-slung, two-bedroom, ranch house, hidden beneath a canopy of pine and scrub oak trees. He rolled over and saw that the clock read nine o'clock. He fell back into the soft comforter and stared at the AC/DC poster on the ceiling. Dimebag Darrell and Metallica stared at him from the walls opposite his small closet. The thrusting music of Tool pulsated out of his speakers and rattled the windows. It gave him energy. His friends would be at first period by now. He grinned. Not him. He had plans for the day.

Reluctantly he rose from his bed and began to dress: black jeans, a black tee and some heavy black boots, which came halfway up his scrawny calves. The boots were laced with a silver chain that ran from the top down to the toes. The toes themselves were covered with a silver hood that morphed into a skull. There was a silver cap over his heels, as well. He grabbed a black leather jacket, only because he felt cool when wearing it, even though it was warm outside that morning.

He took a quick look in the mirror and ran a comb through his thin hair. He would be bald by the time he was thirty. *Fuck it. I'll never live to thirty,* he thought.

In the kitchen he rummaged through the near empty pantry and found a lone breakfast bar. In the refrigerator he got a can of Dr. Pepper and left out the rear door. His midnight blue Ford Mustang Hatchback with a 500 liter V8 awaited him. It had been a gift from his dad, now estranged from his mom.

Dad, whose name is Earl Stevens, lived in Marshall fifteen minutes away. He worked for the local airport and fixed all manner of aircraft engines. Something he was trained to do by Uncle Sam during his time in the Air Force. Upon matriculating out of the wild blue yonder corps, he made his way home to East Texas and found work for a private company who owned three Lear jets and two turbo prop King Airs, which they serviced for oil guys and lawyers who lived and worked out of Marshall.

He met and married Irene Bell, although he is the first to admit he was never really in love with Irene. But they had a kid. A boy named Matthew. He called him Matt. The boy wasn't very good at school and was even worse in sports. He was a scrawny kid and was picked on by the bigger boys. And at times by the girls who found him slow and very unattractive.

He got into trouble from time-to-time and Earl was always close at hand to bail him out. There were fistfights. Drunken outburst. Drugs. Matt had stolen a car once (he claimed they were just joy riding) and it took about six months of Earl's salary to buy him out from the man's anger and his pressing charges. And when the guy started to renege on the deal he had made with Earl, the airplane mechanic showed up on his doorstep with three big buddies ready to take the poor guy apart. It scared him so much that he gave half of the money back to Earl and no charges were ever filed against Matt. Earl then used the money to buy Matt his Mustang. It was used, but with the help of his dad and some elbow grease applied by Matt, (who it turned out, was also fairly adept with a wrench in his hands) the car was a shining example of muscle and steel. And it sounded like a freaking freight train coming at you.

Matt got in behind the wheel of the Mustang, started its big engine. And then roared past his mother's tiny hair salon and onto U.S. 59, spraying gravel from the driveway up and onto her porch. She hated it when he did that. He'd catch hell about that tonight. *But what the fuck*, he thought *what the fuck*.

He headed north toward Marshall. He took out a pack of cigarettes from the glove compartment and put one behind his right ear and then one into his mouth, between his thin lips. He just let it sit there. He thought it made him look tough.

Crossing over Interstate 20, he headed into the small city and then turned right on to U.S. 80 and ventured east toward the airport. He spotted his dad's red SUV parked next to the jet hanger. He knew his dad was there, so he could continue on with his mission. Reversing his course, Matt drove on U.S. 59 until he reached Hwy 43. There he headed toward the country club until he found the county blacktop street leading to his dad's house. Up a long hill, the road curved as it wandered into a dense grove of pine trees. Matt found the driveway off to the right that plunged sharply down the hill onto a flat plateau where he could see the one story brick house. He killed the Mustang's engine and silently coasted across a soft carpet of dry pine needles. He got out and went to the front door. He inserted the key his dad had given him. "Think of this place as a safe house if you need it, Matt." His father had once told him. "Just in case."

Once inside he went to the kitchen and found a box of cereal and a carton of milk in the refrigerator. He helped himself to a quick breakfast and took another soda from his father's stash in the fridge.

He wandered down the wood paneled hallway, stopping to look at a picture of his dad and him at Grand Lake on a fishing outing the year before. They had each caught rather large bass and were holding them up proudly for the camera to see. For the life of him, he could not remember who had taken the photograph. He ventured on until he came to his father's bedroom.

He opened the top drawer of the cheap, cherry dresser and found fifty dollars, which he pocketed. Next, he walked to the far wall and into the closet where he found the steel gun case behind hanging clothes. The case is where his father kept his arsenal of weapons. He had the combination for the electronic lock memorized. It was his father's birthday in reverse. 767040.

Slowly he opened the heavy steel doors and peered inside. He raised his cell phone and activated the flashlight on it so he could see better. He reached in and took out a black AR-15. Checking the magazine he saw that it was fully loaded. Looking to the drawer below, he found another magazine, this one empty. He picked up a box of shells and moved, with the rifle and the bullets to his father's bed. There he loaded the second magazine.

Matt returned to the gun safe and withdrew a 9 mm pistol, also black with a carved wooden handle. It had been a gift to his father from one of the wealthy attorneys in Marshall who traveled extensively to courts across the South on the planes that Earl maintained. He checked its magazine, finding the handgun fully loaded and ready for use; he grinned.

Matt retraced his steps out of the house and back to his car. Opening the hatchback he placed the guns and their clips carefully down on a blanket he had brought from his mother's house. He heard a car coming down the road. It stopped, then entered Earl's driveway and began to descend the hill as it wound through the forest. Matt could make out the black and white markings of the county sheriff's department on the car. Matt closed the hatchback and walked toward the bend in the circular driveway in front of the house.

"Morning, Frank," Matt said as Frank Rawlings rolled his window down.

"Matt." He spat a big load of brown tobacco juice on the pine needles about ten feet from where Matt stood. "What brings you out to these parts?"

"Dad. He wanted me to run a couple of errands for him. I've got a pass in school today. Teachers are in training."

"I see. Well, I saw a car come down here and I didn't know who was here. Just checking to make sure everything is cool."

"Everything is cool," Matt assured the officer. With that the deputy sheriff's patrol car headed back around the circle and up the driveway and out of sight. Matt slowly relaxed. He stood motionless staring at the pine trees. Waiting until he could hear the sound of Rawlings car moving away down the county road.

Matt returned to the house and placed his cereal bowl in the sink and went back to this father's closet and closed everything back to how he had found it. He then walked to the garage and secured a long length of rope and coiled it around his arm and carried it back to the waiting Mustang. He dropped it into the back seat and proceeded to head out of the driveway, up the carpet of soft pine needles and onto the blacktop road, which led him to state 43. He turned left and drove into Marshall.

There was a rumbling in the pit of Matt's stomach. He couldn't tell if it was nerves or hunger. He opted for hunger. He decided not to stop at the Bluebonnet Café and grab an early lunch. He would have plenty of time to eat after he carried out his plan.

Within an hour the fun would begin.

3

The Parkers

On the grassy plain that stretched away from Lincoln to the southwest, were two ranches that dated back to the 1800's: The Greer Ranch and the Ledbetter Ranch. After the Vietnam War, Junior Ledbetter ceded twelve hundred acres to Eduardo Parker, a young man who had served as the ranch's foreman before and throughout the Vietnam years. Ledbetter gave him this land in appreciation for his service to the family, while he and his younger brother, Mike Ledbetter, were away fighting Ho Chi Minh and the 'commies'.

As luck would have it, the land ceded to Eduardo had none of the underground treasures found on the remaining acres of the Ledbetter spread or those under the Greer Ranch. There was no oil or coal beneath the dry land and little water on top of the spread that Eduardo surveyed, as he ran his small cattle operation. As if to add insult to injury, the gravelly land was far from fertile. About all it could grow was wild Texas grasses, barely edible by the scrawny cows Eduardo attempted to herd.

Eduardo and his wife Rosa were first generation decendents from Mexico. They had three children. A son, Roberto, who was away at college in Lubbock, and two daughters. One was a senior in Lincoln High School, Ella, and the other was Cynthia, an eighth grader.

Cynthia Parker wanted a horse. A pony to be exact. Something diminutive in size, just as she was. "I want a small horse," she had told Tio, her uncle - Uncle Jose on her father's side of the family – she wanted a horse to ride. She loved animals. She had two dogs and three cats and somewhere a rabbit, but it had not been seen for several days. But a small horse – that's what she wanted– that's what she told him.

Cynthia wasn't very tall. In fact, she was the shortest girl in her class in the eighth grade at Lincoln Township Middle School. (Originally the school had been named the Jefferson Davis Junior High, but court orders and parental objection to the name caused the reluctant school board to adopt a more generic moniker for the sprawling one-story school.) But what Cynthia lacked in height, she more than made up for in her brainpower. She was number one in every testing score every year. She was tops in GPA in her level and in everything that had to do with reading, math or science she was at the head of the class. Truth be told, Cynthia was going to be pushed ahead two full years, so she could graduate early. Rumors circulated around town (fueled by Tio Jose and his wife Anna) that Cynthia was going to get a scholarship to Yale. The university had been to her house on two separate occasions to visit with the young lady and her parents. All that was waiting was for the state of Texas to approve her matriculation out of high school in a year and a half.

Yale was a long way from Lincoln, Texas. But that didn't bother Cynthia. What bothered her was that she still did not have a horse to ride. Not one of her own. Sure, she could saddle up any number of the steeds on the Villalobos Ranch (the name Eduardo gave to his spread in honor of his great grandfather). She could carry on with her equestrian training on the ranch's horses, but she wanted a horse all her own. She wanted to command it with her touch and care for it with her love.

"Did you water the livestock?" asked Eduardo, at dinner.

She nodded. "Yes, Papa. The pump is still acting up."

"Drought is getting worse and worse. I thought the rain in October was going to end it…but no…I may have to cut some of the cattle and horses loose. Take them to market."

This made Cynthia grimace. She knew that meant bringing another horse onto the property would be difficult if they couldn't keep up with the ones they already had.

"Yale called yesterday," her mother said as she passed a plate of rice to her younger daughter. "They want to come see the school play in March…and the science fair. They are pleased that you excel at both."

Cynthia shrugged. No horse this year. That is what she thought about.

Cynthia would get a horse – a small horse, one just her size– the year after she entered high school. She would ride it every afternoon and was soon excelling in the riding ring as well as in the classroom. Tio took notice and offered to take her to Lexington, Kentucky to the Rolex World Equine Show and competition, where equestrian showmen from around the world would come and perform. She agreed, as did her mother and her father. It would be good for her to get out of Texas for a while and see some of the country. After all, in a little over two years she would be in New Haven, Connecticut and would be spending most of her hours in class and in a chemistry lab.

Three years would pass and she would graduate with honors and immediately apply for and be granted admittance into a graduate program in microbiology at Johns Hopkins University in Baltimore. There she would earn both an MS degree and a Ph.D. in molecular chemistry. And perhaps more importantly, she would meet and marry Jerry Caldwell, a graduate assistant in chemistry who was working his way toward a medical degree.

Two years would pass after her doctorate had been awarded and after her honeymoon with Jerry when she would come upon something quite spectacular. Cynthia and two fellow researchers, one in London, the other in Tokyo, would discover that by stripping apart certain amino acids and placing them back together in a new order, they could build a genetic sequencing system that could actually be trained to attack immune deficiencies in humans. It was as if they had created AI inside the human body, by lining up a genetic string, just so, to fight almost any disease they placed in its way; then once cured, the line of defense could be shuttered – turned off– until such time as it was needed once again. Cynthia's unique part in this discovery was to find out how to 3D print the new amino acids into a programmable gene.

The entire science and medical worlds sat up and took notice. Papers were written. Peer reviews were given. Competing labs tried to replicate her groundbreaking work. Cynthia and her two colleagues were talked about in very hushed tones as potential candidates for the Nobel Prize.

The head of the CDC said that her findings were "...game changing. Countless lives will be saved. Diseases that we had never had the means to even attempt to control, would now be eradicated." The new antigen process was given the name of Parkeratic Programming. Named after Cynthia and her discovery.

*   *   *   *

But on this day in November, during the lunch break at her eighth grade school, her mother pulled her out of class and took her shopping for a dress she was to wear at the Fall Festival in Longview. She was going to represent Lincoln Schools with her uncanny ability to quote Shakespeare and do complicated mathematical problems in her head. "Tio and Anna will be there. You will want to look pretty for them. And for your father."

"Why do we have to go during school hours?"

"I have to work a second shift at the refinery tonight. It's the only time I have, and we must get this dress business settled, no?"

"Okay."

"Fine, I will pick you up at eleven thirty. I have cleared it already with Principal McMichaels. I'll bring your dress shoes so we will know a good length."

"I will need new shoes, Mama."

"We can see about that. Money is tight, Cynthia. If you are

going away to college in a few years, we will need to save as much as possible."

"There will be a scholarship." Her voice pleaded.

"True. True, but it will not cover everything. If your current shoes work, we might save some money there."

"And I guess no horse this year?" Her voice was laced with a timber of dejection.

"We'll see, Cynthia, we'll see."

It was always the promise of futility. "We'll see. We'll see."

The Lincoln Mall sat on the northwest side of the town, along a bending curve in U.S. 59. The shopping complex made a giant Y in the middle of a vast asphalt parking lot. At either end of the arms of the Y, sat a department store; although one of the stores was no longer in business and had been converted into a meeting area for community activities. A non-denominational church met there on Sundays and the space was rudely referred to as the Jesus store. The other two department stores were Whittlings and Kavenders, both regional brands that excelled in secondary markets. In the middle of the Y was a food court complete with burger stands, ice cream shops, a pizza parlor and a salad bar. There was also some playground equipment for little kids. The playground was lined with wooden benches for tired parents and even more exhausted grandparents. A popcorn kiosk sat just outside the north end of the food court area, and its aroma colored the shopping center with its buttery scent.

A slim, dark-haired man approached the two Parker ladies in the mall. He wore a black coat, and black shirt, black trousers and old, scuffed black shoes. He also wore the collar of a Catholic priest. It was was their pastor: Father Richard Mise. Originally from Fort Wayne, Indiana, he had attended seminary in South Bend. Upon graduation and ordination, he was assigned to Mexico to a medical clinic and mission for migrant workers there in Michoacán outside of Morelia. After sixteen years, he was reassigned to a small oil town in East Texas called Lincoln. It was Baptist country. True there was a sprinkling of

Methodists and Presbyterians, but one had to hardily shake the bushes to get any Catholics to fall to the ground. His presiding Bishop, who was in Tyler, instructed him to take the foundering Catholic church in Lincoln and grow it into a vibrant parish. He had been working on that very task for the last five years. Little progress had been made. "Spinning my wheels," is what Father Mise felt most of the time. "Stuck in a protestant rut – more like evangelical quicksand."

"Como estas? Rosa, Cynthia. Good to see you two," he said to the Parkers.

"Father Mise, what brings you to the mall?" asked Cynthia, who was one of the priest's favorite young parishioners.

"I need new shoes," he said, looking down at his old, scuffed ones. "These have seen their better days. I'll say last rites on them soon." They all laughed. "I have a wedding mass this weekend, plus the Bishop is coming to town for baptisms and first communions week after next and I need to look sharp. For the bride and groom and for the Monsignor. And right in the middle of all of that, my sister is turning forty. I need to get her a nice birthday present. Busy, busy, busy. What would you suggest?" He asked.

"A horse." She laughed, as did her mother and the priest. They all knew how much Cynthia wanted a pony. She had even asked in confession once if it was a sin to want something as badly as she wanted a horse. Father Mise had responded to her by saying as long as it did not change her values, wanting something was, in itself, not a sin.

"I'm afraid her horse riding days are over," said Father Mise, referring to his sister. "She would prefer something more mechanized, I would imagine. So, what are you doing at the mall today? Shouldn't you be in school?"

She looked at her mother and blushed slightly. "Yes, but we need to get me a dress for the Fall Festival. I'll be on stage quoting Shakespeare and doing math problems against the boys math club from Longview."

"Really? How does that work?"

Cynthia was proud of her mathematical accomplishments and

she was equally excited about the chance to compete with the boys in the math club from Longview's high school. It was a school more than twice the size of her school. Plus these were tenth, eleventh and twelfth grade boys. Much more senior than she was. "We will all sit at a table on the stage at the fair grounds and a proctor will give us a sheet of paper with five problems on it. Three algebra problems and two geometry problems. They will be able to use calculators, but I will work with pencil and my brain only. We have ten minutes. The two who finish the most problems in that amount of time, win round one."

"There is a round two?"

"Oh yes, Father. We then stand and face the proctor and he or she gives us a problem we must solve totally in our heads. No paper. No calculators. No slide rules. Just our brains."

"I see. And you think you can beat the boys from Longview?"

Cynthia smiled and nodded. "I'm sure going to try."

He rubbed her hair and nodded at her mother. "I bet she gives them a real run for their money."

"She's going to quote Shakespeare, as well," added Rosa.

"Where does your sister live?" asked Cynthia.

"Joplin, Missouri. She teaches school there."

"What subjects?"

"Cynthia, enough questions, we need to let Father Mise go about his business and we need to get you a dress and then back to school," said Rosa.

"She teaches math, Cynthia. Tell you what, I'm going to add the festival to my calendar and come and watch you win a ribbon." He smiled at her.

"Get her a very nice pen. A metal one. Made out of gold or silver," said Cynthia, thinking about the priest's sister.

"That's a great idea, Cynthia. I just might do that."

The priest headed off for the escalators that would take him upstairs to the stationery shop and Cynthia and her mom continued toward the Whittlings department store where a dress for the Fall Festival awaited the young lady from Lincoln.

As Father Mise walked away he began to think about the Sunday sermon. He wanted to talk about potential. About opportunity and reward. About challenging ones self with reaching higher and higher for goals just beyond your grasp. For extending yourself. For challenging yourself to do more. To exceed expectations. Yes that was it. That was the phrase he would hang the words of the homily on – Exceed your Expectations. He thought of Cynthia as the words formulated in his mind. Cynthia Parker was a prime example of Exceeding your Expectations. She had been the inspiration for his next sermon.

Now he needed a fancy pen and pencil set for his sister's birthday and a nice pair of black shoes to replace the worn-out pair tied to his feet.

Twenty-five minutes until the deadly commotion.

4

Perry Reynolds

It was ten in the morning before Perry got his first cup of coffee. He had been on the run since five. It was going to be a long day. Again.

Having grown up in Altoona, Pennsylvania, he had attended and graduated with a masters in food sciences from Penn State University. Immediately following school he married Jane Craig and they almost at once had kids. Now the brood numbered four: two boys, Wayne and Seth – and two girls, Judy and Liz.

Perry's first job was with a major food conglomerate for whom he traveled the eastern seaboard. Somehow he got lost in their constant shuffling of managers and dizzying labyrinth of reorganizations and soon he realized he wasn't going anywhere fast in the giant company. And with as many mouths as he had to feed, he needed to find a more enterprising situation in which to work. He found it at Patriot Farms. A company out of Tulsa, Oklahoma that had three large processing plants in East Texas. One plant was poultry and two were beef. One in Marshall. One in Lincoln. And one in Henderson. He was sent south to manage all three. The pay was good and the land and the people fit his personality to a tee.

He and Jane bought a small farm (ten acres to be exact, but to him it was his piece of the American Dream- owning a small farm.) He had chickens and a couple of goats on the property. They had, at one time, a cow, but it had been sold to buy Jane a new car. Plus, Perry was kept running at his job so much, that he didn't have time to oversee any livestock of his own, even if it was but one cow. In fact, he barely had enough time for his children, which was something he and Jane fought about constantly.

At eleven sharp he left the Henderson plant and headed for an appointment at the poultry facility in Marshall, a half hour away. He knew he had time for a quick bite for lunch. The Bluebonnet Café, halfway between Lincoln and Marshall, would be just the place.

He called his secretary in Lincoln and told her to tell the plant foreman in Marshall he would be about ten minutes late. And he asked her what she would recommend for Jane for their eleventh anniversary.

"I saw the most beautiful sweater at the store in the mall the other day. It was a gorgeous pale blue. Cashmere, I believe. She would adore it."

"Which store?'

"Whittlings." She said.

"Upstairs?"

"You can enter upstairs or downstairs. It doesn't matter but the women's department is downstairs."

"Thanks. Call Grant and remind him I'm ten minutes late."

"You going to get the sweater at lunch?"

"Maybe why?"

"Well, I could move Grant's meeting a half hour and you could grab lunch or keep the meeting where it is and I'll go get the sweater for you."

"No. I'd better do this on my own. If Jane found out I had you shopping for her anniversary gift, she'd skin me alive. I'll go. Tell Grant twelve thirty."

Now Perry's only decision was whether to get lunch at the café or at the mall. He pondered it for a moment then settled on shopping first, and grabbing a burger at the food court. That would give him time to make it to Marshall at twelve thirty. Settled. He headed for Lincoln and to the mall. A cashmere sweater for eleven years. She would love it.

He turned on the radio in his sedan and settled back listening to some soft country music out of a Shreveport FM station as he cruised the blacktop back roads toward the south end of Grand Lake. At Tatum, he would catch U.S. 43 and then over to U.S. 59 and head north to Lincoln and right into the mall. It would be quick and easy. Perry was, if nothing else, a man who controlled a busy daily calendar with precision and ease.

He had been away from the plant in Henderson no more than fifteen minutes when his phone rang with the Lincoln plant foreman on the line. A fire in one of the processing sections had burned an electrical relay station out. He felt Perry needed to see it and help him decide what to do.

"Can it be repaired?"

"It will have to be replaced. Pretty well gone."

"How long for a replacement?"

"Not sure. We're on backup power now. I've got the electric company coming by to see what they will need to do on their side of the meter."

"I'm on my way to Marshall for a meeting with Grant that I've postponed three days now. You get all the information from engineering and from the electric company and let me know the costs. And the timing. How long can we run on backup power?'

"Twelve hours at most."

"Fine. Keep in touch." He hung up and turned the radio off. The music was now interfering with his mind as he thought through his options at the plant. An entire section shutting down for a few days for repairs could mean as many as fifty people out of work. And productivity would fall. Again. He shook his head. Damn, he just couldn't keep the Lincoln plant up and performing at peak capacity – it was always something. Always. Tulsa was not happy with the way Lincoln was running. And it was his job to turn it around.

He nearly passed the entrance to Lincoln Mall as he was deep in thought about the situation at the plant. He parked next to a dark blue Ford Mustang hatchback. Maybe a tad too close. Fuck it. He was in a hurry.

Just inside the mall's main door he stopped and called his secretary. "Tell Grant we've had a fire at Lincoln. I need to go and check on it and I'll call him to reschedule."

"He won't like that. It'll be the fourth time this week."

"I'll reschedule for later this afternoon. Tell him to stand by his phone...keep it near...I'll call him."

Somebody down the hallway popped a balloon.

"What was that?" his secretary asked.

"Some kid in the food court burst a balloon. I gotta go now. You said bottom floor for women's department right?"

"Yeah."

He hung up the phone and headed deeper into the mall. He had thirty six seconds to live.

5

July Williams Bell

Her name is July (pronounced Julie, but spelled July for the month in which she was born). In Forrest City, Arkansas, July Williams had been the first black girl to be elected homecoming queen in the school's integrated history. Her picture made the newspapers all across the Mid South. She became something of a local celebrity. She had been interviewed by TV stations from both Memphis and Little Rock. A man named Everett Wright Bell having seen her picture and watched her on television, went and called on her. He was ten years her senior. He had a good job working on John Deere tractors at the local dealership and was single and could afford to buy July a good college education.

So, like a lot of young girls across the South did, she got married right out of high school. And almost immediately realized she had made a terrible mistake.

She pleaded with Everett to get their vows annulled, but he would have nothing to do with the dissolution of their marriage. He wanted children. And he wanted them in a hurry.

She asked him about her plans for college. He told her to put them on hold and make babies for him. This led to terrible fights. Bell would get worked up, then get drunk and take his frustrations out on July. She, quite often, showed the scars of their battles.

In tears, she went to her parents one night– late in the evening – and told them of her torment. Her father had never really liked Evert Bell but had given his permission to the marriage only when Bell had offered to pay for four years of college for July. The night of the latest skirmish, her dad gave her three hundred dollars – all the money he had – to buy a bus ticket out of town. He drove her to Jonesboro, where she boarded a bus headed for Little Rock. At the last minute, she got off and went back to the ticket window and exchanged her ticket for one to Memphis. She rode alone to Memphis, worried the entire trip that Evert would come home and find her gone and somehow follow her.

In Memphis she used part of the remaining funds her father had given her to secure passage to Houston. It seemed like going to a whole other country. Texas. So big. So vast. So far, far away.

In Houston she found her way to a downtown church where she met a Methodist youth pastor named Edward Wren. Over coffee in the church's family center, she told him her story and he offered to get her a place to live and a job. The apartment wasn't much to speak of: one room with a lumpy bed, the room included the kitchen and a bathroom about the size of a closet. But it was home and it was hers. And she didn't have some foul-smelling man trying to thrust himself on her at all hours.

The job, on the other hand, was something quite promising. It was a clerical job for a major oil company where she was taught to read topographical maps, mark certain holdings on them and then file them in large drawers according to leases held by the firm. They recognized her organizational talents and sent her to junior college where in a year and a half she graduated with an associate's degree. Next, she was offered a part time enrollment at the University of Houston. The oil company paid for that as well, and in two and a half years she earned a college degree: a bachelors of science in land management. She was the first woman of her entire family to go to college and the first person in her family to finish with a degree. But the family never knew anything about it, for she was too afraid to write or call home in case Evert somehow would discover her whereabouts.

For six years she worked for the oil company, then one day her boss, Mr. Jenkins came in and told her he wanted to take her to lunch. Ralph Jenkins was from Kilgore, Texas originally and was a good manager and treated his employees professionally. At lunch he confessed to July that he was leaving the company and going to Tyler to start a new oil venture. And he needed a good office manager to help keep the "ducks in a row," as he called it. He was offering her the job.

The pay increase was intoxicating to her. The move away to a new place where she could have a real home and have a real professional job, it was more than she could even imagine. She said yes almost before Ralph had even made the offer.

The move to Tyler worked out great. The office grew and soon the small oil company had a dozen or so employees and July was made a vice president. Her job was to go into the field and help secure leases from folks who owned small farms and plots of land. Most were poorly educated blacks and Ralph thought July could connect with them – which she did. She was able to secure leases from folks that white land men had been trying to wrestle away for decades. July did it in no time – usually over lunch: collard greens and cornbread in exchange for oil and gas.

Her status in the company grew. And so, too, did her salary. She built a house on Grand Lake, which was her retreat from work. During the week she lived in a furnished apartment on the south side of Tyler. Her neighbors were an elderly Jewish couple named Hoffman, who she kept an eye on and assisted in their weekly shopping. She even had them over to her lake house during the holidays. It was as close to family as she had since leaving Arkansas.

July was also giving to others in her community. She donated a portion of her bonus each year to the Boys and Girls Clubs of East

Texas and was a cabin sponsor at their summer camps. She had started a scholarship to the local junior college for girls of color to study science and math.

One Friday in November, Ralph Jenkins came into her office and said, "July, we've got a lease in Harrison County … we're having a bit of trouble with. And old man named Dudley has given us his verbal permission to drill on his property outside of Marshall. But his adult kids, who live in Los Angeles and in Detroit are balking. There's a family reunion on Monday afternoon. I want you to go over there, get the lay of the land and see if you can get this thing settled once and for all."

"In Marshall?"

"No. Mr. Dudley and his son Wilton have agreed to meet you at the community center at the Lincoln Mall. The mall's got meeting rooms for private conferences there and I have reserved one for you and the Dudleys."

"What time?"

"Two-ish. They want to have lunch with the relatives first, then come and sit down and talk with you."

"What seems to be the hold up? Money?"

"It's always money. But this is also they don't want the father's homestead destroyed with all the equipment and noise. We have offered to move him into an assisted living home for three months while the work goes on. All on our dime. But they don't like that idea."

"How close is the well site to his home?"

"Quarter of a mile. Maybe a tad more."

"What if we were to get him a temporary house? Maybe even a mobile home and put it right there on his property. Not an assisted living place. That kind of place might be sending the wrong message to them. Like it was a nursing home or something. Like he was being put away."

"Whatever. You find a way to bring this to a close. You've got full rights to sign any agreement for us. Just get it done."

July got in her car and drove out of Tyler east toward Kilgore. She stopped at the lake house to get some comfortable clothes. She wanted to dress casually for the meeting. No airs – no putting on the dog for these folks. She needed to be one of them. Earn their trust and take their side when and where necessary. She had done it a hundred times over. It was second nature to her. Once the families realized the money they would be making from the leasing of their mineral rights, they would be more than happy to comply, as long as their father was taken care of – and July would be there to make sure he was most comfortable.

At eleven forty, July pulled into the mall parking lot and ventured into the wing that had at one time been a national department store. It was now a community center. One large room dominated the area, it was the home of Lincoln Community Worship. Off from the worship center were a half dozen glass-front conference rooms, in the middle of which was the office for the center. July entered and checked in with Deloris Hays, the director of special services. Deloris was a large woman, who had not missed many meals in her fifty-nine years on Earth. Deloris and her double-knit stretched pants waddled down a hallway and opened the door to a darkened room. When the fluorescent lights came on July could see that it looked out onto the second level of the mall shopping area and away from the worship center. "Will this do?" Asked Deloris.

"I think so. It's quiet and we can do our business peacefully here."

"I'll have some refreshments brought in. Soft drinks and coffee."

"Maybe iced tea – sweet tea," suggested July.

"Sweet tea it is. What time do you expect your clients?'

"Around one thirty. Maybe a bit earlier."

"We'll be ready for them; make yourself at home and if you need anything you let me or Clare know. Bathrooms are down the hall and to the right."

Deloris left and July noticed a woman's store at the bottom of the escalators away from the food court. She could grab a sandwich and try on a pair of new shoes before the Dudleys arrived. Perfect. She left and headed downstairs.

At the bottom of the escalator she noticed the food court was quite busy. Someone popped a child's balloon. She had fourteen seconds.

6

Texas Ranger
Will Little

Abank robbery the preceding Friday had Will Little in East Texas doing detective work as he assisted the FBI in their manhunt for two young men dressed in dark jeans and dark hoodies who had entered a bank in Hallsville, Texas on the outskirts of Longview, pulled guns and got away with fifteen thousand, five hundred dollars. There were videos from about every angle of the two men, as well as an accomplice in a gray Toyota get-a-way car. The car's tags had been covered over with what appeared to be black duct tape.

Will had been a Texas Ranger for more than sixteen years. He began his career in law enforcement in Killeen, Texas and then moved to neighboring Temple, Texas where after two years he took the Department of Public Safety (DPS) test and was made a Texas State Trooper. In the Lone Star State they are referred to as DPS officers. In other parts of the country they are called the highway patrol. Seven years in that role, he got the chance, after receiving a master's degree in law enforcement and forensic science at Baylor University in Waco, to matriculate to the elite services of the Texas Rangers. Will was stationed out of Tyler but worked an area from Lufkin to the south, to Texarkana in the north and as far west as Corsicana. He was a senior officer in the exclusive force and had a rather stellar record at solving crimes, especially bank robberies. That is why the FBI had called on him to assist them in this latest heist. The number of bank robberies in the region seemed to be growing as the economy seesawed back and forth between robust and crumbling dry. Economist had told Will that those with jobs in the oil fields and related industries seemed to be safe from the constant rumblings of unemployment, but those without jobs were having great difficulty in locating work. And like the bunch that had held up the bank in Hallsville, some job prospects were less legal than others.

"One of these guys has a limp. Reminds me of a guy we caught a few years back breaking into businesses after hours to rob their vending machines. He spent a spell in Huntsville, if I remember correctly. Might have a look in on him."

"Got a name?" asked the FBI agent.

"Phillips, Wayne Phillips," said Will. "Used to live out by the Greer Ranch entrance. Down near Henderson. His dad is a welder. Carl I think his name was." Will had a mind like a steel trap. A name, a face, an address, a phone number, once he heard it or saw it, it was locked in his gray matter for good. He was as close to a walking – talking Google source as anyone around. He said it was called eidetic memory. "He has a sister over in Jacksonville. Think she's a schoolteacher. Not sure what her married name is. But her maiden name was Carly Phillips."

"We'll check it out."

"Great. I'm heading to Lincoln. There's a young man down there who has been in and out of trouble with the law a few times. Might sniff around his place."

"Let us know if you find anything interesting."

"Will do."

Little got into his unmarked car and headed for Lincoln some twenty-five miles away. It was close to lunchtime so he thought he'd just stop in at the mall and grab a burger. Maybe even get a new belt. His old belt was a tad worn and Will Little was a fastidious dresser – creases in his dress khaki trousers ironed just so by his lovely wife, Karen, his life partner for over twenty-five years and mother to their three kids, and his buttons were always in place on his starched white shirts also complements of Karen; and a belt that was shinny and new, to match the brown boots he wore with pride, as he did his felt Stetson. But recently, the belt had fallen victim to too much use. It needed to be replaced. Will Little reached to the sun visor in the car and retrieved a pair of aviator sunglasses. He was not only a good Texas Ranger, he looked the part, too. You didn't want to fool with Will Little. Not unless your life depended on it.

There was a story that circulated among the Rangers and the DPS officers in that part of the state that Will Little busted up an entire motorcycle gang of more than thirty bikers single handedly. For a long time Will deflected the story saying that there had been others present who assisted him with the takedowns; but after a while, he simply let the story grow. It did great things for his image and prestige in the community and in the eyes of those who might try and cross him. His six foot, five inch frame needed little endorsement and the air about him was all authority, especially with the gold star on his left breast pocket. His job as a Texas Ranger was as much to stave off trouble, as it was to find it and bring it to justice.

Will entered the mall from the south side and passed a man on a cell phone call. He overheard him changing a meeting time to that afternoon. He smiled, knowing that his schedule was his own to make and to keep. He too, heard a balloon pop in the food court. That was the last thing he ever heard.

7

Alice Dixon

Alice Dixon checked the walk-in freezer again. The third time that morning the co-owner of the Fresh Freeze Ice Cream Palace had looked at the dial on the freezer's control panel. It was starting to read closer and closer to 30 degrees. That was the critical zone. Something was wrong. Alice feared it was the compressor.

She called her husband who was the other co-owner of the franchise store in Lincoln Mall. "The store was like a printing press —printing money," he once told friends. "And in the summer it is almost a crime how much we can make." He had bragged. Todd and Alice owned two other franchise locations for the Fresh Freeze, one in Nacogdoches across the street from Stephen F. Austin State University and another in Longview near Le Tourneau University. College kids loved their ice cream. They were planning a fourth location in Tyler, but the franchise committee had yet to approve the new site for them. They wanted it directly across the street from the sprawling junior college. The phone rang three times before the sleepy voice of Todd finally answered.

"Todd I think the main freezer is about to go out." She said it with conviction in her voice, but without alarm. Todd had been up all night with a problem at the Nacogdoches unit and hadn't gotten home until well after one in the morning, so his brain was spinning up slowly.

"Did you call service?"

"Not yet. I wanted to talk to you first."

"Call them. ETEX refrigeration in Longview." He paused. "No. No. It's in Kilgore. And get a tech over there ASAP. I'll get Gene to close for me in Longview tonight and I'll be over right after lunch. See if the guy at Burger House can store some product for us. He owes us one after he lost power last year."

"Will do." Alice hung up and checked the dial again. The needle pointed just above 30 degrees now. She had to act fast. A college boy named Randy White who dipped ice cream part time, was there with her and she told him to mind the counter while she went across the food court to seek out the manager of Burger House about moving ice cream product to his freezer unit. "Put as many cartons in the display cases as will fit comfortably. I don't want to lose any product." He nodded and got busy as she left the ice cream shop and moved through the throng of people who were gathering for lunch in the food court. The crowd was bigger that day than she had expected, and that was good. More sales. More money and maybe if she were lucky, less spoilage of ice cream. She noticed a class of preschoolers having lunch with their teacher and chaperones. That would be business coming her way in no time. Another smile.

The owner of Burger House was a Greek man named Kiloskous. But very one called him Jerry. She didn't know why nor at that moment did she even care. "Jerry. Jerry I need a word with you," she said over the orders to and from his kitchen being shouted as burgers were being flipped and potatoes being fried. Kiloskous looked up and nodded her back behind the Dutch doors that separated the ordering line and cashiers from the cooks and the kitchen staff. "We're about to lose our big walk-in freezer. Was wondering if we can move some product over. For a few hours until service can fix it?"

"Sure, Alice. Sure." He turned to a young Hispanic boy named Raul. "Raul, go with Mrs. Dixon and help her bring some ice cream over here."

"Thank you, Jerry, you are a life safer."

"No problem, Alice. No problem. More fries up. And two more cheeseburgers. Let's go guys."

Alice left the chaos of the burger place followed by the Mexican kid in a white tee shirt and white slacks, the uniform of Burger House – that along with a bright red paper hat with the store's logo emblazoned on it. Once at the Fresh Freeze, Alice showed Raul where the walk-in unit was and which round, cardboard containers to deliver first. He stacked them on a hand dolly that was inside the freezer and started back across the food court as Alice dialed her husband again. "Todd, Jerry's going to let us store our product there. And I've got the service guys on their way." At that moment, she too heard the kid's balloon explode in the food court. She didn't think to look up but instead, stepped around a corner where she could hear Todd's instructions clearer.

"What's the thermostat say now?' he asked.

She looked at the wall unit. "Thirty three."

"Damn. Get the stuff out of there as quickly as you can. It will stay fairly hard for an hour, but with the temp falling that fast, we'll be in trouble unless he get it back below twenty-nine soon. It'll stay fresh and hard at twenty-nine and below. That's the safe zone. Of course I'd prefer closer to zero, but I'm not going to be a beggar. What's Kiloskous's unit set at?'

"I don't know. I didn't ask him." She could kick herself for not noticing.

"That's okay. With hamburger meats and what not in it, I'm sure his freezer unit is well below twenty – maybe even closer to zero, as well. That'll have to do."

A second balloon exploded and she heard someone scream. Alice had less than a minute to live.

8

The Pre Schoolers

- Terry Brooks
- Cindy Reynolds
- Shamiqua Jones
- Missy Jackson
- Linda Watts
- Kee Kee Williams
- David Perez, Karen Ray
- Cammy Elliot
- Bobby Joe Marshal
- Ellen Henry
- Judith Davenport
- Hal Davenport
- Robbie Owens

Eleven preschoolers and four chaperones all scarfing down hot dogs and hamburgers (along with an intermittent French fry and catsup fight) were just about to move to the Fresh Freeze for some ice cream when they heard the first pop of the balloon. Hal Davenport jerked his head around and at once realized there was a problem. People coming from the community center end of the mall were running with a terrified look in their eyes. Another pop sounded. Now Hal was sure it was not a child's balloon.

A young man dressed in all white with a red hat from Burger House crossed in front of his view pushing a cart of large ice cream cartons, as a young man in all black came around the corner and began shooting at the crowd milling about the food court. Hurriedly he grabbed two children closest to him. Shamiqua Jones and Missy Jackson. He placed them under his torso at the edge of the long table. Pop. Pop. Pop. The explosions grew louder and louder. Their frequency became more and more accelerated. Pop.Pop.Pop.Pop.

Judith Davenport, Hal's wife of twenty years flung herself over Karen Ray and a young boy named Carl Washington. Judith and Hal had met on a blind date at Baylor University when they were juniors. Judith had received her MFA in piano and was in the Shreveport symphony, as well as the East Texas orchestra and taught music part time at Lincoln Senior High school. Hal was an engineer at Patriot Farms processing plant in Lincoln. His phone had been ringing all morning, but because he was off that day, and helping his wife and her friend with the class outing, he had left the cell in his car's glove box. He knew nothing of the fire at the plant. He didn't even know his director was coming through the east door of the mall walking directly into the line of fire of the young shooter.

Raul Garcia spun around as the bullet entered the left side of his head and exploded out the right, sending blood and gray matter across a table of three elderly women having lunch together. They immediately screamed and ran toward the back wall. Pop.Pop.Pop. Pop.Pop. Now the explosions were sounding like a drum roll they were coming so fast.

Terry Brooks, Cindy Reynolds along with Robbie Owens, the teacher of the preschoolers, all went down in a barrage of gunfire coming from the young man dressed in black. His gun was smoking from the heat of the escaping shells. Robbie had been in Hal and Judith's wedding in Waco two decades before and they had returned the favor at her wedding the following year. They were also godparents to her two daughters.... Pop.Pop. Pop.Pop. Pop.Pop... Twin girls named Crystal and Clarice.

Pop.Pop.Pop.Pop.Pop.Pop.Pop. Hal Davenport took three shots in the back of the head and in the spine. Shamiqua Jones and Missy Jackson were no longer protected by Hal's body and they were shot several times. Missy once in the head and once in the heart.

July Bell turned at the bottom of the escalator and saw the young man in black walking briskly toward the food court. He fired down the mall at the east opening. She jerked her head around and saw a man in a Stetson and fresh khakis with a crisp white shirt go down. He had a silver revolver drawn and was apparently about to fire. A pool of blood flowed from beneath him. She looked up right into the young shooter's eyes. Pop.Pop. She fell dead at the base of the east escalator. The gunman aimed and fired again down the mall to the east, away from the food court and caught Perry Reynolds who was approaching the scene right between the eyes. He was still talking on the phone with his secretary, who was about to make arrangements to change his calendar yet again for the day.

The shooter turned his attention once again to the food court that was now a panic zone. He opened fire at the long table, which had hosted the preschoolers. He shot quickly and deadly killing Carl Washington, David Perez and Karen Ray. Two other children, Bonnie Hart and Millie Rivers lay motionless under the table with ketchup splattered all over themselves, which the gunman took for blood and walked away assuming he had already gunned them down. As he walked he tossed the magazine to the side and reloaded the AR 15. During the brief lull, the last remaining child from the preschool outing was grabbed by Randy White, the young college boy at Fresh Freeze. He and the child barricaded themselves inside of the warming walk-in freezer. Just outside the door, Alice Dixon was screaming into the phone as her husband listened on in disbelief. She was shot with the first few rounds of the second magazine.

The commotion was drawing attention in other ends of the mall. At Whittlings Department Store, Rosa and Cynthia raced from the store toward the food court, not knowing where the shooting was coming from, but their car was in that direction. Others were right behind them, running in that direction because someone had come in yelling there was a gunman in the department store on the second level. The food court seemed like a safe place to go and hide. Cynthia, was shot immediately upon entering the bloody scene. Mrs. Parker was shot also but she kept running and threw herself at the gunman and knocked him to the ground. Cynthia tried to get up but her leg had been hit in the thigh and she couldn't stand. The kid clothed in black regained his balance, raised the rifle and Pop.Pop.Pop.Pop. Shot Rosa at point blank range then turned the gun on Cynthia Pop.Pop. Pop. The last shot pierced her heart and she bled out on the cold, mall floor. There would be no pony. There would be no Yale. There would be no great microbiological discovery. That had been taken away with three rounds of ultra-high velocity brass. The ripple had begun.

Upstairs in the Community Center, Deloris Hays who was bringing refreshments into the room for the meeting, looked out the glass window of the conference room and saw the commotion unfolding along the escalator and into the food court. She immediately went to the office and evacuated all the staff out the side door. As she moved into the parking lot, she spotted four black men and a woman walking toward the south mall entrance, the entrance for the community center. Instinctively she knew this was the family coming there for the business meeting. She yelled at them to get back into their cars and drive to safety. "Shooter. Shooter. Go away. Get in your car. Shooter. Shooter. Get into your car and drive away." She was frantically yelling at the Dudley's as they returned to their cars and drove off hurriedly. Deloris Hays slumped to the black asphalt-parking surface and clutched her chest. She was having a massive heart attack. As she was passing out, she heard one of her co-workers calling the police. "We have an active shooter at…" All she saw after that was white. Then darkness.

Father Mise was slipping into the second pair of black shoes to try on for size. The first pair had been too tight. He had always been a ten, now the young man waiting on him suggested a ten and a half or even an eleven. "Not all shoes fit exactly the same – some sizes are quite different brand to brand," the young man explained. Father Mise nodded. He thought that lesson might fit well into Sunday's homily. Then he heard a child's balloon pop. It sounded as if it came from the food court. He didn't give it another thought.

Then he heard another pop. Then another pop. Then a series of pops. And he realized it wasn't a balloon but rather gunfire. A woman came running through the men's shoe department screaming that there was a shooter loose in the mall.

Another woman and a man came along right after the first one, also confirming the shooter story.

Father Mise slipped back into his old scruffy shoes and thanked the startled young clerk, "Son, you had best find a safe place. Go, get your co-workers and get out. Protect yourselves. This could be real. It might be a drill, but if it is real you want to be far, far away from this mall. Go. Go now."

The young clerk ran toward the back of the store and disappeared behind a curtain marked employees only.

Pop. Pop. Pop. Pop. Pop. Pop. The sound echoed throughout the mall. He could now hear screaming. He stood and moved cautiously toward the entrance of the store. Looking toward the food court he could see people fleeing and others falling to the ground.

The priest reached into his pocket and felt for his rosary beads. Then he stepped into the mall with his back against the wall and slowly headed toward the melee, which was unfolding. Smoke was starting to rise and mix with the sunlight from overhead frosted windowpanes in the ceiling, giving the scene a strangely foggy feel. More gun fire. Pop. Pop. Pop. Pop. Pop. Blood curdling screams of children and old people. A man came running out towards the east entrance and was gunned down. Suddenly a young man in all black came racing from the food court and ran right past the priest. They exchanged glances momentarily. The gunman never paused and never aimed his rifle at Father Mise. But the pastor could see the young man's eyes. They were wide and glistening. He had the look of a wild animal. He disappeared outside into the bright light of the November morning. Father Mise reached into his other pocket and dialed 911 on his cell pone.

"Where's your emergency?" asked the clam voice.

"Lincoln Mall. Food court. There's been a shooting … many down. Many wounded… many may be dead. Lincoln Mall Food Court. This is Father Richard Mise. Send police and ambulances. The shooter I believe just ran out to the parking lot. He may have gone to reload. I don't know." With that, Father Mise hung up and raced to the food court.

The carnage was almost more than he could stand.

9

Hail Mary full of grace...

Father Mise was dumbfounded as he watched the shooter sprint past him: their eyes making instantaneous contact. Then he was gone. He never slowed or even lowered his weapon toward the priest. He simply ran past him, out into the bright lights of the mid-day sun.

The priest continued toward the chaos in the food court. The first person he came to was a young Hispanic man in a white outfit with a bright red cap. He knelt, feeling for a pulse. He had been trained to do so at the clinic in Mexico. Triage was a side venture for him at the mission, which had always been shorthanded. Often he had been summoned to the clinic to assist in times of great emergencies.

He found no pulse on the body that bore a nametag over the right breast pocket of Raul. Ice cream crates were strewn about him as blood and gray matter covered the floor and intermingled with melting chocolate cream around him. There were screams coming from the storefronts of people in hiding.

The next victim brought an immediate pain to his heart. It was Cynthia Parker. She still clutched in her hand the plastic covered dress her mother had purchased for her moments before. A gaping hole in her chest let the priest know time was of the essence. He lowered his head next to Cynthia's ear. Placing his thin stole over his neck and kissing it, he whispered, "May our Lord and God, Jesus Christ, through the grace and mercies of his love for humankind, forgive you all your transgressions. And I, an unworthy priest, by his power given me, forgive and absolve you from all your sins, in the name of the Father and of the Son and of the Holy Spirit. Amen" Tears ran down his cheeks as he turned to Rosa, afloat in a pool of her own blood. He repeated the petition, as he made the sign of the cross over her. Then he moved to two children who lay next to a man. All still. All dead. He began to weep as he crossed himself and said the last rites over and over and over.

A young man and a girl emerged from the walk-in freezer and saw Father Mise. "Is it safe?" The young man asked. The father shook his head and motioned them back into hiding.

He then pulled his cell phone out and called for help again. "We need ambulances, doctors and police at the mall. There's been a terrible shooting."

The next young girl he came to was Cindy Reynolds. She was still breathing. Several wounds were openly pouring blood in giant spurts onto the floor. He grabbed his coat and forced one of the sleeves into the largest hole. He removed his belt and made a tourniquet for the wound in her upper arm.

From a distance he could hear sirens approaching the mall. "Hurry," he said under his breath. "For God's sake hurry."

Looking up he caught the eyes of Judith Davenport. She was mouthing something as he moved to her. "My children. My children. Tell them…" she died. He began to repeat the rite once again, not even knowing if the woman was Catholic or not. It didn't matter to him. He had a job to do for anyone there who needed the prayer of salvation – he was there to surround them with love. But there was so much carnage he felt it was hopeless.

A woman came to his side dressed in the green and yellow apron of The Salad Bar. She pulled at him. "I've got two still alive, Father. Come quickly."

At the back of the food court were three elderly women. Two were still alive and a third one lay motionless in their laps. There was so much blood covering them he couldn't tell who had been shot and who had not. He knelt in front of the ladies and quickly assessed their wounds. He felt for a pulse in the third one, but she was gone. Quickly he ordered the salad lady to bring paper towels. He began to pray aloud for the comfort of the ladies as they wept. A hand tapped him on the shoulder and he looked up and into the eyes of a young, shocked-looking EMT who was ready to take over. "I've got this father. You tend to the dead."

Police were searching the stores nearest the food court and talking to others who had seen the shooting occur. Father Mise recognized one of the officers and called him over. "I saw him leave out the south door. He was still carrying a rifle. He looked right at me ... right into my eyes... but he didn't shoot."

"Did you recognize him, Father?' asked the patrolman.

"No. He was Caucasian. I'd say about sixteen or seventeen. Dressed in all black. Maybe five nine or ten."

"You didn't happen to see a get away car or if he had accomplices?"

"No. I'm sorry I didn't. After he fled out the doors I came straight here to begin helping people."

At just that moment the radio clipped to the officer's uniform squawked that a second shooting had just occurred at the Bluebonnet Café. Witnesses said they saw a blue, late-model Ford Mustang race off. Last three digits on the Texas plate were X15.

The officer called to other policemen in the area and gave orders to fan out and search the parking lot. Yellow tape was being stretched around the food court and two policemen were busy taking photographs of victims and shell casings, placing numbered markers down by each. Father Mise asked if he could continue. The officer nodded, "Just don't touch anything. Leave them as you find them. It will help us in our investigation."

The priest nodded and began to move to each of the victims and say a short prayer over them. Each time he passed Cynthia, he cried a little harder.

"There are two hiding in the ice cream store freezer," he said to one of the cops passing him. The officer walked into the Fresh Freeze Ice Cream shop and opened the door to the freezer, which was now registering close to forty degrees. A young college-aged man and a small girl came out. As soon as she saw the scene with the scattered bodies of her school buddies in the food court she burst into tears. The college boy held her as she collapsed and he called for Father Mise, who came and took the girl in his arms and began to soothe her. He knew it was an image that would more than likely be baked into her fragile memory for the rest of her life. "Hail Mary…full of grace…"

As he prayed, she wept.

10

Matt Stevens
(again)

Matt got into his Mustang and pulled away. He drove straight to U.S. 59, which was less than a block away and headed north. He was famished. He would stop at the Bluebonnet Café and have a chicken fried steak that was his plan. In the distance he could hear the wail of sirens racing toward the mall. He grinned. He had done it. Just as he had planned. He had done it. He was a fucking genius. Pulled it off all by himself.

He counted three black and white state units pass him. Then two more sheriff's cars. Lights ablaze and sirens blistering the fall air – heading south as he drove north. He pulled into the parking lot of the Bluebonnet Café and was blocked momentarily by an eighteen-wheeler trying to navigate a short turn around. Matt grew restless. "Fuck it. Fuck it." He yelled. Stopping his Mustang and throwing it into park, he hopped out and raced to the cab of the truck where Milton Owens was maneuvering his rig. "Hey, you need some help driving that thing, old man?" he yelled up at Milton. The truck driver looked down and then ignored the young, redneck hothead. He had come across dozens of them in his time on the road. Patience, he believed, would win out in the end. He slowly eased off the clutch as the truck jerked backwards when a bullet whizzed through his windshield, shattering the glass. Milton stopped the truck and grabbed his trusty baseball bat he kept on board for situations just as this, and started to climb down from the rig when two more shots rang out from the 9 mm pistol the young man in black was holding. A fourth shot caught Milt in the head and ended his life. His limp body fell backwards releasing the parking break and the truck slowly began to roll down the lot toward a gully.

Matt thought for a moment, then decided that lunch at the Bluebonnet might not be the best idea of the day. He returned to his Mustang and drove off in a tear, burning tire tread for fifty feet or better. At Interstate 20 he headed west away from Lincoln and away from Marshall. He would circle back around and visit a friend's house on Grand Lake. It would be a good place to hang to let things cool down.

11

Car 7

"Attention all cars. We have a shooter at the Lincoln Mall. Repeat there's a report of an active shooter at Lincoln Mall." Darrell Hampton stirred. The crackle of the radio awakened him. "Repeat there is an active shooter…Lincoln Mall. Food Court. All cars… Proceed with caution. Multiple victims."

Suddenly sleep left him as the adrenaline kicked in. He started the patrol car, switched on the emergency lights and activated his siren, he pulled out of the short asphalt cove where he had napped and headed up Park Road toward town.

The radio crackled again. "Car 7. Darrell come in."

"7 here. On my way to the mall. Just crossing Park and 17th."

"Head to the Bluebonnet. There's been a shooting there, as well. Blue Mustang. Texas tags…Last three digits are X15. Shooter is believed to be the same one from the mall earlier. Just happened, so be on the lookout."

"Ten-four…Heading to Bluebonnet." Darrell made a sharp turn east bound off of Park road onto 17th street and floored the Charger. Up ahead in the distance he saw a blue Mustang hatchback turn onto the road from the Interstate exchange. It was approaching him at an alarmingly fast speed. He swerved into its lane to get the attention of the driver and then back to his side of the road. The Mustang never slowed down. It sped past. Darrell braked hard and spun the Dodge patrol car around and gave chase toward Grand Lake.

The Mustang was starting to pull away from Hampton. The local police had a policy of not exceeding eighty five miles an hour in a chase unless it was on the Interstate, then they could go up to 100. The Mustang began to disappear from site.

"Car 7 in pursuit of blue Mustang. Headed west on 17th toward Grand Lake. Request backup. You might notify DPS and Gregg County...I'm losing him." The Mustang disappeared over a rise in the distance and Darrell felt hopeless until he heard his chief's voice.

"You are go to use any speed you need to catch the SOB. Hurry." The voice was from police chief Weldon Charles.

With that Darrell floored the patrol car and the muscular engine sprang to life as gallons of petroleum poured through its veins and exploded into sheer energy. The car leapt down the road eating asphalt hungrily in its path.

Darrell crested the next hill and the blue Mustang was stopped across the road. A thin man draped in all black stepped out of the driver's side and produced what looked to Darrell like an automatic rifle. Before Darrell could even stop his car, the young man began to pepper Officer Hampton's patrol car. Pop. Pop. Pop. Pop. Pop. Pop. The officer's windshield exploded in front of him and he lost control of the Charger as it careened off the side of the road and rolled a half dozen times coming to rest on the driver's side, wheels still frantically spinning. A cloud of red dust filled the air. The young man raced to the car, looked inside and saw Hampton struggling with his seat belt and reaching for his gun that was holstered below him. Matt fired three times at point black range at Darrell Hampton.

Matt raced to his car and headed back toward town, to a turnoff that would take him to the lake's large public park.

12

Where's my daughter?

Claris Robinson heard it first from a report on the radio from a Longview FM station. She had been casually folding clothes she had neglected from the night before. She had the radio on for company. It was a quick break in the news. A shooting at Lincoln Mall. Nothing more than that. "Details as soon as we get them." That was what the announcer promised. But a mother's heart shifts into overdrive. She tried calling her daughter, Crissy. No answer. Fear began its march up from the pit of her stomach to her throat.

Through her den's open windows, she heard her next-door neighbor over the fence speaking with the mailman, Mr. Rugger; she was saying that a shooting was in progress at the mall. He had heard it, too. Claris stepped out onto the front porch and interrupted their conversation to see if either had any details. They did not. She went back inside.

She returned to the radio. Just music. She tuned up and down the dial, but could not find anyone else talking about the events at Lincoln Mall.

She called Crissy again.

No answer.

Her daughter was at the mall at work that day. It was part of her degree plan from the high school – 'distributed education' the district called it. It was business. Sales. Marketing. Learning your way around a store. It was worth three hours credit in a pre-college grading system.

She phoned Crissy a third time.

Still no answer.

Fear turned to panic. Grabbing her car keys she went to the garage and started her car, and began backing out into the bright mid-day sun. A bulletin came on the radio stating that Lincoln Schools were under a lock down. There was a shooting in progress at Lincoln Mall, only a few blocks from the expansive campus. The newsman said that details were sketchy at this point, but it was believed that the shooter or shooters were in the food court area of Lincoln Mall. Crissy worked at Beverly's Women's Apparel – right across from the food court – just on the other side of the escalators. Soon a report interrupted the music and said that there were multiple fatalities. Tears were beginning to swell behind her sunglasses. She drove like a possessed person.

Aloud in the car she said, "I'm coming, Crissy. I'm coming."

The Robinson's home was on the far side of Lincoln – away from Highway 59 and the mall. She could make it to the mall in ten minutes, if she caught every light green, but as fate would have it, she was catching them all red. Cursing out loud, she floored the accelerator each time a light turned green and her car tires squealed along the warm streets. She passed traffic on the right and the left, she didn't care that they were honking their horns at her recklessness. As she neared the school, she could see patrol cars at the exits and entrances of the parking lot. There were no students in sight. She continued on Lincoln Drive toward the mall, which now loomed ahead, just past a short row of pine trees. As she attempted to turn into the parking lot a sheriff's deputy stopped her, his patrol car blocking the driveway.

He yelled, "Halt."

"My Daughter."

"I don't care. You can't drive in there."

"My daughter's in there."

"So too are others…but we're working to get everyone out alive. It is a mad house down there just now. You wait here."

"Can you see if she's okay? If she's been released?"

"What's her name?'

"Crissy Robinson. She works at Beverly's."

He repeated the information into a lapel microphone and a voice came back with a negative response. No Crissy.

The tears gushed forth. "My Crissy."

"Ma'am, I need you to park your car over there." The young officer pointed to a shady spot under a pine tree that sat behind a row of neatly trimmed hedges and then told her to wait in her car until he could get further news.

She did. And as she parked her car, her cell phone rang. "Mom!"

"Crissy. Where are you?"

"We are okay Mom. We're in the storage area…we're locked down. We're safe."

"Are you sure?"

"Yes. There's been a shooting, mom. A lot of people are hurt."

Claris could see down the parking lot toward the mall, emergency vehicles, their flashing lights going off and EMT's pushing gurneys to and from waiting ambulances… "You sure you're okay?"

"Yes. Mother. We're waiting for a signal from someone that it is safe to come out."

For some reason, Claris Robinson began to ball uncontrollably. "Mom. I'm okay. I'm okay. I love you."

Through her tears she said, "I love you, too, baby."

13

Royce Hursh and Eve Kholemann

The NBC Nightly News team had just finished with their second editorial meeting deciding the order of the evening news. The oscillating economy was taking center stage; that, and trouble at the White House securing votes for farm funding, which many thought could jeopardize the President's reelection.

The anchor for the nightly news was Bob McAdoo, but he was gone on a sabbatical with his wife, to visit her sister who was dying with cancer at M.D. Anderson Hospital in Houston. Royce Hursh was his temporary replacement. Eve Kholemann was the executive producer for the nightly news. She had been on the desk for five years as the exec producer and six years before that as nightly producer. Royce had been the network's chief Washington correspondent for four years, after more than fifteen years in other capitals around the globe, so both were tried and true veterans of the broadcast news industry; although, it was Royce's first gig at the main desk in New

York. They knew the stories they had just talked about could change two or three times before the six thirty air time.

The two were finishing up their coffee and sharing some notes for the evening's program, when a production assistant came in and said there was an emergency phone call from both the Longview and Shreveport affiliates. There had been a mass shooting at a mall in East Texas. Dozens killed and the shooter was still at large.

Eve was patched through simultaneously to the two news directors at the stations. Over the speakerphone in the conference room, they both confirmed the stories and told New York they had trucks and reporters already rolling to the scene. Longview would be there first due to proximity, but Shreveport had the more experienced crew, especially with satellite uplink.

"How many killed?" She asked.

"We don't know yet," said the news director from Longview.

"Reports range from six to more than a dozen. But there were school children involved," this from the news director of the Shreveport station, which also served a combined license with Texarkana.

"How many shooters?" Eve wanted to know, as Royce hastily began to make notes on the back of news copy he found on the table.

"Nothing official yet but it is believed just one. And he ... (a pause) or she is still on the loose," said the Longview newsman.

"Keep us posted. We're going to bulletin. I want you two to work together and we'll use you as a network hub. We've got David Rawlings in Dallas, we'll fly him in. Where's the closest airport?"

"East Texas Regional just outside of Longview," again the Longview news director spoke.

"Operations, get David Rawlings on a jet to Longview...East Texas Regional. Tell him to call in when he is air born. More than likely he is over at Channel Five right now."

Royce looked at Eve. "We should tell Bob McAdoo...I know he's in Houston with his sister-in-law and all..."

"Yes." Said Eve, who immediately turned and yelled into the newsroom. "Someone find Bob McAdoo and get him on the phone.

It's an emergency. Tell network ops we've got a bulletin ready in four minutes."

Royce handed Eve his hand-written lead and she nodded. She called for a P.A. to come and type the words into a teleprompter. "Shreveport and Longview, stay on the line with me. I might need you to feed me lines for Royce Hursh who is going live in three minutes." Eve started out of the news conference room handing the phone to an assistant, "Get this call transferred to my cell." She headed for the control room outside of the news studio. Royce moved into the studio and had donned a coat and was straightening his tie. Make up was quickly moving in, placing a paper towel around his neck as they began giving him a quick powder and touchup. His hair was combed and lip gloss applied. He took a sip of water and placed an earpiece into his right ear. He could hear Eve delivering quick and sharp orders in the control room. "You got me in there?" He asked Eve.

"Yes. We're live in two minutes. Graphics I need a map of this area. It's in a town called Lincoln. Southeast of Longview. Southwest of Marshall. Dallas is to the west by two hundred miles. Shreveport to the east by fifty. Houston is south by bout 150 miles. Got the area?"

"Got it." shouted someone in the distance.

"Get me a Google map of the mall as well...I need graphics to give me a bulletin lead in and a crawl. Shooting in Texas mall. Multiple fatalities. Shooter still on loose. Someone find out how many mass shootings in Texas this year? I know of two in El Paso. They were also in malls. And there was a big school shooting..." she paused.

"In Uvalde," added Royce.

"In Uvalde," she called out to the newsroom staff. "Get me stats on all of those. And there was a church shooting in South Texas, as well. Get me stats on it, too."

"Sutherland Springs," said Royce into her headset, which was now firmly in place on her gray and black hair.

"Right. Sutherland Springs. Get me stats on it... I want Lynda Risson at the Capitol to track down the Texas Republican Senators who just voted to oppose gun control and get interviews. And get someone over to the gun rights lobby. I want them to pass along their fucking thoughts and prayers and call for more control of crazy people."

There was a pause. Eve caught her breath. She turned to the director. We're live in thirty." Again a Pause. "Welcome to the evening news, Royce." He nodded, keeping a very somber face. When this many had died and especially with children involved, it was very serious business. A P.A. came in and pointed to the teleprompter that now had his words typed neatly in all caps so he could read them. He scanned the lines twice then nodded. He was ready.

"After you do your intro we may feed you some stats and even send it live to Texas, but if they are not ready, we'll do a quick close and wrap up with a promise for more details as soon as they become available."

"Got it." He said.

"Thirty seconds. Stand by," said the director, Sheppard Green, a twenty-year veteran of the newscast.

"Ops ready? Intro Ready? Graphics ready?" Eve was calling the troops to be on top of their game and to be set. "Don't start the crawl until Royce has gotten to his second sentence."

"We're at three, two, one…"

Sound effects were up and pulsating music came in under it as a graphic appeared on the screen with the NBC News logo and the words Special News Bulletin. A voiceover repeated those same words. "From NBC News Central in New York, here's Royce Hursh." Eve quickly glanced at the CBS and ABC monitors along with the feeds from Fox News and CNN, as of that moment they had not broken in with the story. NBC was first.

Royce, calmly and forcefully began, "Word is just in to NBC News from Texas that there has been another mass shooting in the United States. This time at a shopping mall in a town called Lincoln, Texas…"

"Lincoln sits between Dallas and Shreveport…north of Houston…" Eve said into her headset microphone, as Royce repeated the words almost as soon as she had spoken them. "Graphics. Map."

A map appeared to the right of Royce on the screen. "It is not known at this time how many victims there are, but reports of multiple fatalities and among them school children…the shooter is believed to be still at large and a rather extensive manhunt has begun…"

"This is the third major mass shooting in Texas this year…and the thirtieth in the country…" Eve said it slowly and clearly.

Again Royce repeated her words adding, "By rough count, so far this year more than 300 Americans have lost their lives to mass shootings in public. That is a number not counting those victims of today's mass shooting in Texas. Again, in this case it is not known if the shooter acted alone or if there were multiple shooters involved. For those just joining us, there has been a mass shooting in a shopping mall in the city of Lincoln, Texas just to the west of Shreveport, Louisiana and to the east of Dallas. Authorities are looking at this time for a suspect they believe to be driving a blue Mustang… he is to be considered dangerous and heavily armed."

Eve talked to him again in his earpiece. And Royce told the nation, "We are going to Longview to speak with Gregg County Sherriff, Terrance Cook."

A rather plump-looking man in a ill-fitting suit appeared on camera and began to speak. "At this time what we know is … we believe… a single individual entered Lincoln Township Mall just off of U.S. 59 and opened fire around noon in the mall's food court." Cook's name and title appeared below him on the screen. "The shooter then fled and is believed to have shot a truck driver north of town before fleeing toward the west, according to eye witnesses.

"At this time, we do not know how many victims there are, but we have early reports that there were school children caught in this horrible scene. Texas Rangers and Department of Public Safety officers along with my office and staff and the city police of Lincoln are coordinating efforts in tracking this shooter or shooters down. We remind the public that this individual or individuals are armed and should be considered most dangerous." A person handed the chief a note, he read it and looked up into the camera. "The last three digits on the Mustang believed to have been used by in the get away are X 15. That's a Texas license plate ending in X15. If you see this car, call the Gregg County sheriff's office or the Lincoln police, but do not approach it on your own."

The camera light in front of Royce turned red and he was back on the air. "Again to repeat the news, there has been a mall shooting in Texas in the town of Lincoln, not far from the cities of Marshall and Longview in East Texas. The shooter is believed to be still at large and a manhunt is under way at this time. As more information comes into our NBC News Center we will break into network programming and update you. For NBC News, I'm Royce Hursh."

"Good job everyone Now let's get organized. I want Linda Risson on the line ASAP. Steve Wallace is covering the White House at this time, get him over there and find out what the administration has to say about yet another shooting on their watch. Let's go people, we've only got two hours to evening news time."

Eve looked at the competition's monitors. Only ABC was starting to break into programming with a special news bulletin. "You motherfuckers are five minutes late," she said with a smile on her face.

14

Bob McAdoo

The M.D. Anderson Hospital waiting room was full. Families from around the globe waited on word from the doctors about their family members under the care of one of the world's best oncology centers. Bob McAdoo paced back and forth with a cooling cup of coffee in his hand. At this time, he would normally be prepping for his evening news show. Perhaps his nervous energy was simply a refined response to his conditioning of more than a decade to be ready for the Nightly News. His wife Elaine moved to his side and pointed to a TV monitor at ceiling height. There on the screen was NBC with a special news bulletin. The sound was turned down so as not to disturb families in the waiting area. Royce Hursh was speaking into the camera with a most somber-looking face. A type crawl started across the bottom of the screen. A mass shooting at a mall in East Texas in the Township of Lincoln. Multiple fatalities including school children. Shooter still on the loose. Wide area manhunt.

He turned to speak to Elaine as his cell phone rang. "This will be Eve," he said.

Elaine nodded. "Take it. They'll want you there."

"Eve?" He answered his phone.

"Bob this is Melinda Griffin." She was Eve's assistant producer. "There's been another mass shooting…"

"I just saw your bulletin."

"We were the first on air."

"Good job. What can I do?"

"Eve needs you in Lincoln."

"Where is David Rawlings?"

"He's in Uvalde covering a hearing about the police inaction during their shooting. Then he was scheduled for a story tomorrow on the border. Near Laredo. You're it."

"Who's on the ground with me?"

"I've asked for Bruce Tunney of Channel 2 in Houston or Ellen Watt from Dallas. They are both excellent producers. Ellen covered the last mall shooting in El Paso…Bruce anchored our Uvalde coverage with Rawlings."

"Do you have my wife's phone number?"

There was a short pause. "Yes…"

"Good, Text her Tunney's info and I'll call Jerry in Ops. I've got to get to Lincoln ASAP. Is there an airport near?"

"Wait, Bob." She paused talking to someone near her, then returned to the call, "Channel 2 is going to send a chopper to Lincoln. They said there's room for you."

"Okay. I'm at M.D. Anderson in the medical district…"

"Hold on…"

He looked up at the screen, which showed NBC returning to its on-going programming. The next voice on the phone was Eve joining Melinda.

"Bob, I take it Melinda has briefed you?"

"Yes. And congrats on being first out the gate. Now lets get a team up there and cover this thing like a blanket."

Melinda spoke next. "Channel 2 says they can pick you up across the street at the Texas Heart Institute. There's a heliport there."

"Got it. Listen, all I've got on is what you get. Slacks and a blue cotton shirt and blue jacket. No tie."

"You're covering a shooting in a mall. Go in a buy what you need, for Christsake…or steal it." said Eve.

"Right. On the run now. Will call you from the air." He hung up and turned to leave, as Elaine kissed him. "There's a number on your phone for Bruce Tunney of Channel 2. Text him and tell him to bring me a road kit. He'll know what I mean. I'll meet them at the heliport at Texas Heart." He kissed his wife. "You text me if anything changes with your sister." She nodded and hugged him.

"Be careful, Bob."

"I will."

"And pretend it's not a chopper," she called to him as he stepped into an elevator.

Bob McAdoo hated helicopters. Hated them with a passion. He had flown in them covering both Gulf Wars and the battles in Afghanistan, as well as numerous stories of wild fires in California and illegal border crossings along the Rio Grande. No matter how many times he went up in a chopper, he hated it.

Bob raced across the street into the Texas Heart Institute building and security was already waiting for him. They rushed him upstairs on a secured elevator and then up a flight of metal stairs to the heliport. It was blistering hot for a November day and the heat was only surpassed by the oppressive humidity of the city. From the southwest he could hear the all-too familiar chopping noise of the TV station's helicopter approaching. It circled the building then slowly lowered onto a giant red cross painted in the center of the landing area.

Bob ran to an opening door as a hand reached out to assist him on board. It was Bruce Tunney, a long time friend and one of the best news producers Bob had ever worked with. Bruce, who had a very bright future at the news headquarters in New York City had opted to move to Houston after marrying a local girl, name Sally Cumby. Bob and Bruce had traveled the world together getting into as many tight scrapes in bars in foreign lands as they did with rogue governments and dictators. But with few scars to show for it, both men had settled comfortably into the roles as anchor and producer. And they respected one another as only true professionals could– with unyielding trust in each other.

"Good to see you again, Hound Dog," said Bob to Bruce as they placed headphones on to block the noise of the chopper and to communicate easier. The nickname came from the fact that Tunney was a native of Memphis, home of Elvis Presley who made the song "Ain't Nothing But A Hound Dog" a world-wide hit.

"Likewise. Sorry to take you away from Elaine in this hour of need."

"Her family is there. They are strong and will pull through. Plus she's been on this ride a hundred times before. She's used to it by now."

"How are the kids?" asked Bruce.

"Jenny's at NYU and Bill is …well… he is still trying to find himself. He's building guitars in Quebec with a guy who pays him minimum wage but gives him a cabin to live in."

"Oh, to be young again." said Bruce.

Bob nodded. "At least he's learning French. How long is this ride to Lincoln?" Asked Bob.

Bruce shrugged and turned the question to the cockpit to the pilot. "What's our ETA in Lincoln?"

"It'll take just at an hour," said the pilot, as the giant Gulf Coast city began to recede beneath them and the buildings became toy-like objects on a game board.

"Did you get my text about the remote kit?"

Bruce patted a carry-on suitcase at his feet. "Got everything my prince requires. Even your shade of makeup powder."

"You are the best, Hound Dog. You are the best."

The radio crackled and Eve began to address both newsmen. "We just got word that the count is at least nineteen dead. At least seven of those were preschoolers out on a field trip. This number also includes a Lincoln policeman who apparently gave chase to the shooter and was wrecked and then shot to death following the accident. She began to read off the names and titles of the officials they were to get in touch with when they were on the ground and the names of the news personnel from Longview and Shreveport TV stations with whom they would be syncing their broadcast to satellite. " You need to get to a Father Mise. Catholic priest who was there during the shooting. Eye witness and very credible from what we hear. Tell your pilot you have permission to land your helicopter on the high school football field. It is south of the mall and we'll have a Longview news van there to assist you with equipment and transportation. Tell your pilot, after he lets you off to go to the East Texas Regional Airport outside of Longview and wait there. Don't have the name of the FBO for you yet. But other networks are flying folks in and they want to keep the football field open for others to land. Looks like we're first, so let's get on it."

Both Bob and Bruce looked at each other and nodded. They thought in unison, but Bruce voiced it aloud, "At least we don't have to jump into a fire fight," He knew how much Bob hated this type of air travel and reminded him of their deployment when embedded with troops in Afghanistan.

"The guy is still on the loose. Don't be too sure there won't be a fire fight."

15

Father Mise
(in a daze)

He made his way through the carnage. It appeared that a war had been waged in the mall. Civilians lay sprawled out on the floor and plastered against the walls, blood and body remains splattered about like a giant blender had been turned loose in the food court.

He stopped and knelt beside each victim, not knowing their religion or creed, but with all the faith he could muster, he prayed over each corpse. There were people weeping and officers trying to interview witnesses, who were still in a state of shock, as the pastor himself was.

Father Mise took special care praying over the small children, torn to ribbons by the penetrating bullets that ripped their soft flesh away from tender, young bones. Beyond the gathering of the preschoolers, were the bodies of three elderly women clutching each other against a wall. Two were still hanging on, bandaged by the triage of the EMT's who were busy assisting others in need. The two elderly women still alive were crying over the body of their friend, who was draped across their laps.

Father Mise arose and went back to the opening of the food court and found Cynthia's bullet riddled body and he knelt and wept. He openly cried, as he thought of her on the stage taking on the Longview Boys Math Club and showing them her mental might. He thought of her getting her own horse and learning to ride and show in equestrian events around the state. He cried and began to pray and as he did a shadow fell across him. Looking up he saw the figure of a plain clothed policeman starting to kneel beside him.

"Know her father?" He asked.

Mise nodded. "She was a parishioner. A good girl. Smart as a whip. And very kind. That's her mother, there." He said as he nodded toward Rosa's body. "Cynthia and Rosa Parker."

"We're going to have to ask you to clear the area. This is a crime scene now and we'll need to get in here and investigate with as little disturbance as possible."

"I saw him."

"Who?"

"The young man with the guns."

The cop pulled a small notebook from his breast pocket and detached the pen that was with it. "Give me details."

"He looked right at me. I was coming down the mall from over there." Father Mise nodded toward the path he had taken into the food court from the shoe store. "He stared right at me and kept going."

"White?"

"Yes about sixteen or seventeen. Caucasian. I've told the other officer all of this."

"Tell me again."

16

Earl Stevens

Two mechanics aligned the jet engine's frame with the bracket bolts that would secure it to the pylon on the side of the Lear Jet's body: one driving a forklift holding the engine, the other giving precise hand signals as to where to place the powerful engine; the team worked in harmony, a precision dance of brute force and minute moves. Slowly the third member of the crew threaded the bolts and began to tighten the placement of the engine to its holding. Next a series of hoses and pipes were attached to the engine. It was slow, precise work. It had to be done just so. People's lives depended upon it.

A man came out of the hangar's office and walked toward the workers. "You guys hear about the shooting?"

They all looked up and in unison said 'no'.

"Some guy shot a bunch of folks over at the mall in Lincoln."

"Damn, " said Earl Stevens, "…when is this shit going to end?"

"When we give everybody a gun," said Wallace Meter, who was standing against the forklift that remained stationary under the Lear's replacement engine.

"Naw, I don't think that's the answer. Too many nuts will have guns then," said Earl.

"Like they don't already…" said Wallace.

At just that moment, Hal Kingsly and Tommy Rupert, two of the highest paid trial lawyers in the United States came into the shop. Marshall was a mecca for personal injury lawyers. And the really good ones, like Kingsly and Rupert, lived quite well off their ventures. "Our bird about ready?" asked Kingsly in his deep baritone voice, a voice that had swayed juries all over the South in litigations on chemical fires, big rig wrecks, and most recently on tobacco and opioid cases.

"You bet,' said the manager. "Earl, let's roll it out for these guys."

At that moment two aviators dressed in black pilot uniforms appeared and entered the circle of men. "Shooting over in Lincoln this morning. A bunch of folks killed," said one of the pilots.

Earl looked back as he walked toward the diesel tug that would connect to the front wheel of the King Air he was about to pull out and into the afternoon sun. It was fueled and inspected and ready to go. "How many?" He called out.

"Don't know, but the radio said a bunch of the victims were school kids."

Everyone shook their heads.

"There was a day when Tommy and I would be racing down there to find us a client or two. I'm glad those days are behind me. Gruesome stuff." Said Kingsley.

"To be sure," said Tommy.

When the King Air was situated on the ramp outside the giant hangar, untethered from the tug, the two pilots boarded followed by the lawyers. The door closed behind them and after a few minutes the props began to spin under the power of the turbojet engines.

Earl gave them the thumbs up and the plane, under the direction of ground control, began to roll toward the far runway and then into the air to parts unknown.

Earl returned to the immaculate shop with its polished concrete floors, as everyone was about to take a break for lunch. He moved into the office and sat in front of the television set on the edge of the pilot's lounge, to catch the latest news of the shooting just down the road.

Just before 1:30, as he was rising to return to the shop, two uniformed policeman entered the office.

"Help you?" He asked.

"Looking for Earl Stevens."

"You got him." He said and extended his hand.

The officer quickly shook it then asked, "Do you know where your son Matt is?"

Earl shook his head.

"Have you talked with him today?" asked the other officer.

"No. What's this about?"

"He has a Ford Mustang. Blue. Texas Tag A7X15?"

"Yeah I guess. Not real sure about the plate number. Has he been in an accident?" Earl was now starting to worry for the safety of his son.

"Mr. Stevens, we believe your son's car may have been used in a get a way from Lincoln Mall. A shooting occurred there and we are looking for Matt."

"Did you try the high school?"

"Yes. He hasn't been to any of his classes today."

Earl's head swam. "Did you try him on his cell?"

"It just rings and rings then goes to voicemail."

Earl pulled his own cell phone out of his pocket and dialed Matt's number. It rang six or seven times then finally he heard. "Matt here. I'm away from the phone. Leave me a message at the beep."

"Same thing we got. Any idea where he is?"

Earl assured him he did not.

"Could he have gone to your house?"

"Not that I know about, but from time to time he does go there. Just to get away and cool his heels. You know how teenage boys can get."

One of the cops stepped outside and radioed the Marshall police and told them to check out Stevens house off of 43. "Kid might be there. Dad says he goes there from time to time."

'Ten four, we'll send a unit over there."

"Don't bother. We're around the corner. James and I will cover it. We're at the airport talking with the father now."

After they discussed his son with Earl, the two policemen left. They immediately drove towards Earl's house, when the sheriff's radio called them.

"Marshall 22, This is Sherriff base."

"This is Marshall 22. Go ahead."

"We had a car up at the dad's house early in the day…about ten or so… Frank Rawlings…said he saw the Stevens kid at that time. Dressed in all black. Said he was running an errand for his dad. Nothing out of the ordinary. Said he had a day off from school. Something about a teacher's training day."

"That's a lie. We'd better go to the house."

"Take the father with you."

"Ten four."

The two patrolmen circled back to the airport and retraced their steps into the hanger. They explained the latest information they had received and Earl agreed to go with them to his house. He grabbed a light jacket and the three started out the door.

"Take your own car. We'll follow you," said the elder policeman.

He nodded and got into a Chevy truck and they drove off.

Five minutes later they were pulling up to the house, the soft carpet of pine needles silently and softly welcoming them.

After inspecting the outside of the house, Earl said he couldn't see anything missing. The three went inside the house, the officers had their weapons drawn just in case. Earl thought that was totally unnecessary.

The first thing he noticed was a cereal bowl and spoon had been left in the sink. "He's been here. Or somebody has. I didn't eat breakfast this morning. We had a jet to overhaul and I didn't have time. That bowl has been used since I was here."

"Sherriff deputy said he saw Matt come from the barn."

"It's a shed. Not a barn. Let's go look." Earl was beginning to be a bit nervous. What had Matt done? What had he gotten himself into this time?

Earl missed the length of rope that had been taken, but once back in the house he did not miss the guns and the ammunition that were gone from his safe.

An APB was put out immediately for Matthew Stevens, sixteen… from Lincoln, Texas…Driving a blue Ford Mustang hatchback…Texas license plate A7X15. Considered armed and dangerous.

17

Julian Meadow

He was in the mall picking up a present for his niece who was turning twelve. He was, after all, the favorite uncle. Julian had already been up early covering a story. He was the chief photographic stringer for the Dallas, Houston and San Antonio newspapers in the East Texas region. After school at Grambling University, where he majored in business, he decided that chasing the almighty dollar by working for the man was not what he was about. He wanted more freedom out of life. So he turned his hobby of photography into a profession. And he was good at it.

Already that morning he had covered a plant fire at Patriot Farms processing plant in Lincoln. When he got there most of the activity was over, so he shot a couple of cover shots of fire engines at the scene and first responders wrapping hoses up and loading back onto their bright red rigs, then he radioed his coverage into a dispatcher who said to send the shots in and he would disseminate them. "Never know when they'll need a shot to cover a hole in the news," said his dispatcher.

He drove to the mall and locked his camera equipment away in the trunk and then set off for the south entrance of Lincoln Mall – to

Kavenders, where he hoped to find something that a twelve-year old girl would just love. After all, he reminded himself. He was the favorite uncle.

He no sooner entered the store then he heard the report; one explosion right after another, echoing loudly coming from the store's entrance into the mall. Pop. Pop. Pop. Pop. Immediately Julian knew what it was.

Gunfire.

He had lived with that sound growing up in the fifth ward of Houston, an area of that city notorious for gun violence and death. He had three buddies gunned down in a blaze of bullets during a robbery attempt at a convenience store just before high school graduation. It left a lasting impression on him. And a fear of guns.

Julian turned and started ushering people out the door towards the waiting parking lot. Some were screaming. Others were frantically pushing. He tried to calm the melee. He also moved onto the warm asphalt lot and opened the trunk of his car. He removed his camera and a lanyard with a yellow tag attached, which simply read PRESS. He placed the lanyard over his head and around his neck. He also brought the Nikon camera strap around his neck and then began to sprint back into the department store, knowing the whole time the risk he was taking.

Like a salmon swimming upstream during spawning season, he fought the crowds of shoppers flowing out the doors to escape the dangers inside. Kavender's was mostly empty now. A few managers hung back, checking dressing areas and restrooms. But soon, they too were gone. He eased out of the store and into the mall. At the center of the giant Y, he could see a haze of blue dust filtered in the air coming from the food court. He moved toward it. There were no more sounds of shooting.

Simply screams and sobbing. Instinctively he pulled the Nikon to his eye and began to document the horrors that lay in front of him. A Catholic priest was moving from body to body, as others emerged from hiding spots in the fast food court – coming from the small restaurant kitchens and freezers, where they had sought refuge. The priest looked up at him, fearfully at first, as if Julian might be a shooter, then seeing his PRESS tag relaxed and went back to his prayers.

Julian moved carefully amidst the carnage and came upon two elderly ladies, covered in blood who clutched to the limp body of their friend. An EMT approached them and knelt.

Julian recorded the moment.

He turned as a young man and a small girl emerged from a refrigerator compartment in the back of the ice cream store. Again his lens capturing the instant they saw the horrors before them.

Police were starting to flow in. A commander was issuing orders. He saw Julian and recognized him from previous encounters. "How many?" Julian asked.

The cop shrugged. "Just got here. Your math is as good as mine."

"No. How many shooters?"

"One, we think."

Julian walked toward the east entrance of the mall and came upon a downed Texas Ranger with a shiny silver pistol still in his hand. His Nikon captured the moment. Later, Julian would win a Pulitzer Prize for the photograph.

Further toward the door was a man with a cell phone in his hand, he had collapsed against the wall and bled out.

Julian returned to the food court, which was now being taped off by police. It was a crime scene and had to be protected. He moved up the staircase that ascended beside the escalator to an overlook and began to shoot down into the food court. The entire eating area was strewn with bodies. Blood was everywhere. Bullets had torn gaping holes in the food vendor's facades, as well as ripped apart large chunks of the mall's walls. He followed though his eyepiece the movement of the Catholic priest as he went from body to body, kneeling beside each and saying a prayer. He found himself photographing each stop the priest made.

Julian's cell phone went off. "Jules, get to Lincoln Mall. There's been a mass shooting," it was his dispatcher, who was headquartered out of Tyler.

"I'm there already. I was here while the shooting was still an active scene."

"Get me a lot of coverage. This is huge."

"Will do." Julian hung up, but strangely didn't feel like interloping into the scene with his camera any more. It was too sad. To horrific. He simply bowed his head and let a tear fall from his eye.

His last photo of the day were two small school children a young black girl and small white boy, no more then four or five years old, covered in blood– survivors of the massacre, exiting the mall with a policeman.

They were holding hands.

18

The Manhunt

The police and the sheriff's office began the manhunt. Three counties were involved. Hundreds of uniformed officers and plain-clothes policemen were summoned to take part in the passive search. They assumed a lone shooter, since nobody had identified more than one male suspect. They knew the get-away car from the Bluebonnet Café shooting matched the description of the car leaving the mall. A blue Mustang. It was heading west along Interstate 20.

Helicopters were dispatched to survey a vast area of networking highways and farm roads. Roadblocks were set up along major arteries, snarling traffic between Longview and Tyler.

They were looking for a sixteen year old, white male, Matt Stevens; considered to be armed and very dangerous. Might be high on drugs. Use caution. But get him in to custody ASAP. The orders were clear. This guy had to be brought down.

Officers on the lake began to motor along the jagged shoreline looking for a car matching the description of the blue Mustang. From overhead the pilots looked down also searching for the car.

On foot and in patrol cars, the police fanned out in an area that was as big as Rhode Island. "This guy could be anywhere," said one highway patrolman.

Then came the news on the radio that made the manhunt even more personal. Officer down.

Back at the mall, Father Mise finished his interview with detectives and his information was radioed to the search parties out looking for Matt Stevens. Father Mise asked if he might return inside the mall to the food court and finish administering final rites; the detective, a Baptist, shrugged, "Sure. But for God's sake don't touch anything."

Father Mise re-entered the food court and looked up at the landing on the staircase and saw a photographer from the news agencies watching the whole thing. Their eyes connected and Father Mise nodded at the young black man. They had met once before, but the priest could not, at the time, remember when and where it was. For now, he had to turn his attention to the dead and giving them a peaceful send off to whatever was on the other side.

By the time he ventured back outside, the sun was setting and Father Mise found a policeman and asked if the shooter had been caught yet?

"Not yet. Big dragnet out looking for him. We'll get the bastard. Sorry Father."

"That's okay. I agree with you after seeing all this carnage."

"Father, there's a young college by from the ice cream shop over at the command center. He's pretty shaken, You mind sitting with him and helping him a bit?"

"I'd be glad to, Officer…"

"Holloway. Thank you Father." The cop walked back into the mall and Father Mise approached the command center and found the young ice cream clerk and sat next to him.

Mise didn't say anything for a time, but soon he spoke, "When I waved for you to get back into the freezer I didn't know who was still there and not knowing what was happening. I hope it wasn't too cold."

"No. Funny thing is that our freezers were out. It was not cold at all." And as he said this, father Mise noticed the young man was shaking like a freezing person. He took off his blood-splattered coat and draped it around the young man's shoulders and the young man placed his head onto Father's Mise's chest and began to weep.

The priest firmly hugged the young man and allowed the tears to flow in silence. Sometimes words are not needed. Just time and a gentle hug. That is what the Mother Superior in Morelia had taught him during triage training in Mexico. "Sometimes just let them know you are there and you care about them…and you can do it with a hug." In Mexico the instructions had been given him to help overcome his deficiency in language. At Lincoln Mall it was applied to the young man to simply let him know he was not alone in the suffering he was feeling.

19

The last to die.

Matt drove to Park Road and then past the county park at the top of a tall hill overlooking the giant body of water. Down an unnamed asphalt street until he got to Clayton Blvd. It had been named after Dixie Clayton a famous stock car racer from the area.

He soon found the red brick house with the garages in back. Sammy Hall's place. Sammy wouldn't be home. He worked the morning shift at the refinery that was over twenty miles away. So Matt stopped the car, making sure it was hidden from the street, opened the garage door and helped himself to Sammy's four-wheeler. But before he did, Matt entered the house and grabbed some chips and another can of soda. He searched the pantry for something else to eat, but when he found nothing that interested him, he started to leave. Then he went to the freezer. There he found a microwavable pizza.

He cooked the pizza, ate it and washed it down with a beer from the refrigerator in the garage.

He loaded the guns onto the four-wheeler and then drove off to the end of Clayton Boulevard to where the woods began, separating the home sites from the rugged cliffs of the eastern shore of the lake.

He knew the area well. Once off the asphalt street, he drove the four-wheeler deeper and deeper into the forest until finally it could go no further in the dense woods with its impassable underbrush.

He got out, grabbing the guns and walked a few more minutes until he struggled to the edge of a giant cliff overlooking the lake. He sat on a rock and enjoyed the view. He lit the cigarette that was in his mouth and inhaled. It felt good. He felt good. His body was calming down now. He was coming off the highest high he had ever experienced.

His head felt light and was spinning. Weed or pills had never made him feel this good.

This excited him.

This was powerful.

After a few minutes he found a soft patch of grass and pine needles and lay down. Sleep would feel good.

When he awoke, the afternoon light was beginning to fade. The sun was setting over the western edge of the lake and the fall air had a slight chill to it. It felt nice – an escape from the end of Summer's last attempt to bake everything below it alive. He sat up and toyed with the pistol. It felt strangely heavy in his thin hand, something he had not noticed before.

"You will never feel that kind of rush again.

"I know.

"You will never get that kind of high – ever again.

"I know. I know.

"You were the king, man. You were the fucking bomb. You did it. And now it is over. And that high is gone. You will never feel that good ever again.

"I know. I know." The conversation with himself ended. It was quiet again.

Matt raised the gun to his mouth and pulled the trigger.

The report echoed across the lake and reverberated off the rock cliff upon which he now lay quite still.

20

Officer Hampton and Captain Morris Littleton

A truck driver came upon the wrecked patrol car. It's carcass crushed on all sides. He stopped his long rig, climbed down from the cab and approached the smoldering twisted steel wreckage. It wasn't the first car accident scene he had driven upon in his career. He knew that there would more than likely be carnage inside the car. Inside, he saw a body. It was a wounded patrolman. He ran back to his truck, grabbed a fire extinguisher and doused the flames that had sprung up from a leak at the engine compartment.

He tried to free the officer from his entangled seat belt, but could not get to the release button. Officer Hampton was hanging virtually upside down and the angle to reach any controls on the safety harness was next to impossible. He pulled a pocketknife from his pants and began to saw at the broad belt. It took him forever to cut through the safety material. He felt for a pulse and there was a faint tick in the man's neck vein. Immediately he got on his cell phone and called 911. He gave the operator the vitals and went back to work on the downed officer. He was scared to move him in case it would do any more damage to him. At that time, Officer Hampton was covered in so much blood and the windshield was blown out, that the truck driver didn't realize it was from a shooting. He thought it was the result of the massive rollover.

Within minutes Texas DPS cars rolled up to the scene and state troopers went to work trying to free Hampton from his wreck. By this time it was too late to save his life. He was dead.

He finally got his rest.

A state trooper radioed in the report. Only then did the truck driver learn of the shootings at the mall, at the Bluebonnet and now here on the highway.

"Blue Mustang Hatchback, you say?"

"Yes. We've got an APB out for the driver."

"Young white kid. Sixteen or seventeen?"

"Yes."

"He pulled in front of me and crossed over to Park Road. Not more than ten…fifteen minutes ago. He was flying. I thought he was going to roll that Mustang he took the turn so fast."

The state trooper thanked the truck driver for the details and for his attempted assistance with officer Hampton. He then radioed in that the shooter was more than likely headed for Grand Lake.

*   *   *   *

"Roger, command center. Blue Ford Mustang. I may have spotted it. It is behind a house in The Cliffs Estate neighborhood…east side of Grand Lake…on Clayton drive. Pretty near the woods."

"Roger, Morris. Will send back up. How long can you stay overhead?"

"I'm good. I'm full…plus reserve."

"Remain above location. But be careful. Shooter has some high-powered guns."

"Roger that. I'll go up a few thousand feet."

Morris Littleton circled the Bell Jet Ranger around the site at an altitude he felt safe and out of the range of the shooter, if there was an attempt to bring the bird down. As he circled, he made wider and wider loops searching for signs of someone who might have tried to escape on foot. The late afternoon was fading fast.

A Lincoln police patrol car pulled into the driveway. Two heavily armed officers in SWAT fatigues got out and approached the car. Carefully they looked inside. "Garage door closest to street is open."

"Who's house is it?" asked the other cop.

"Base, we're at 1558 Clayton. Right before the cul d' sac. Just to the south of the woods."

Squawk. "Give me a second." There was a pause while the police staff at the station looked on a plat map for the name of the owner of the address. "House is registered in the name of Sammy Hall. Works at the refinery."

"Give him a call and put him on our line."

"Stand by."

The copter pilot, Littleton, radioed, "I'm going to take a run up and down the lake shore and along the cliffs. I'll get back to you in five."

"Ten four, bird." The two officers carefully circled behind the Mustang, using it as a bullet shield in case the shooter was inside waiting for them. They didn't want to get caught in an ambush.

Their radio crackled and a voice came on. "This is Sammy Hall."

"Mr. Hall, I'm officer Draper of the Lincoln Police Department. We are at your house on Clayton Drive. There may have been a break in here."

"A break in?"

"Yes sir. The garage door closest to the street, on the right hand edge of your house, by the back drive…it is standing open."

"That's where I keep my four-wheeler."

"Does anyone else live there with you?"

"Yes. My wife. But she is in Santa Fe on business."

"Does anyone else have access to your house. A key or a pass?"

"No. No one...Wait. Yes. My hunting buddy, Matt Stevens. He has a pass. He uses the four-wheeler from time to time."

"There's a blue Mustang hatchback parked in your back drive..."

"That's Matt's."

"Mr. Hall, how much longer before your shift is over?"

"About an hour. I had to double-up and work the afternoon here because a woman didn't show up for her shift."

"Okay, sir, I do not want you coming home. Instead, go to the city hall in Lincoln...to the police station and we'll check with you there. There may be a crime going on here and it may be part of a crime scene. Understand?"

"Yes. I'll go straight to the police station. What's going on?"

"You haven't heard?"

"About?"

"There's been a mass shooting at the mall. We think this Mustang is tied up in it..."

"Jesus. Not Matt. Please, tell me it's not Matt."

"You know him well?"

"Since his mother and father divorced, I've kind been like family to him. Like a big brother."

"Has he been angry or moody recently?" Asked the cop.

"All the time. He is angry about something all the time."

"Mr. Hall, we have to go now, but please, remember and go to the police station. You can be a big help to us there."

With that, their conversation was drowned out by the roar of a low flying copter that circled and began to rise again. "Base we need back-up. Suspect's name is Matt Stevens."

Morris Littleton made another giant sweep of the area. And soon ventured out over the large body of the lake, returning to get a good look at the shore line with its steep, rocky cliffs. He could see nothing moving and no one camped out. He repeated the procedure several times, using his bright sun lamps, as well as infrared displays, to dig deep into the shadows of the pines, before returning to the house with the patrol car parked outside, now with three other police vehicles assisting it. "Bird here, I see nothing along the eastern shore. The cliffs look clear."

"Check again. We're missing a four-wheeler. It is camo in color, so it may be hard to find. You have a heat-seeking camera on board?" asked one of the state troopers now joining in the search of the house.

"Ten four. Will do." With that, Littleton turned on a device that allowed his camera to find infrared patterns and show them on a screen. He again began his wide-arcing circle around the property.

It took the copter and its experienced pilot five minutes to locate the four-wheeler via the infrared equipment. "Bird to base. Found the four-wheeler."

The police at the house immediately stopped their search to listen to Littleton. "It's about a half mile from you to the north. In dense woods. Leads to an overlook that has pine trees all about. I can't see anything on my scope in the clearing. Shooter may have moved further into the woods for hiding.

The five officers began to fan out from the house. Soon two more patrol cars – from the county sheriff's squad– arrived with two officers apiece. Now all nine policemen began to comb the woods surrounding the house. The going became harder as the denseness of the undergrowth increased the deeper into the woods they pushed. They had to go slowly, knowing that the shooter was heavily armed and had shown he would shoot at anything, including policemen and children.

At a slight rise the copter flew over them and radioed that they were less than a hundred yards from the four-wheeler. Slowly they crept to it and found it still warm– not hot– but warm.

"We need canine back-up," radioed one of the county deputies.

"Ten four. Will send them to you."

"I'll go and meet the dog boys," said a deputy whose name was Patrick. He slowly worked his way back from where they had just come and out into view at the end of the street.

The light was starting to fade in the denseness of the woods. "We need to work fast. He'll have the upper hand in the dark," said one of the state troopers. The copter made another pass over them and radioed that there was nothing along the lake to their north, but he could not penetrate a signal into the woods and underbrush to their west. "Too much interference. Might look that way. It would be a good hiding spot for him…Wait. Wait…I see him. I've got the shooter spotted."

The copter circled to their west. They could hear its giant blade whipping in the air. "He's below you. To your west."

All the officers immediately turned direction and started down hill toward Grand Lake's steep edge. They knew it was treacherous going with the cliffs ahead. From behind them they could hear the canine patrol arriving. The dogs were approaching quickly with their handlers calling out from behind them.

Soon the dogs came to the patrolmen and sniffed around then moved past the officers, deeper and deeper into the undergrowth and toward the lake.

One of the county deputies arrived with a towel in his hands. "It was in is car, we gave the dogs his scent from this. They'll find him if he's still out there."

The copter again made a low pass and then swooped out over the lake; turned and dove back toward the search party that was again starting to fan out in a wide pattern.

Suddenly the pitch and cadence of the hound's barking changed. "They found something," said the deputy who seemed to know the animals quite well. Let's go this way. He led them on a more southerly route. "There's a clearing down on the cliffs this way. We used to come out here with girls when I was in high school. The lake has a cove there and is heavily wooded. Good protection if you're hiding from something or someone."

The searchers moved carefully. Everyone expected the suspect would start shooting the dogs at any moment. They listened carefully as they approached the shoreline as silently as possible. The dogs continued their bay until finally the troop was upon them and they saw the grizzly sight of the suicide.

"We've got Stevens. He's dead. Self-inflicted shots."

*   *   *   *

Eleven miles away, the police chief of Lincoln along with the county sheriff, Cook set up a make-shift news area and held the first of many press conferences.

"This evening on the edge of Grand Lake officers from the Lincoln township police, the DPS and county deputies found the shooter who had apparently committed suicide. His name is being withheld until notification of next of kin. The manhunt for the shooter is officially over." Cook spoke rather solemnly.

Bob McAdoo was the first to ask a question.

"Bob MacAdoo, NBC News. Do you believe this shooter acted alone?"

"We do."

"And do you know how many victims there are in this shooting?"

"At this time our numbers show there are eighteen inside and a truck driver at the café north of town and a patrolman on Park Road who encountered the shooter shortly after the killing spree took place here."

As the sheriff and police chief fielded questions the copter flown by Morris Littleton, passed overhead on its way to the landing pad just north of city hall. Darkness was draping quickly over the scene, only it would be hard to tell, with as many police and news unit lights illuminating the nearly empty mall. The only thing left inside were police investigators from numerous crime labs under the direction of the county corner Dr. Phillip Smith, the F.B.I. and twenty dead bodies. The sheriff had failed to include a woman found next to her car outside the community center who had died of an apparent heart attack.

Even as the day slowly came to an end, the work for law enforcement officers was really just beginning. The hard part of the job. The notifying of next-of-kin.

21

A few questions. Please?

Father Mise received a call on his smart phone and was informed that the authorities were heading to the Parker residence to notify the family of Rosa and Cynthia's deaths. The church secretary, who was working late that day, took the call from the DPS dispatcher who thought it would be a good idea for Father Mise to be there with the family.

Mise agreed. He headed for his car in the parking lot, which was bathed in the floodlights of police units and EMS vehicles. The press was adding candlepower to scene as well. It was hard to tell that nighttime had fallen and that the sun was long gone from the early autumn night sky.

From the curtain of bright white lights, stepped Bob McAdoo, "Father a quick word…"

"I'm on my way to comfort a grieving family."

"Just a few questions…please."

"Very well," said Mise. He was disturbed to have been interrupted in carrying out his mission.

"Bob McAdoo, NBC News."

"Yes Bob…I recognized you…"

"I'm told that you saw the killer. Face-to-face?"

"Yes. Kind of. I mean I was coming down the hallway going toward the food court and he was exiting the food court heading for the mall's doors. We made eye contact. Just for an instant."

"What made you head to the food court?"

"I heard the shooting. I thought I might help."

"How did you know it was shooting?"

"I have heard gun fire like that before. In Mexico. Drug gang wars."

"Were you…did you not fear for your own life?"

"To tell you the truth it happened all so fast, I didn't think about me. I thought about the others. Those who were shot and who were dying…who were hurting."

"Did the shooter say anything to you?"

Mise shook his head. "No. But we stared at each other for the briefest of moments. Like I am looking at you now. Eye-to-eye. Then he turned and fled outside. He looked very young and there was a wild look to him. Like a caged animal who has just been released from his captivity."

"Did he appear to be on drugs to you?"

"There is no way I could tell that. I mean the entire encounter was a second or two at the most. He was there and I was here and then he was gone."

"And what did you find as you entered the food court?" McAdoo moved the mic closer to the priest as the cameraman pushed in as well.

Father Mise hesitated. He felt a lump rise in his throat and his lips began to quiver. A tear rolled down his cheek. "It was horrible. Bodies everywhere. Some were still alive. Hurt badly and in great pain. Confusion with those who had escaped the shooting but had witnessed the tragedy. I remember the smoke still hung in the air… like a cloud. And then there were those innocent children…" He stopped. His voice trailed off as he looked away from the camera that was pointed into his face. He took a deep breath, returning his stare at the lens. "It was like a war zone. Like a mass killing field. I've never witnessed anything quite as brutal in my life."

"Did you personally know any of the victims?"

He paused. "Yes. Quite a few." Again the tears returned. "I really must go now." Father Mise tried to turn, but Bob McAdoo moved with him and asked one more question.

"Why do suppose the shooter spared you?"

Father Mise stopped, thought for a second and then said, "Perhaps it is God's will. That's all I know. All I could prescribe it to." Again he turned as McAdoo stepped away, this time Mise halted and turned back to the newsman. "I will tell you this Mr. McAdoo, I will make it my life's mission to see that this type of senseless killing comes to a halt in our country. I think that is why God allowed me to live."

"So you are angry?" Asked McAdoo.

"It is part of the grieving process. One of the many steps. And yes. I am moving toward anger at every moment. Even a man of God can be angry. Remember our beloved Lord and Savior, Jesus Christ got angry with the moneychangers and merchants in the temple and drove them out. And his servant – me – I am becoming angry. I have pain. I have sorrow and I have anger. It is part of the process. Thank you, I must now go and comfort a grieving family."

Father Mise exited the lighted area and dissolved into the darkness. This is Bob McAdoo For NBC News in Lincoln, Texas. The mass shooting today has touched many lives in this community and communities around this country."

The TV lights went out the cameraman lowered the camera and Bob McAdoo stood staring into the darkness at the spot where Father Mise had just left.

"I want to get to know him some more," said the newsman.

"He is an interesting fellow…" It was Bruce Tunney, who had walked up and stood next to his friend. "I don't think we've heard the last from the good father, Bob. Not by a long shot.

22

Eduardo Parker

The lights from the rusty, faded red International Harvester tractor were about the only illumination Eduardo had as he worked to repair the water pump at the bottom of the hill behind the house. Its main job was to fill the tank that fed the house and the run off would go into a pond for the livestock. If he couldn't make the pump work, he was going to have to sell livestock. And sell quickly. He was sure of it now. He was also sure others in the county were feeling the same pressures as he was and that would mean more heads of cattle at auction and the prices would be driven lower and lower. It was not a good cycle to be in as a seller.

He ran the numbers over and over in his head as he tightened the bolts securing the last seal on the pump. He hoped that was all it needed. A new pump was not in the budget at that time. He still owed the last payment for his older daughter, Ella's braces – plus he was contemplating buying a pony for Cynthia. But this was not the best time to add to the livestock of the farm. But again, prices might be in his favor. The numbers circulated in his tired brain.

A set of headlights approached him at the bottom of the two-wheel rutted lane, which led between the barn and the first fence line to the nearest pasture. Dickey Lawrence his neighbor got out. "Eduardo, there are policemen at your front door."

"Police?"

"Yes. They want to talk with you. They sounded urgent."

Had something happened at the refinery to Rosa. Was there a problem at school with Cynthia. Had Ella forgotten to pick her up. Where was Ella?

"Come along, Eduardo. They are waiting for you."

He climbed onto the tractor and settled into its scratchy, rusted steel saddle. He cranked the diesel engine and backed it up and turned around as Dickey also began to drive away. At the top of the hill, Dickey paused and said to his older neighbor, "I'll get the gate. You go on."

Eduardo drove the tractor to the edge of the open barn door, which he was using as an equipment shed. It was going to be a fall and winter of rebuilding the fences along the highway and down to William's Creek, so he had his supplies stacked inside the weathered gray barn – out of the elements that would rust and rot them before he could get to use them. Fence wire, wooden slats and creosoted poles stacked six feet on either side of a pocket into which he backed the tractor. He killed the engine as two patrol men, state troopers he noticed, approached.

"Eduardo Parker?"

"He nodded. "Si. That's me. What can I do for you?"

"We need a word. Perhaps inside?" Said the taller of the two officers. He looked a tad older than the other. Both had dour faces.

Eduardo showed them into the house, as a lone light washed the kitchen in a pale yellow glow. They sat at the kitchen table, refusing the offer of a glass of tea from Eduardo, who washed his hands in the sink.

"Mr. Parker, we come here tonight with some tragic news. Both your wife Rosa and your daughter, Cynthia have been killed."

There is a blanket that is draped across scenes such as this –it has been repeated time and time again in living rooms, around kitchen tables, on front porches all across America. Tragic scenes played out almost daily. The blanket seems to suffocate those under it. There is little sound. Nothing under its presence makes any sense. Logic and value and truth and knowledge are all, momentarily suppressed. There is just emptiness. Then the blanket is lifted and emotions flood back in.

"My Rosa? My Cynthia? Dead?"

"Yes sir. There was a shooting at the mall. They were in the line of fire and were victims of the attack."

"Oh my God," He began to weep. His entire body shook. "May I see my girls?"

"Not just yet. The county coroner is preparing a place where families can come and identify their next of kin and see them. A private place. We will send an officer to you to bring you there. We just wanted to notify you. Our deepest sympathies go out to you."

"Have you told Ella?"

"Who is Ella?" asked the younger officer.

"She is my other daughter. She goes to high school…"

"It's been locked down since the shooting. Students are just now being released. The gunman has been located and is dead. So it was safe to release them. She should be home soon."

At just that moment a car pulled up into the driveway. Ella came running into the kitchen "Daddy, did you hear about the shooting?…"

She paused as she entered the room and saw the officers now standing, hats in hand. "Daddy?"

She began to cry before they even told her what had happened. And when the words did reach her ears she wept. Eduardo held her. He thanked the officers and told them to quickly bring an escort so he and Ella could have a final visit with Rosa and Cynthia.

The two state troopers showed themselves out of the house, behind them the sounds of a young woman and her father crying in each other's arms.

It was the hardest part of being a peace officer.

As the officers retreated into the dark of night, Father Mise stepped onto the front porch and knocked gently. Eduardo saw him and motioned him to enter. It had already been a long day for the tired priest, but now the real work began. The work of consoling the living.

23

Todd Dixon

Todd already knew something terrible had happened at the mall. He had heard it over his phone as his wife fell to the floor, gaping holes in her; draining life from her small body. He could hear the screams and Pop. Pop. Pop. Pop. of the rapidly firing rifle in the background as he drove toward the mall from his home at Grand Lake Shores, a comfortable gated community on the western side of the large body of water. He was a good half hour away, but the sounds coming from the phone Alice had dropped as she slumped to her death, were conveying the nightmare as it occurred in the food court. It was as if he was there – or was listening to some sporting event transpiring live on the radio. He began to weep as he yelled his wife's name into the phone over and over, but when no response came he feared the worse.

A train at the Spicewood Hill crossing, delayed his advance. The long coal train came to a halt. It stayed motionless for about five minutes. Todd was going crazy inside his SUV. The car radio was just now starting to warn people of the dangers transpiring at the Lincoln Mall. Shelter in place, the police were saying the shooter is still on the loose. As the last car of the train finally cleared the road, Todd floored his SUV and sped northeast toward the town and toward U.S. 59, which he knew would take him to the mall. Or at least to the proximity of the mall if police had it cordoned off.

At Park Road he turned right, passing 17th Street and headed east away from Grand Lake and into the north side of Lincoln. He was being passed by emergency vehicles racing in the same direction he was traveling. He could still hear people in the distance over his phone crying and yelling. The shooting had mercifully stopped.

As he topped a hill on Park Road, he could see the mall. It stood out, its pearl-white walls gleaming in the brilliant afternoon sun. The solar panels on its saw-toothed roof reflecting sunlight in all directions. Police and fire equipment and ambulances lined the giant shopping center. All entrances to the parking lot were sealed off with police cars. He pulled up to the western most entrance and rolled his window down. "I'm Todd Dixon. I own the Fresh Freeze Ice Cream Parlor. My wife is inside. I fear she has been injured."

"Wait here," said the female officer who immediately got on the radio. In a moment she turned to his window. "Drive toward that yellow fire engine. Over there." She pointed to a group of vehicles all clustered together at the south entrance to the mall. "Behind it we have set up a command center. Ask for Captain Rick Turner." He repeated the captain's name, thanked the officer and drove onto the mall property and aimed at the yellow fire truck, its lights still flashing red. As he approached the hub of activity around the fire truck and a rather large van with the words Crime Scene stenciled on its side, two officers came to him and motioned him to park his car behind the fire equipment. "I'm Todd…"

"We know who you are. Get out. Follow us."

Todd exited his SUV and followed the two officers who were retreating from the protection of the fire truck with great haste. A uniformed man approached Todd and introduced himself. "Mr. Dixon, I'm Captain Turner. Lincoln Police. It is my sad duty to inform you we believe your wife was one of the victims of today's mass shooting. We are still checking out the facility for other suspects and for other victims."

Just at that instant, Todd saw Randy White, his employee, emerge from the door facing the command center, escorted by two guards. He moved toward him. "Randy. Randy." He was almost in tears.

The young college boy saw him and opened his arms to hug him, "She made me and a young school girl hide in the freezer when all the shooting started. I saw her, Mr. Dixon. I am afraid she didn't make it..." His voice fell off and he also began to weep heavily. His entire body shook in Todd's arms. They remained in a tearful embrace for several long moments.

"Mr. Dixon these two officers will escort you inside to identify your wife. We ask you not to touch anything. It is a crime scene and an on-going investigations is taking place." The Captain was directing the officers to take Todd inside the mall, as he showed the young man a place to rest by the command center. A doctor and nurse came to his side to examine him.

As Todd and the two officers entered the darkened mall, a schoolgirl in the hands of a fireman walked out toward the sunlight. Todd looked at her and thought she couldn't have been more than five years old. He had no idea at that time she had escaped death in his broken down ice cream freezer.

The scene in the food court was one of mass destruction. A war zone. A killing field. Bodies were everywhere. Walls of the food shops were ripped apart by powerful bullets. He recognized the young man in the white uniform of the Burger House as Raul. He had interviewed with Todd for a position, but Todd wasn't hiring, so he had sent Raul to speak with Jerry Kiloskous at The Burger House, who hired the young man. Everyday, Todd would see him dressed in his all-white uniform with his red paper hat and he would nod to him as the young man would wave appreciatively, constantly thanking Todd for helping him find a job. Now the same young man lay in a pool of blood. Dead on the mall food court floor Todd's ice cream melting around him.

The officers continued to escort Todd toward the ice cream parlor. There he found the freezer door open and he closed it out of habit and saw that the temperature was at fifty degrees. The warmest he had ever seen it get. Then he looked to his right, behind a concrete pillar Alice lay crumpled on the floor, a cell phone at her feet. He closed his eyes and began to feel faint. Tears flowed from his eyes as he reached for her, but the patrolmen stopped him. "Crime scene, Mr. Dixon You can't touch her. Not yet."

"That's Alice. My wife."

"Thank you for ID-ing her for us, but now we have to escort you back out. It's the law, sir. I'm terribly sorry for your loss and for you having to see this carnage. But…"

Todd stood and cut the officer off. "Do you know who did this?"

"Not yet, sir. We have a manhunt out looking for the shooter."

Then Todd did something strange. He would recall later he had no idea why he did it, but he took the wall phone off its cradle and called ETEX Refrigeration and told them not to come today. There had been a shooting and he was afraid his store was going to be closed for some time." As he stepped out into the food court, carefully making is way around fallen bodies, he spotted Jerry Kiloskous. He went to him and the two men hugged.

"I'll get the rest of your ice cream moved over…"

"Oh don't bother, Jerry. Don't bother. For god's sake…go home…"

"But it will melt."

"I don't care," said Todd. "I really, truly don't care anymore."

24

Jane Reynolds

As soon as she came to the door and saw two detectives from the Longview Police department on her porch, she knew that the news she was hearing from the radio was not good.

"Mrs. Reynolds?"

"Yes."

"Is your husband Perry Reynolds. Patriot Farms...Perry Reynolds?"

"Yes. Why?"

"May we come in, Mrs. Reynolds," asked the detective in the kindest, softest voice he could muster.

She opened the screen door and showed the two men in. They instinctively looked around and found seats on two overstuffed chairs as Mrs. Reynolds sat on the edge of a rose-colored sofa.

"Ma'am I'm afraid we have some sad news for you. Your husband, Perry is one of the victims of the shooting at Lincoln Mall. We identified him from his Texas driver's license and he had a Patriot Farms business card in his wallet, as well."

She sat there facing the two seasoned policemen, her bottom lip beginning to quiver. A tear rolled down her left cheek then one on the right side found its way to her lap, as well. Before long there was an entire river of tears gushing forth as she just sat there and cried, not saying a word.

One of the detectives produced a clean handkerchief and offered it to her, but she declined. From where, neither detective later could recall, she produced her own tissue. She looked at them and said, "I bet he was at the store buying me an anniversary present. He always waits to the last minute."

"Yes. Well, ma'am, your children are more than likely in lock down at their school. All the area schools are sealed off until the suspect or suspects are found. There is a number you can call to get a message into them." He handed her a card with a hand-written phone number on it. "Give it a call, and operator will take their names and relay the message. When the time is right and the lock down is lifted, you'll be able to go and get them."

She wept hard. Her thin body shook like a rag doll being shaken. She buried her face into her hands and wept even harder. The policemen stood and excused themselves. They had three more of these calls to conduct. "If you need us for anything, my information is on the back of that card," said the shorter man.

They closed the door behind them as they retreated back to their unmarked car and drove off. The next call would be to the home of Officer Darrell Hampton. One of their own. Tragically lost in the line of duty.

25

Robert and Pella Williams

The Saint Francis County sheriff, Benny Lloyd drove west out of Forrest City, Arkansas into a small community called Palestine. There he found the home of Robert and Pella Williams. It was a plain white board house: one story and no paved driveway. It was in need of a grass cutting; the old tree in the shaggy front yard could well use a pair of sheers itself.

He stopped the squad car in front of the house and started up the sidewalk with grass growing between its concrete squares. There were at least five other houses in the neighborhood that looked exactly the same, only this house was in need of more care.

He knocked on the door. An elderly black man, with a deeply wrinkled face appeared on the other side of the screen. He looked past Lloyd at the squad car then spoke, "You tell Wallace we done paid our rent. Social Security come last week and we sent him his money order jest like he axed us to."

"Mr. Williams?"

"Dat's a me."

"You have a wife named Pella?"

"What's she gone and done now?"

"Do you have a wife by that name?"

"I do." He turned his head into the room and yelled, "Pella get over here. De police come fo you."

"No sir. I'm not here about you or your wife. I'm here with news about your daughter. You have a daughter named July?" He pronounced it like the month and Pella, who had joined her husband at the door, corrected the sheriff.

It's spelt dat way cause she were born in July, but we call her Julie."

"I see. Might I come in?" The sheriff asked removing his Smoky the Bear park ranger hat.

Williams opened the door and the sheriff entered the small house, which was little more than a run down three-room cottage.

"What kinda news you got 'bout my July?" asked Pella.

"She, I'm afraid to tell you… she is a victim in a mall shooting in Texas. It happened right at lunchtime this morning. Her identification had a card in it with your name and address listed as next of kin. It was at a mall in a city called Lincoln. Its all over the news right now."

The old Black man got up off the sofa with his wife and turned on the small black and white TV and there, on the screen, was a man that the title said was Royce Hursh. NBC News.

"So far authorities have not been able to reach all of the next of kin, but it is believed that as many as nineteen souls were lost today at the Lincoln Mall in Lincoln Texas…as well as a patrolman giving chase to the shooter as he attempted to escape. Included in the dead are six preschoolers and their three adult chaperones…all on a field trip. One of the classmates was rescued by a young man who hid her and himself in the freezer of his ice cream parlor. From Lincoln here is Bob MacAdoo…Bob…"

"Royce, the night's darkness is starting to descend upon this community, even though the darkness of this horrible event has preceded it by several hours. As many as twenty are feared dead but two who survived it are with me now. Randy White and you are young lady…" He placed a microphone in front of a little girl who said her name was Terry Brooks. "Tell us Randy, what you saw inside today."

"I was getting ready for the lunch traffic. Getting our freezer stock moved out to the counters, when suddenly I heard shooting."

"How many shooters, Randy?"

"I only saw one. A guy dressed in all black. He had an automatic rifle and was firing at everyone. Not randomly, but aiming at people as if he wanted to kill them. I grabbed that young girl and we hid inside the freezer until the shooting had stopped."

"Fast thinking there, Randy." McAdoo turned back to the camera. "Police have confirmed that the gunman has been found. A victim of a self-inflicted gunshot. His name has not yet been released awaiting notification of his next of kin, but it is believed to be the work of a juvenile from the local town."

The camera panned the scene, which had been cleaned up by police making it at least slightly more acceptable to the viewing public. "From Lincoln, Texas for NBC News, I'm Bob McAdoo."

"Thank you, Bob. Another gruesome shooting. That's the twenty-first mass shooting in the country so far this year. More than 300 lives so far have been lost to gun violence this year…and that is in mass shootings alone. Individual deaths or incidents involving less than three, are not included in those numbers…and neither are suicides or accidental shootings.

"After the break we're going to the Hill and to The White House for reactions from congressional leaders and from the President about today's massacre."

The screen faded from the NBC newsroom to a countryside where a woman on a bike and a kid with a kite were playing outside because of their allergy medicine.

Mr. Williams turned off the set. "Dat where it happened?"

The sheriff nodded.

"Dey done kilt my baby. Kilt her dead," said Pella, as she began to weep. It had been ten years since they had seen their daughter. And three since they had heard from her. She still lived in fear of the man named Bell, from Forrest City who might come after her.

"You gonna tell that Bell fellah she dead?" asked Robert.

"Got to. By law. He's still her husband. On record anyway. I understand they have been separated a long time."

"Close to twenty years."

"Even so, I gotta go find him and tell him." The sheriff stood to leave and surveyed the front yard. "Mind if I send some kids from my church by to mow your yard this weekend?"

They both said it would be good and thanked him for coming. They moved to hold each other on the sofa as the officer left. The little house seemed a lot sadder than when he arrived, and that was saying a lot.

26

Earl Stevens

The police showed up at his house at seven, told him the news that his son was dead and was believed to have been the lone shooter at the mall. They needed to search his house, since it was the next-to-last known whereabouts of Matt before the shooting and before he took his own life.

Earl sat on the bed of his pick-up truck and waited while the sheriff's officers flowed through his home, turning it inside and out. He described, on three occasions to three separate officers, the types of weapons missing from his home.

On the fourth time, he told the plain clothes cop to go fuck himself. "Get the notes from the other three guys I told that very same thing to."

"I'm with the FBI," the man said.

"I don't care if you're from the fucking moon get out of my face."

"We're just trying to understand the big picture of what happened today…"

"I'll tell you want happened. My son came here got an AR-15… got shells…got a 9mm handgun then went and killed twenty people, then turned it on himself and killed himself. There. That what you want to know?"

"Where did the guns come from?" asked the FBI agent.

"My gun safe."

"No, I mean where did you purchase them from?'

"I don't remember...let me think." He paused. He was about to throw up he was so upset. At his son. At these fools tearing his house apart. At being asked the same questions over and over and over. And he was mad at himself for allowing Matt such open access to the guns in the first place. Even having them here pissed him off at that moment. He was – he felt– some kind of accessory to this horrid crime. "Rudy's gun shop in Houston– The rifle. The handgun, I don't remember. I've had several over the years. Not sure which one that one was or where it came from. It may have been a gift."

"You have serial numbers on them?"

"What? No. I don't have serial numbers on them. Who does?"

"No need to get defensive, Mr. Stevens."

"No? Listen, you are here asking me these stupid questions. What are they on some FBI form you have to follow? The real thing you should be asking is after I went to his school counselors and asked for evaluations of Matt...what the hell did they do? And his psychiatrist ...what good was she? He was mad...angry all the time. And the only time he was calm is when we went out and did things together. We'd go shooting. We'd go fishing. We'd go... I don't know... we'd just get away and he'd settle down. Now you tell me, where is all my backup as a parent? I can't be with him 24-seven. Where are the professionals who are supposed to watch for these traits? Tell me that. Where is that on your fucking FBI questionnaire form?"

The FBI agent thanked Earl and backed away. Now was not the time to confront a grieving father. And Earl was in the stage of grief that was all anger. He was torn up inside. He was blaming himself and others and he could not see the world through sober eyes at that moment. The more he felt grief the more he raged, and the fire was not going to be doused by a bunch of questions from a cop. As the

FBI agent passed one of the sheriff's officers he said under his breath, "Keep an eye on that guy he's about to blow."

It took the officers two hours to conduct their search of Earl's house. The FBI made sure the local cops put things back in an orderly manner. Earl was upset enough without having him go off the handle because his house was ransacked.

Earl was called at around nine-thirty to come to the Lincoln police station. He was to enter through the sallyport at the rear of the building. There, he saw the county coroner and a body on a covered gurney. The cops standing nearby pulled the white sheet back and the remains of Matt were lying there looking up. A gaping hole in the left side of his head was proof enough that he had placed a gun barrel in his mouth and pulled the trigger.

"It's Matt," That was all Earl said. He got back in his truck and drove off. He pulled into the driveway at the beauty shop that sat out by U.S. 59 and drove down the gravel driveway to his old house. He got out and approached the front door. It was open and light from the living room came through the screen door. "Irene." He called.

She came to the door, her eyes swollen and red. She opened the screen and he stepped inside. For the first time in ten years or better, they hugged. They stood in the doorway and held on to each other as if the world depended upon it. She stepped back and said, "I just brewed a pot of coffee, want some?"

"Sure, I ain't gonna sleep anyway."

She poured two cups and got out the cream. She remembered Earl liked cream in his coffee. She drank her's black, with a packet of sweetener stirred in it. For the longest time they just sat there and stared straight ahead. Finally he spoke. "It's my fault."

"What is?'

"This shit with Matt."

"To hell you say. You pull the trigger?"

"No but…"

"Then don't take on his demons. You didn't kill no one. He did. Not you."

"But they were my guns."

"Well, hell…it was my gasoline in his damn car. But I sure as hell didn't drive him to the mall and let him out and say go kill some folks and I'll pick you up at two."

"Irene…"

"No listen, Earl. You've pampered that boy and so have I. And now he's gone and broken our hearts. He has ruined about twenty families…ruined their lives. Broke their hearts. Ended dreams and just trampled all over everything good about our community. Our boy did that. But we didn't. You didn't and I didn't. So quit putting that shit on your shoulders and carrying it around. You got too much to worry about than trying to carry his sins around with you.

"I got a salon up there that'll stay damn near empty 'till Christmas next year, cause folks will be talkin' this shit up and not comin' in and what have you. No. It is not right. It is not fair. But he did it. He did it to us, as well as to all them innocent people at the mall. He might as well have shot us, too.

"But you know what Earl, he didn't. He didn't shoot us. We're alive and well. And we have to keep on going and live like we're well… even when it hurts we're going to have to rise up each morning, open the door and step out into that world and breathe that air and continue to live. We owe it to those who died, Earl that's what you and I owe. To keep living.

"So I don't care if he got a gun from you or money and gas from me or anything else. It was his sin. Not yours. Not mine. Now get out of my house. I got a bunch of crying to do.

Earl was a bit in shock at the attack Irene had just levied at him. "You want to have dinner later this week? Go over to the boats in Bossier City?"

"Sure. Thursday. You come pick me up and don't bring that filthy pickup truck. You bring your dating car. You hear?"

He nodded and drove away in his filthy pickup. Thursday they would talk about plans to bury their son.

27

Bob McAdoo with Father Mise

A day past and the armada of journalists and their vanloads of equipment remained camped out in the mall's parking lot. The shopping center was shuttered. Closed until further notice by the police and especially by the FBI who wanted a complete investigation into this crime.

Bob McAdoo was tired of the scene. Waiting. It was all waiting now. Waiting on press conferences, which seemed to stretch on and on, hour after hour with nothing really important to add to the story. Twenty dead. Killer caught. Killer dead. He was ready to return to Houston to be with his wife, Elaine, who's sister had taken a turn for the worse at M.D. Anderson. She didn't have long.

David Rawlings, the southwestern roving correspondent for NBC News was heading toward Lincoln. He would replace Bob on the front lines and the McAdoos could be together for their own tragedy that was unfolding in a hospital in Houston.

That evening, while Bob awaited Rawlings arrival, he slipped off in an NBC staff car and drove to Marshall for a bite to eat. There was a catfish place near Caddo Lake in the small town of Uncertain, Texas, outside of the Harrison County seat, that used to be a hangout of Bill Moyers. The famed PBS TV journalist and LBJ pressman had grown up in Marshall. He was one of the reasons Bob had gotten into broadcast journalism in the first place. If the catfish place was good enough for Moyers, it would be good enough for him, or so he reasoned. He entered the dark eatery and found a table for two facing out onto the swampy lake, it's knobby cypress trees and the gray moss that took refuge in their branches, created a dark canopy for the eerie body of water. It gave the restaurant the feeling of being a lost riverboat in some horror show.

But located two seats across from him was a face he recognized. Father Richard Mise. In plain clothes. Incognito as it were. He invited the priest to join him and the father did.

Wine, catfish and hushpuppies flowed. So too did their conversation.

"Ever been through something like this, Father?"

"Yes," said the priest, which surprised Bob.

"Really? Where?'

"I was at a medical mission in Michoacán, in Mexico, not far from Morelia. On a couple of occasions we had drug gangs warring in our backyard. Figuratively of course, but close enough that we had to take in civilians caught in the crossfire and treat them for very serious injuries. I was coached quite thoroughly by the nuns in triage. So a battle zone or two doesn't alarm me."

"No?"

"No."

"What does then, Father? What alarms you?"

"The shape our country is in today. The killings in what is supposed to be the most sophisticated, most advanced society on the planet."

McAdoo rolled his eyes. "Really? You think that?'"

"I did at one time." The priest took a bite of the crispy catfish and chewed deliberately for a long time before he swallowed. "Coming from the slums in which I was working, to the States, one could see the vast economic differences. Yet, we are a country that, I am afraid, is of poor spirit."

"That must be disturbing to a man of the cloth," said McAdoo. He poured them both a glass of wine from a bottle of Merlot. "I mean, you work your life to corral sin and turn people's lives around and yet you face a scene like that at the mall. It has to be discouraging."

"Christ was never discouraged when one sinner turned his back on him, for he knew another would come to him. We cannot win every lost soul. We try, but we will never convert all. Our job is to place the good news – the gospel – out there and allow mankind to experience its soul-changing power for themselves."

"Still, though, it has to feel – what shall I call it – a defeat of sorts, when such carnage explodes before you – at your feet."

"I try not to look at it like that. But I will confess to you, Mr. McAdoo..."

"Call me Bob, please."

"Bob, I am tired of the killing. Tired of the slaughter. We are a better people than this. In my heart I know it. It is just that too few have stood up and had their voices heard, so we continue to put up with this mayhem."

McAdoo nodded and then changed the subject. "Where is home?"

"Indiana. Fort Wayne."

"No kidding. I'm from Muncie."

"How did a Muncie kid make it to the top in network news?"

"I slithered between the cracks."

Both men laughed.

"No really," said Mise, "how did you advance so high?"

"After high school, where I worked in radio at a local station doing high school sports and covering the local city council sessions and getting paid next to nothing because the station manager was such a cheap ass; I went to college in Kentucky. UK. Had an uncle who lived in Lexington, so I could room at his place and attend classes there. It helped stretch the scarce dollars, if you know what I mean."

"Good basketball…"

"Yes. Very good. In those days all football was, was a fall activity to keep us occupied until basketball season could fire up again.

"I got a business degree, but never gave up my love for broadcasting. After college I went out west…to Salt Lake City first, then to San Francisco. I was very lucky. The anchorman at the NBC affiliate left suddenly for health reasons and I was put in the afternoon news chair – the early edition we called it – and it was only supposed to be temporary. Next thing I knew, five years had passed and I was promoted to chief anchor and then two years later, was swept up in a new management change at the network in New York and was given a correspondent job. I covered the Gulf War and then Afghanistan and other skirmishes in the Middle East. Then it was back to New York and the role of weekend anchor at the network. Two years of doing that and I was crowned the man on nightly news."

"Impressive."

"Not really. I'm no different than that young man covering city council meetings in Muncie. Just more seasoned now. But at heart and talent, the same guy as I started out being."

"Why news?"

"I wanted to give people the truth. The whole story. The big picture. That's my gospel. An informed society is a society armed with the truth."

"Doesn't always work does it?'

McAdoo shook his head. "No. And the more we get outliers spreading doubt and innuendo about the news and the people who deliver the news, the less and less people want to listen to what we say. They second guess it…second guess us."

"So you turn to shock value?"

"I would say that there is some shock value. I mean we are, after all, trying for greater and greater numbers in our audience. That's what pays the bills. That is what advertisers are buying. And if a bit of shock and awe can convert into eyeballs and ad dollars, I guess so be it. " He paused and raised a finger, "So long as the shock and awe are legit.

"Not entirely different than the headlines coming from the pulpits of America's churches…am I right?"

Father Mise slowly nodded. "Sure. Not all… but a few. No. More than a few are in a game to grow the biggest churches money and fame can buy. But that is not why I was called into the priesthood. Not way back when…"

"So, what called you? I mean I'm sure God called you, but what got your button pushed?"

"Eddie Phelps."

McAdoo shook his head. "Don't know the name."

"No. And there's no reason why you should. Just a kid from the neighborhood who at the ripe old age of sixteen, was shot in the back as he walked into a grocery store in the middle of a robbery. My best friend.

"I was devastated. My life stopped as I learned the news. It was as if a portion of my heart had been ripped out. Eddie and I played basketball together. And baseball in the summers…and we smoked our first cigarettes together and had our first stolen booze together – from his dad's bar at home."

"Scotch?"

"Yes. It was terrible. I couldn't understand why adults swilled the stuff."

They both laughed.

"But his death left a gaping hole in my life. And emptiness I could not fill with any activity or anyone else. I started drifting. I even tried to fit into a gang, just to belong to something beside myself– something bigger than I was. But it didn't take.

"My father, sensing I was adrift, called on Father Pete at our local parish and told him of the problems I was going through. And Father Pete took me under his wing and led me out of the darkness and into the light. Say what you want about Catholic priests and their wayward ways with young boys, and believe me we have some that are way out there…but Father Peter was a saint. I became a regular at masses, became an alter boy and joined the choir and before you know it, he had arranged an interview for me at Notre Dame and I was off to college and then to seminary and here I am, dressed in a collar – well, not tonight – I became a priest, as much to find peace inside my head and heart as to actually help anyone else. But in Mexico that changed. I found my calling. I began to serve others. And it changed my view of the world."

"Why Mexico?"

"The Monsignor who was in charge of our cadre of priests at seminary recognized in me an emptiness. He knew I needed to find a purpose bigger than myself. He was a bright man. A man of deep insight. And he knew of the mission – the medical mission– starting up in Mexico and got me assigned to it. I had to hurriedly learn Spanish and the customs of the people and soon I was lost in their world. Trying to help them out of their problems and suffering and soon I forgot about my needs and wants and concentrated on others. Just what the Monsignor knew I needed."

"How did you get to Lincoln?" McAdoo ate some more catfish and washed it down with a sip or two of wine.

"A few years ago a new diocese was started. A spin off from Dallas and Shreveport. The new bishop planted several missions about in the eastern portion of the state. He had a small church already here in Lincoln, but no one full-time to grow it. He found me on a trip to Mexico and got permission to move me here to grow the flock in Lincoln and to oversee a few of the outlying missions. I spoke Spanish and there is a growing number of Spanish speaking folk here, farmers and migrant workers. It is the second language of the state. So I got a flock. We hold bi-lingual masses and we are slowly – key word, slowly – growing."

"How slow?"

"We'll get a new family every quarter. If we're lucky. I have a small, but very loyal flock. Hey, it's Baptist country. I'm lucky to get fifty at Sunday Mass. More for the Spanish mass."

McAdoo, a Methodist smiled. He knew what the priest was saying. "Some people like ABC some like CNN and some like NBC. It is the flavor you grew up with, I suppose. Personal taste."

"How do you explain FOX?" Asked Mise.

"Some people have no taste."

Both men laughed and continued their meal.

"So in all of your network travels, you found time to find a wife and start a family?" Asked Mise.

"Yes. I was in Frisco and the network had started a show called Profiles. I was sent to Texas to interview Lady Byrd Johnson, Lyndon's wife, for the show. He had already passed, but she was still active – mostly behind the scenes–still a powerful woman. I was having dinner in Austin one night and the people next to me kept borrowing chairs from the table where this lovely young woman sat studying. Little did I know at the time she was in seminary. And, like you, was deep into her theological readings."

"Seminary?"

"Episcopal. In Austin."

"Go on."

"I told her she might as well join me or else she was going to be out of a chair soon. She did and two years later we were married. She was working for a center for battered women in Houston. I moved to New York City and she followed and we had our three children there. I was away from home a lot, covering the news around the globe; so raising the kids fell to her, but she was a pro at it."

"The seminary training no doubt?" Mise grinned, as he sipped his wine.

"I suppose."

"First marriage?"

McAdoo shook his head. "No. Sorry to say. I married a girl right out of college, but it didn't stick. Sorry Father, guess I'm an adulterer."

"My son, adultery is not real high on God's concern list at this moment, I can assure you that. Not in this part of the state. He's got bigger fish to fry." With that the priest ate another bite and grinned at McAdoo. It was a grin that said, don't worry I'm not here to pass judgment.

After a few minutes of trading baseball stories and examining their favorite big league teams, McAdoo asked, "When do you have your first funeral – you know, from the mall?"

"Day after tomorrow. Mother and a daughter."

"The Parkers?"

The priest nodded. "Yes. It will be the first of many. And the hardest for me. I had just spoken to Rosa and her daughter Cynthia in the store just moments before the shooting. Such a waste of life. Did you know the young lady was going to compete against the high school math club from Longview at our local festival? She's an eighth grader and she had no fear or misgivings about going up against high school boys: they equipped with calculators and what not and she only with a pencil and paper."

"My, she sounds exceptional."

"She is – was. Now gone. Taken from us. Her promise. All she could offer this land. All she could bring forth and teach us. All she could accomplish with that intellect she had. And her mother...the most loving woman on earth. Worked at the refinery to allow her husband to run his failing farm. Why? Because she loved him. She wanted him to get to live his dream. His farm was never going to make a lot of money. Not until the land is sold. But his dream was to own a piece of America and to make a life of it. And her job, her hard work, allowed him to carry on that dream.

"Those are the kinds of stories that guns snuff out. That the senseless killings end. It is the type of story that organizations like yours, Bob, do not cover. You can't. You don't have time to get to know the depth of lives that twenty corpses represent. But I'm hear to tell you that each of those bodies in the morgue in Longview has a story as diverse and rich as yours or mine. And a gun – a bullet– snuffed those stories out."

"I would like to tell Cynthia's story and Rosa's to America. I'd like to share the moment you just shared with me; share to the viewers of our newscast."

"Then cover their funeral. Cover it live. It will be the first of many, and maybe that way, their stories will start to disseminate across this land. And who knows, maybe their deaths will help heal what ails us."

They finished their fish and hush puppies and had another glass of wine, and then they each drove back to Lincoln. But along the way, Bob McAdoo was deep in thought about an idea.

The next morning he shared it long distance with Royce Hursh and Eve Kholemann.

"I want to cover the first two funerals of the victims live on TV."

"You crazy?"

"No. In fact, I already have permission from the parish priest who will officiate the service."

Eve Kholemann thought on it for a moment then said, "You'll anchor it from there, Royce will back you up here and we'll get Rawlings to work the crowd. I'm sure state and national dignitaries will poke their vote -seeking heads into this crowd. Anything for a photo op. He'll grab their sound bites."

"I'll get started setting up here. We might have to share air time with the other networks..."

"Fine. The more people who see this suffering the better it will be for the country," said Eve. "Get busy, we've got a lot of work to do."

28

The home of Texas Ranger Will Little

Karen Little came downstairs and started the coffee pot. It had the makings for ten cups. That was by habit, even though she realized she would be the only one in the house drinking coffee that day.

Will was gone.

That is as far as she allowed her thoughts to go:

Will was gone.

The kitchen and its tile floor, newly laid by Will and a friend, felt cold to her bare feet. They had plans to tile the downstairs bathroom, as well, but as of yet had not gotten to it. The knotty pine cabinets seemed awkwardly foreign to her as she opened and removed the sugar and then the breakfast cereal for the kids. She went to the refrigerator and retrieved two bottles of milk. The kids preferred whole milk and she used 2% milk on her breakfast flakes. Everything seemed detached from reality.

She looked out onto the front yard that was being painted a

pale yellow by the early morning sun – the newspaper rested on the moist lawn, the evening sprinkler having misted the thinning grass. Will would have retrieved it by now and had it opened and would be commenting on the day's stories.

Her children dribbled down the stairs, the smallest, Linda eight, was still in her PJ's and was half asleep, rubbing her eyes trying to awaken to a new bright day. Next was her older sister, Betsy, twelve and she was already dressed in the uniform the school district was mandating that year. It was a test to stem the ever-increasing inflationary costs of dressing for school – especially public school. It was their idea to lesson the divide between the haves and the have-nots.

The last to enter the kitchen was Ralph, a senior at Lincoln High, who was on crutches due to a football injury. He had played defensive back on the team and was being eyed by both Kilgore and Tyler junior colleges as a scholarship possibility. He hoped this set back would not hurt his chances to play either for the Rangers or for the Apaches.

"Where's daddy?" asked Linda, missing their father's large presence at the table. Normally he would have been sitting at the head of the table, legs crossed in his starched and neatly pressed khaki trousers, reading the newspaper. And if he had time, he would work the crossword puzzle, often asking the children for help when a clue concerned the latest rock and roll or movie star that he didn't know, or when he thought they could add to their vocabulary with a new word.

"Was he working the shooting?" asked Ralph, knowing that often his father would not be at the breakfast table if he had been called out for some investigation or stake out. He had a huge area to cover. Most of East Texas.

Karen's eyes watered and she began to cry. She caught herself and tried with all her might to halt the tears, but they were already set loose and all she could do was let them flow. She didn't even have a voice to speak to her children. It was gone.

Will was gone.

She wept.

She had cried on the front porch when Ranger Captain, David Mitchell and an assistant officer came to the house late in the night to pass along the sad news. She had cried in her bed, a pillow resting over her face so she would not disturb the children. She wondered how she would face them and tell them the tragic news.

Will was gone.

Now they were to find out and her emotions were spilling out of her and down her cheeks onto the cold tile floor.

Will was gone.

Both Betsy and Ralph sensed something terrible had happened. Maybe because of his age, Ralph came to the conclusion first. He stared at his mother's eyes and they told him everything he needed to know.

"Dad's gone, isn't he?" Ralph asked.

His mother nodded and wept more, as she grabbed for her younger daughter and hugged her. Soon Betsy realized the magnitude of the words and joined in the family embrace. Ralph stood apart from the girls and began to cry on his own. He and his father had been so close, more like friends than child and parent. Just the day before, they had planned a father-son fishing excursion on Grand Lake. Rent a boat and spend the day hunting the giant bass, which lay along the tree-lined banks of the west shore. It was going to be fun. But…

…But Will was gone.

The kitchen seemed to draw in on them. Its walls seemed to squeeze them together. Where there had been five, only four gathered in tears now.

Will was gone.

29

Randy White

He sat up all night. Shaking. There was no way he could close his eyes and fall asleep. He kept hearing the shooting and the screaming on the other side of the freezer's door. The report of the rifle going off and off and off some more. Faster and faster as the shooter squeezed the trigger ever so quickly and deadly. The screams. The yelling. The mass stampeding of feet and then the silence.

And then he had opened the door and looked out. There was carnage everywhere. Mrs. Dixon lay in a pool of blood, a cell phone at her feet. The young girl he had hidden inside began to cry and a man – a priest– moved past them motioning them back inside the freezer.

Again they waited, not knowing what was to happen to them. The young child began to cry and ask for her mother. Randy, took her in his arms as he squatted next to her.

"Shhh. Quiet. We don't want the bad man to hear us." The young girl stopped her crying – a whimper or two, but no more crying. "What's your name?" He asked her in a whisper.

"Terry Brooks," whispered back the small child, mocking the way he had spoken, the way children will do to follow an adult's lead.

"Terry, we are going to be okay. Trust me we are. They will send for help – for us. The police will come soon. I know it."

He held her tightly and she whimpered some more. She was shaking excessively with fear, because it wasn't that cold in the freezer any longer.

"Why is the bad man so angry? Why is he shooting at everybody?" Her whispered question came to Randy who had no answer for her.

"I do not know, all I know is if we stay in here we will be safe from him. Okay?"

She nodded and then buried her face in his chest and the whimpering became quiet sobs.

This scene kept repeating itself on the move screen of his mind. Over and over the feature ran. It played in slow motion. It played in full color. It had stereo sound. It was as if he were still there in the freezer and on the other side of that steel door was a mad man with a machine gun killing everyone in sight.

He kept seeing Mrs. Dixon dead at the side of the ice cream counter. Her cell phone at her feet. She had been talking to someone. Maybe calling for help. But she had died.

And little Terry Brooks in his arm; he kept feeling her shake from fear and torment. And he remembered he kept telling himself he had to be strong for her. He had to be brave for her. He had to act like it was going to be okay, even though he expected any moment for the door to be flung open and for them to be shot. At that moment in his life, Randy had to be an adult.

Randy even planned to lie on top of the child to protect her before the onslaught of fatal bullets. He closed his eyes and asked God to forgive him. He wasn't even a church-goer. Nor was his family. But at that moment he needed the strength of a higher power.

Then it all went silent and he and the young girl crept out, but the priest waved them back inside.

The movie ran like this over and over and over until the sun came up in the morning. Randy didn't know what to do or where to go.

So he hid under his bed.

He stayed there until two o'clock in the afternoon, when his roommate, Jimmy found him and coaxed him out from under the bed. Jimmy, whose father was a doctor in Longview, called his old man and told him what had occurred and what was happening to his friend, Randy.

Jimmy's father immediately told him, "Load him in a car and drive him here. I'll meet you at the hospital. And don't drive by the mall. Go the long route. Drive along Grand Lake."

For seven days, Randy stayed in the hospital under the care of Dr. Selma Lawrence, a psychiatrist trained in the Army in trauma recovery. Slowly the movie faded. It became stills – moment-by-moment photographs in his mind. And slowly, they began to fade like an old Polaroid picture that hadn't been dipped in the preservative bath. There, but slowly dissolving away with time.

30

The First
Funeral

Grief was setting in.

The shooting had occurred at noon on Monday. By Wednesday afternoon the town was beginning to settle. The dust clearing, as the locals say. The mall was still closed, of course, but schools were back in session and most folks tried, as best they could, to get on with their lives. In small groups at shops or along the streets, and over the phone and in offices, in garages, and in shops, at Wednesday night pray meeting at the Baptist church, there were whispers of the event.

At first, the talk was in hushed tones out of respect for the dead. But soon the conversations turned more to the event as an event– like a sporting event being discussed – who won and who lost. What was the final score?

Quickly the scab was heeling and the façade of everything is all right in the community returned, even if it did feel slightly uncomfortable. *It didn't happen to me or to my family, therefore I'm okay. I'm saved from this horror show.* But deep underneath, there was a notion – a gut feeling– that somehow the terrible act that had transpired there in their city had mysteriously tainted them all.

They were all stained with the blood of the victims. And it didn't seem fair and that caused a great deal of resentment and anger.

It was taken out mostly on the visiting army of media folk who inhabited the small community, but it was also taken out on authorities of all kinds –'*how could you have let such a thing happen to our city?*'

To be sure, the town was ripe for some self-analysis and even more ripe for a heaping dose of self-forgiveness.

Father Mise decided neither was appropriate.

On Friday, Father Mise lead the processional into Saint Elizabeth's, which normally seated about two hundred people, and at the best of times, fifty of those places would be occupied by worshipers. But this day, there was a capacity house and many more standing outside. A choir from the Cathedral in Tyler had been sent to offer music and a lone broadcast camera joined the choir in the upstairs loft; there by an agreement Father Mise had worked out with the five networks and their producers. "I want only one camera and I want it in the choir loft and I want no cameras focusing on the grieving family members. Is that understood? Agree with me, or you'll get no access." All the news producers agreed, except FOX, but the other networks persuaded the lone holdout to sign on, as well.

"It will limit our first amendment rights," argued FOX News. But everyone ignored them and finally the network was on board with the rest of the organizations, all agreeing to take a single feed from CNN and rebroadcast it via satellite to their audiences.

The processional was slow and solemn. Crying was the only sound that echoed in the small Catholic church, which had been built in the late 1950's. Little effort had been exerted to refurbish it since that time.

The caskets of Cynthia Parker and her mother were wheeled to the teak fence separating the maroon carpeted alter area from the congregation. Father Mise in his white cloak and stoles with golden trim stood at the bottom step to receive the pair of plain wooden coffins. Flowers were everywhere. Later, the priest would confess he had never seen such an outpouring of flowers in the church.

"In the name of the Father, the Son and the Holy Spirit. Amen."

"Amen." Echoed back to him in unison from the gathering.

And so began the very quiet and reverent Requiem Mass. After the two readings from the bible, Father Mise ascended the short circular steps to an elevated pulpit on the left hand side of the sanctuary. As the choir finished the Alleluia hymn, he looked out at the parishioners and guests gathered to say their goodbyes. He then read the Gospel – Matthew 5:1-12.

"Rejoice and be glad, for your reward will be great in heaven.
A reading from the holy Gospel according to Matthew

When Jesus saw the crowds, he went up the mountain, and after he had sat down, his disciples came to him.

He began to teach them, saying:

"Blessed are the poor in spirit,
for theirs is the Kingdom of heaven.

Blessed are they who mourn,
for they will be comforted.

Blessed are the meek,
for they will inherit the land.

Blessed are they who hunger and thirst for righteousness,
for they will be satisfied.

Blessed are the merciful,
for they will be shown mercy.

Blessed are the clean of heart,
for they will see God.

Blessed are the peacemakers,
for they will be called children of God.

Blessed are they who are persecuted for the sake of righteousness,
for theirs is the Kingdom of heaven.

Blessed are you when they insult you and persecute you
and utter every kind of evil against you falsely because of me.

Rejoice and be glad,
for your reward will be great in heaven."

The Gospel of the Lord."

Waiting for the room to settle from its response, he took in a deep measure of air and slowly let it out. He knew that not only these eyes seated before him were watching him, but perhaps millions around the country – even around the world – were tuned in to see and hear what was being said about the horrible events that had taken such a young, promising life and the life of her dear mother amidst another mass shooting in the United States Of America.

He had even received a cable from Rome, from the Pontiff himself, expressing his sympathy and encouraging Father Mise to carry on the faith in such trying times.

Father Mise began, "I wish I could tell you what God's will in all of this is.

"I cannot.

"It is beyond me to even imagine how he could allow a tragedy such as this – how he could have allowed it to transpire. But we are here today because it did transpire. Just as it has time and time again across our country. Senseless killing of innocent lives. Leaving us to grieve. To wonder. To second guess the very laws of our land written to supposedly protect us and grant us freedom.

"But I fear those rules are now grossly outdated. I know they are for Cynthia and her mother, Rosa.

"Guns and bullets killed these two precious souls. True, a troubled soul pulled the trigger time and time again, but the access to such weapons contributed to their murder.

"Oh, the powers that be will offer their thoughts and prayers and will ring their hands on television and will promise swift action to stop such mass killings, but they will do nothing. The killings will go on.

"They go on because America has no will.

"*You* have no will."

He gave a long punctuated pause.

"You do not wish these deaths to stop. All of you. Those here in Saint Elizabeth's and those of you at home watching. You have lost your will to stand up and be heard. You are no longer brave enough to say 'enough is enough'.

"You just allow it to continue.

"So the blood of Cynthia Parker and Rosa Parker is on your hands. It is on your soul. It is your sin, as much as it is the young man who gunned them down.

"Every politician in the land who has taken money from the gun lobby to protect the killing in our streets has sinned and is responsible for this.

"And your complicit voting for them makes you an accessory to this crime."

He had wrestled with these words for the five days leading up to the funeral. It was the first service of some twenty that would take place in the small city. And he knew he had to voice the dissent against the madness that was sweeping America. Others might not. Others, might sweep it under the carpet and hide their true feelings behind the talk of spiritual redemption and the saving grace of Christ, but he had to take a stand. He might lose his position at the church if the bishop disapproved, but his conscience told him to speak the truth. "Ye shall know the truth and it shall set you free." That's what his scriptures had taught him. So he was going to speak the truth.

"We are a land awash in guns. And their violence has now flooded into our small community. The blood of those we lost at the mall the other day is on our hands.

"Yours and mine.

"And on the hands of everyone who keeps voting for the men and women who turn their back on this disease in America.

"We should all bow down before Cynthia and Rosa, here and ask their forgiveness. We should go and seek the others who fell that day in the mall and request their forgiveness.

"We should look at ourselves in the mirror and recognize how weak we have become; not willing to stand up and say what we all know in our hearts is the truth.

"Perhaps this is why God allowed this illness to flood our streets with innocent blood. So it would awaken us to the task we have at hand. We didn't do it after Columbine or after Sandy Hook. Not after Virginia Tech, not after the grocery store shootings in Buffalo, New York or after the church shootings in Charleston or Santa Fe nor Sutherland Springs, Texas… nor at the night club in Orlando or at Stoneman Douglas High School in Parkland, Florida. The list goes on and on and on and on.

"It is too numerous to even read here. It would take hours. The cities and towns where mass shootings occurred. Where innocence was wiped out with the violence of guns. In schools. In theaters. At a McDonalds! In houses of worship. In our homes…" He paused.

"It is time that we as a nation arise and take back our streets… our schools, our churches. It is time we return our country to a place where one doesn't have to fear crowds or plan an escape route in our local theater just in case gun violence erupts.

"It is time we take away the guns. Put them up…lock them away and realize that guns do kill people. Along with disturbed souls who need help and care. But the gun is their weapon. The gun is their tool of death. The gun is their refuge to some kind of peace to be a salve to the devil they carry inside. But it is the gun…the gun is center to this disease.

"But America is too weak for change. Too scared – too timid to take action. To embarrassed to ask neighbors to disarm. To meek to stand up and admit our founding fathers either got it wrong in the second amendment, or so poorly wrote it that today it can be interpreted in so many openly harmful ways…we can even watch as federal judges allow military weapons such as bazookas and cannons and rocket launchers to be owned by citizens under the tenants of this death amendment. Under the proclamation that it is their right.

"Rights? Where are Cynthia and Rosa's rights?" He was on fire now. 'Pissed off' he would later tell the bishop in Tyler who begrudgingly complimented him on his courage, then placed him on leave for six weeks to rest.

"The death amendment must be repealed."

He took another breath and waited.

"The death amendment must be repealed now. Do you have the

courage to join the fight to end the madness? The death amendment must be repealed now."

There wasn't as much as a twitch of an eye lid in the still church.

"I pray for your forgiveness and for mine in these deaths. In the name of the Father and the Son and the Holy Spirit. Amen."

The NBC News command van parked outside the church was silent as the producer, the engineer and the director all looked at one another. "Jesus son of Sam…he nailed it," said the director, a Texan from Houston who owned two handguns himself.

"You going to give up your guns?" asked his long-time friend the producer.

"I just might. I damn well just might."

31

a private
family service

Matt Stevens was laid to rest on a small plot that had been hastily purchased by his father near the rural town of Bivins, Texas. It was in a far-off corner of East Texas not far from Atlanta in Cass County; off a dirt road deep into pine and cattle country. Little traffic passed by the fenced-in two acre yard of tombstones and grave markers. In fact, Matt's father, Earl, who had seen the small burial ground on a deer hunting expedition years before, had a hard time locating anyone to dig a grave. He finally found the owner of the small facility and paid six hundred dollars for the plot and another six hundred for a small head marker. On a brass plaque it simply read:

Mathew Stevens
2008-2023
RIP Son

The two guys with the yellow backhoe stood off to the side and watched. They had no idea who was being buried. A mother was there draped in black and soaking in tears, along with a father in an ill-fitting dark suit and a skinny, young minister they had never seen before.

The preacher read few passages from the Bible, then said a prayer and the three got back into a black station wagon and followed the lone hearse away, red dust billowing behind them. The two guys filled the hole with dirt and then threw sod over the mound. Rain, if it ever returned to East Texas, would slowly lower the mound and even it out with all the other graves around, most of which had been in the small cemetery for over a hundred years.

32

the interview

The slow processional was filing out of Saint Elizabeth's as Bob McAdoo spotted William Wadsworth, the political mouthpiece for the National Gun Association. From the news truck, Bob spoke to David Rawlings, who was moving through the crowd interviewing local dignitaries in attendance at the sad memorial service. In the reporter's earpiece he heard, "David to your right...ten yards...Bill Wadsworth. NGA. Go."

David Rawlings was a seasoned professional. He had interviewed governors, congressmen, senators, and even Billy Graham, once. He knew how to get next to a person and pepper them with questions. He knew when to be tough and when to lighten up. He knew how to turn an interview into a story. David Rawlings was good at what he did.

The NBC News correspondent approached Wadsworth who was looking the other way at just that moment.

"Bill, sad day in Texas, No?"

Wadsworth turned and frowned. He was in no mood for a joust with the press. He was there to bolster the state and national politicians who would be queried about gun control and anti-gun sentiment. He was there to smile in the background and remind them of his organization's deep pockets, into which the politicos had their hands buried. But it was too late. Suddenly he switched on the TV face. Then it was washed away with a sad, sad look, of a man who had just lost his best friend.

"Our thoughts and prayers go out for this family and for this community. Tragic. Simply Tragic…"

Rawlings cut him off, "Will this reignite the talk on Capitol Hill for gun control?"

"I'm not sure this is the time and the place…"

"According to the homily in today's mass, it seems as if people are starting to clamor for saner laws when it comes to guns…"

"Well, we have plenty of laws regulating firearms. And we have a Constitution that allows them in the hands of our citizenry. I think that…"

"So you are saying the NGA is opposed to sitting down and discussing with Congress…with the President …a rational approach to limit the use of high powered, high volume magazine rifles…"

"I didn't say we wouldn't talk…"

"What is holding you back? Even your own membership has been polled and over 65 percent approve of stiffer controls on guns."

"Guns are not the problem, David. Mental, unstable people with firearms are the real problems. The solution is to get these people help – it is a medical problem. Instead of talking to the NGA you should be talking with the AMA…why aren't they up in arms over mental illness and mass…"

He paused just long enough for Rawlings to fill in his last word, "mass shootings?" Wadsworth knew he had used the wrong language. He had set himself up. Backed himself into a philosophical corner. He was way too polished to have allowed that to happen. "Seems that shooting starts with a gun, sir. And these guns – these high capacity, fast-firing guns – are being used in large mass killings …they are of the variety that hunters and sportsmen don't use. They are killing weapons designed for military use…"

Wadsworth did the only thing he had left in his arsenal of public discourse. He walked away.

"Again the NGA shows an utter disregard for the casualties of gun violence in America. For NBC News in Lincoln, Texas, I'm David Rawlings."

The network cut to a commercial. Springtime Bleach Sheets, to make your wash whiter and brighter.

33

the press conference and the barber shop

Pete Pollard ran Pete's Trim Shack on the corner of 17th and U.S. 59, just down the street from Matt Steven's mother's beauty salon. The parking lot was full of cars on Friday afternoon. The mass at Saint Elizabeth's had just let out and the processional was driving slowly past the barbershop toward the city's cemetery on the highway toward Carthage.

Two men sat in the red leatherette barber chairs getting their crew cuts and a shave. Three others waited patiently for their turn. Pete and his assistant, Donna Helms, worked quickly and efficiently getting the men groomed for the weekend. The old air conditioner buzzed under the load, as it dripped into a bucket on the floor. It was an unseasonably warm day. Outside on the short porch, on an old wooden bench, sat three more men and a school-age boy, all waiting their turn to go under the magic of Pete and Donna's sheers.

"Sure is hot this November," said one man whose neck was being lathered for a shave by Donna.

Everyone in the tiny shop all agreed.

"What we need is some rain," said another. Again general agreement around the establishment.

"Gonna be hot at the game tonight." It was Friday and shooting or no shooting football was to be played in Texas.

A television set sat in the corner and two very familiar faces appeared: The Governor of Texas, Jim Salisbury and a United States Senator from the Lone Star State, Rick Cross both Republicans and both staunch gun rights advocates.

The first to speak was Governor Salisbury, with his country preacher twang and quivering voice, "It is a sad day in Texas. Another sad, sad day. Our citizens are suffering yet again. Another of these unfortunate situations. A sick, sick person taking innocent lives and shattering families and communities. It has to stop. It can't go on. We must find a way to get help to the mentally disturbed."

"Here we go again," said Pete out loud. "They're going to blame all of this on the loonies. It's the guns that are the problem."

"Guns don't kill people, people kill people." It was said by the man in Donna's chair. For the briefest of instances she had a notion to slash his throat. But it passed.

"That's what they all say. Every time there is one of these mass shootings that guns don't kill people. Bullshit. They do. And the bullets in them do. You limit the firepower out there and the violence is going to go down. It has in every country that has taken a stand in limiting this kind of armaments."

"You gonna take away my right to have a gun?" Asked another man waiting on the next available seat.

"What about those people who got killed…what about their rights?"

"You put guns on them and that fool wouldn't have come in there guns a blazing."

"Oh so you want all of us, like the old west, to walk around with six shooters strapped to our waist?" Pete hated the gun violence. He knew deep inside there had to be a sensible solution to the madness. Just make the high-powered, high volume guns illegal. And make the consequences for using guns in a crime steep. Steep enough to get people to think twice before pulling the iron out and start shooting. "The problem is guns. Crazy people come into a mall with a knife, he's gonna cut up a few, but he'll be wrestled down and detained. Or he can come in armed with a fruit basket and start throwing apples at everybody."

The entre shop laughed. The silliness of the scene seemed to make its point.

The governor was stepping aside and Rick Cross the mouthpiece in the Senate for the NGA was taking questions from the assembled.

"Senator, you stood up in the Senate and opposed the last administration's attempt to place restrictions on the type of rifle used in the shooting at Lincoln Mall. Why?"

"Easy. Second Amendment."

"So there's no room to even consider limiting certain types of weapons – mass shooting weapons…"

Cross cut the questioner off. "The law is clear…I have the right to and it is not to be impeded…to own a firearm."

Another reporter stood and asked, "But as a constitutional purist, as you call yourself, weren't those guns the second amendment was writing about … weren't they muskets?"

Laughter in the make-shift pressroom that was actually the cafeteria at Lincoln High School, but the Senator seemed disturbed at the question. "You think this is funny?'

"No sir," fired back from the reporter immediately before Cross could go off on one of his political tirades. "In fact, I take it very seriously. But you change your stance on every issue that comes your way. You are a constitutional purist on taxation and on states rights, but when it comes to guns, you waffle more than a bit on the historical interpretation of what a firearm is. Today the federal courts are even allowing citizens to own bazookas."

"And right they should. The second amendment doesn't allow any infringement on the right for a citizen to arm himself."

"What about the well-regulated militia portion of that law?" asked another reporter. Now more and more questions were being tossed at the squatty little man in his tight-fitting suit. He was sweating profusely under the glare of the TV lights.

"What would you say to the Parker family who lost a mother and a daughter at that mall. Where are their rights, Senator? Who is watching out for them?"

"Well the police should…"

A groan went up in the room, clearly audible to the entire watching nation and especially clear in Pete's barbershop.

"There you have it, Harry," said Pete to a customer seated against the wall. "There's your argument. You want rights? Fine. You got to have some responsibility with those rights. That's what we are demanding."

"Already been addressed. Read the second amendment."

"I have. It is a poorly written piece of shit."

Harry got up and marched out of the barbershop. "Let him go. He's a hot head," said one of the remaining men waiting for a cut. Harry's place was taken by a man with a plaid shirt on and a John Deere baseball cap. "You guys watching the press conference?"

"Don't get Pete started. He's wound up this afternoon."

34

Eduardo Parker.

Two days after the funeral, Eduardo called his brother Jose and asked if he and his wife, Ana, would mind looking after Ella. He needed to go away on some business for the ranch and didn't want to leave her alone in this time of grief. Along with her friends, she would more than likely go back to school on Monday. He wanted someone around to keep an eye on her. They readily agreed. Jose told Eduardo that they would do anything he needed. He knew how his brother was hurting, so getting back to ranch business – getting back to work– would be good for Eduardo.

It was a bright, warm Sunday morning. Eduardo pulled his Chevy pickup out of the crunchy, gravel driveway and headed for the eastern shore of Grand Lake. There he would access the state highway, which would lead him to Henderson. From there he drove through the central section of eastern Texas and merged onto I 35 south of Temple.

His destination that day was San Antonio.

He stopped in Georgetown and bought gas and a sandwich along with a soda. He returned to the road and took the bypass around Austin, whose traffic was notoriously horrible. He had discovered as much the day he took Ella to the university for her senior visit.

She had opted to join her brother at Tech in Lubbock, instead of the Austin school.

In New Braunfels, he stopped and called his sister, Maria in San Antonio. She lived on the south side of the sprawling city. "Maria, como esta?" Maria was the youngest of seven children, while Eduardo was older, by almost twenty years.

"Eduardo, I am so glad to hear from you. Jose called me with the sad news, no? He said little Cynthia and Rosa were killed in that shooting. Oh my God in haven... Holy Mother Mary, how can this be?"

"It is God's will," said Eduardo, although he didn't believe that. "Maria, I am wanting to speak with, don Carlos. Do you know how to reach him?"

"Si, Eduardo. I talk to my son almost daily."

"Can you call him for me?"

"To be sure, why?"

"I need a meeting with him. It is business matter."

"Give me your number and I will have him call you. Eduardo I want to come see you ... to visit you."

"Give me some time, Maria. I am not in the best of moods for company these days."

"I understand my brother, I truly understand."

They talked for a few more minutes then he rushed her off the call, saying his business was timely and he needed to talk with her son very soon. Eduardo hung up his cell and waited. He sat in the parking lot of a Wal-Mart as he waited. Twenty minutes passed and then the phone rang.

"Tio Eduardo?"

"Don Carlos. So good to hear your voice."

"Me Tio, I heard the sad, sad news of your loss. How can I be of service to you?"

"I have a business request. But I don't think we should discuss it over the phone, if you know what I mean."

"I do, Tio. I do. Let me tell you this. I can be anywhere in San Antonio in under an hour. Are you nearby?"

"Yes."

"Don't tell me where. I will text you an address. Go there and I will meet you, no?'

"Yes. And thank you don Carlos."

"Anything for my Tio."

A few moments later an address appeared on his text screen from a number he did not recognize. He brought up the map on his phone and located the site. It was less than thirty minutes from the Wal-Mart. He pulled out into the thickening afternoon traffic.

He slowly made his way toward the destination that don Carlos had suggested for their rendezvous. His nephew had the reputation around the Alamo City of being a man in charge of many things. Some legal. Most illegal. He ran a gang. He ran drugs and women and gambling. And yet, he seemed to be above the law. The authorities never seemed to get close to don Carlos. The young man had received a graduate degree in business from the University of Texas at Austin and then immediately went into the import business for himself. What he imported was of constant interest to the Federal Government; although, they could never track contraband back to don Carlos.

He was Mr. Teflon.

The address was a neighborhood of industrial warehouses. One right after the next, forming a labyrinth of concrete walls and metal roofs, closing the outside world away. Eduardo pulled up to the building with the number he had been given. Two men in tan jogging suits stepped from a dark SUV from the other side his nephew, in golf clothes, mostly orange and green, appeared.

"Search him," said don Carlos, as if he had been talking about a total stranger.

"But don Carlos..." Eduardo started to protest.

"Shh. Mi Tio. It is just part of my business."

"One man patted Eduardo down while the other ran an electronic wand around and over him.

They both stepped back. "He's clean."

Don Carlos motioned Eduardo to come close. He did; and as Eduardo came near the tall, handsome Hispanic man, don Carlos. reached out and hugged his uncle. They held the embrace for some time. "I am so truly sorry for your loss, Mi Tio. So very, very sorry."

"Thank you, don Carlos. But today I do not come on family matters but on business."

Don Carlos nodded and led the way inside the giant warehouse, with one of the men joining them and the other remaining on guard at the door they had just entered. They walked up a flight of steel stairs to an office, which overlooked a loading dock and tables upon long tables of packages. Painted delivery vans, made to look like UPS, Amazon and DHL trucks were parked inside, as men moved back and forth loading them with items from the long tables. Other men paid special note on computers to what had been loaded into what van.

"Don Carlos, I can't tell you how indebted I am for you to see me…"

"My uncle is always welcome to come see me. What can I do for you?"

They sat in a small office and the remaining guard closed the door leaving the nephew and uncle alone together. An air conditioning unit ran noisily in a window behind the empty desk.

Eduardo reached into his jacket pocket and brought out a paper bag. Inside it were rolls and rolls of bills: twenties and hundreds mostly. Don Carlos looked at the money then up at his uncle. "Tio, que es este? What is this?"

"I need a gun. A big, powerful gun."

"Mi Tio? But why? Que paso?"

"I do not wish to involve you, don Carlos. It is better I not tell you. To protect you. The less you know the cleaner your hands."

Don Carlos nodded. He understood. In principle, it was how he ran his business. Need to know only.

35

cleaning up the aftermath

The shift superintendent at the refinery needed a replacement for Rosa Parker. He was going to have to juggle schedules around. Vacation time was going to be used. Comp time, too according to the union. He scanned his list for the most qualified to take her role. It would be hard. Rosa was one in a million. The hardest and brightest worker he had ever had. Come to think of it, she had trained him for his job. HR was involved in interviewing candidates and in getting benefits passed over to Eduardo and his daughter. Paperwork was flowing. Massive amounts of paperwork.

At the Texas Ranger office in Austin, decisions were needed to replace Will Little. The FBI had called and requested that the new candidate be experienced with bank heists. No one was more experienced in that field than had been Will Little. But he was gone now and people would have to be moved about. Families uprooted and moved. The management juggling act had begun. His replacement told his family of their upcoming move to East Texas and his two daughters were distraught. They had deep ties to the

Houston cheerleader community and many friends in their schools. This change was upsetting.

At the mall, a construction crew came in and basically cleaned out the entire food court, down to the studs of its interior walls. Where they could, they plastered over the bullet holes. Where it was too violent a tear, they rebuilt sections of the walls. The entire floor was jackhammered apart and the tiles removed. New tiles were brought in and the floor of the crime scene was covered. It was as if the entire battleground was being whitewashed away under a barrage of heavy construction. Yet, as one moved through the facility, it was still hauntingly eerie. Instead of feeling like a shopping experience, it felt like a morgue.

At Russell Pipeline Company, a new driver had to be found to replace Milton Owens. The Russell Company sent a large wrecker to the parking lot of the Bluebonnet Café to remove their rig that had been crippled in the shootout. It was stuck in a culvert along the northern side of the frontage road. After removing the yellow crime scene tape left behind by the police, it took more than two hours to extract the rig from its acute angle.

July Williams Bell's body was flown back to Arkansas at the expense of an unknown party and delivered to the Mount Zion Baptist Church for her funeral and burial in the town of Palestine, where her elderly parents now resided, having left Forrest City more than a dozen years earlier. No one ever stepped forward to be credited with the generosity of flying her home to her final resting spot, but it was rumored that the payment had come from the owner of a John Deere Tractor dealership who had received a phone call from a woman in Tyler, Texas named Hoffman who said she knew July and was in great sorrow for her loss.

Steve Washington was the back-up quarterback on the Lincoln High School football team. And on the first day back to school, he sat on the sidelines, completely uniformed, but did not take part in drills. It was the last week of scheduled games for the team, although an appearance in the state playoffs was not out of the question. Lincoln had to defeat Newsom's Creek in the last game to extend their season.

The Lincoln squad was a six-point underdog. Later that week Steve quit the team, telling his coach "I no longer care about sports." His little brother, Carl had been a victim in the mall shooting. The high school coach, having been trained in depression awareness, notified the school's mental health therapist about Steve's condition. "We should keep a close eye on him. Offer him counseling," said the coach. She thanked the coach and wrote it off as a sad case of melancholy over the loss of a sibling. Hell, he was a football coach, she had a PhD... what did he know? Two days later, Steve Washington hung himself in an abandoned barn two miles from the dam of Grand Lake. He became the twenty-first victim of the shooting, although indirectly.

Bob McAdoo signed off his last broadcast from Lincoln and hitched a ride back to Houston on the Channel 2 copter. His good friend, Hound Dog Tunney, at his side. They were both mentally and physically drained from the week's ordeal in Lincoln. "I've covered a lot of shit in my day, Hound Dog, but something about this got under my skin. It tore at me. At my heart. At my whole self."

"I know what you mean, man. I feel kind of filthy for some reason. Like I've been crawling through the debris of a war zone."

"Yeah but in a war zone you know who the good guys are and who the bad guys are. Here I don't know who is who. I mean I feel like I invaded these people lives. I've never had that feeling before."

"It'll pass, Bob. There will be others. There will be, I promise you that."

Bob McAdoo's sister-in-law died two days after his return to Houston. She was buried in Wimberley, Texas at the edge of the Texas Hill Country. Bob and Elaine wrapped up their business in Texas and returned to New York City, where a week later, he sat at the NBC Nightly News desk once gain, the anchor for the storied network. His first news entry that night was a mass shooting at a college in Southern California. It had transpired moments before they had gone on the air, but in the background Eve was already summoning news troops and organizing coverage in San Diego and Orange County. "There will be others, Bob. There will be..."

Todd Dixon walked among the ruins of his ice cream shop, the construction crew already having come through and basically ripped its façade all away. He opened blueprints and showed the foreman how it was to be rebuilt. Insurance adjusters were everywhere taking photographs and measuring space. The Mall's legal team was on standby, as were the firm's maintenance crews, in case things came up that the construction crews were barred from touching. One such thing was the repair to Fresh Freeze Ice Cream Shoppe's freezer. A firm from Kilgore was there already getting the compressor back on line and into working order, although all around them was still a pile of the aftermath of the killing and chaos.

"Don't know why I need a freezer now," said Todd to one of the insurance men. "Everything is gone."

"You'll rebuild, Mr. Dixon. I know you will."

Todd nodded. He really didn't have his heart in it. He had lost a store once to a tornado, but that was different. Here, he had lost his life mate – his lover – his wife. Screw the ice cream. His heart was what was melted. It might never recover.

The Dudleys never did come to terms with the oil and gas company that July Williams Bell represented. They passed on all offers and the kids returned to their homes in Los Angeles and Detroit. Their father lived out his life, undisturbed on a piece of wooded property that could well have made the entire family wealthy.

But they passed.

Officer Darrell Hampton was given a full color guard burial with cities from across Texas, Arkansas and Louisiana sending officers to honor their fallen brother. In all, more than five hundred peace officers and first responders attended his graveside service officiated by the state police Chaplin Maynard Reese, a former resident of Lincoln. The same afternoon, the Garcia family buried Raul in a neighboring section of the community's cemetery. Eighteen people visited his grave and dropped red roses onto the mound of dirt, below which the young man rested. A lone, red paper hat sat atop a white cross at his headstone.

The town of Lincoln was slowly settling back down. Not to normal. That would probably never occur. Normal. It was a strange and foreign notion. But the town was calming. The nights were long and starting to cool and neighbors walked the lighted sidewalks again, whispering to one another in hushed tones as they passed, as if to respect the peace in their town. They deserved that. Just a little peace.

36

road trip
(part one)

Eduardo was awakened at his motel room two days after meeting with don Carlos. He was camped out on the outskirts of San Antonio in a town called Converse. His cell phone was buzzing.

"Tio. Come to the address I have just texted to you. Come alone. You know the drill by now."

Eduardo got dressed, checked out of the motel and drove to the far south side of the city. He found the street and the address that had been texted to him. It was a low-rent, two story apartment building with four units and a garage downstairs. He pulled into the driveway in the back of the building, as he had been instructed to do. A man in jeans and a Houston Astros jersey got out of a blue station wagon opened the back to the car and retrieved a long newspaper-wrapped package that looked like a cylinder. He also produced another box. He brought them both to Eduardo's passenger-side window and placed them on the leatherette front seat. Without so much as saying a word, the man nodded at Eduardo and the East Texas rancher backed out of the drive and headed home.

He had what he had come for.

Muchas gracias, don Carlos.

The drive back to Lincoln took five and a half hours. Longer than he had planned. He made sure he drove the speed limit and didn't attract any attention. He stayed to small two-lane motorways and rural farm-to-market roads, through the villages and the scattered farms and ranches. Small towns he eased past and kept moving, not wanting to draw notice to himself. Before he reached Jacksonville, night had fallen on him, giving him a dark shroud of secrecy.

He pulled into his home at a minute or two before nine o'clock and went inside, looking around, making sure his daughter was gone and with her aunt and uncle. He called Father Mise at the church.

"Padre, it is Eduardo Parker."

"Eduardo. How are you?"

"Good. But I need to speak with you."

"At this hour?"

"No. Perhaps tomorrow. A confessional."

"Well, Eduardo I am due in Tyler in the morning at the bishop's office. I don't think he liked my homily at your family's service..."

"I can come early," he interrupted.

"I see." Thinking of all that Eduardo had been through, he decided that an early meeting at the church would be the prudent and just thing to do. "I can meet you for confession at say, seven...I have a mass at seven thirty."

"Seven. Fine."

"Eduardo, are you okay?"

"Si, padre. I am fine. Just some things I need to get off my chest to God...looking for forgiveness and direction."

"Very well, then. I will see you at seven."

Eduardo went back to the barn where he had parked his truck and got the long paper wrapped cylinder as well as the box. The box was quite heavy. Once inside he laid the items down on his bed. Inside the newspaper was a black rifle and four clips for ammunition. Two were fully loaded. The rifle resembled the one police found with the shooter who had taken his Rosa and Cynthia from him. A military style weapon. AR 15. He picked it up and fingered it. It felt cold and heavy to him. Solid. Inside the box were more long, shiny brass bullets with red tips at their pointed end. Don Carlos had done well. Very well.

He closed his bedroom door and placed a chair against the knob, to slow any intruder who might chance their way into his room.

He spread out on the bed next to the gun and the box of ammunition and went sound to sleep. His phone's alarm awakened him at five. He showered, shaved, put on fresh clothes, packed a small bag and put a shaving kit inside it, just as he had done for his trip to San Antonio. Deep from the bottom of the hill behind the house he could hear a bull bellow. Somewhere in the distance a crow announced the coming of morning.

He carried the rifle and the ammo box to the car that sat parked on the grass at the back door of the house. It was Rosa's car. It had been returned to him by the Lincoln Police three days after the shooting. It was no longer needed as evidence in their investigation. He placed the gun and the bullets in the trunk.

He went back inside and made a cup of instant coffee. He didn't have time to get the coffee pot out of the drainer and brew coffee. Instant would have to do – Rosa would have never stood for that. But things had changed with her leaving. He poured some milk into the hot cup and sipped slowly. Ever mindful of the time, at six-thirty, he emptied the rest of the cup into the sink, rinsed it out and set it in the strainer to the side of the sink. He used the bathroom and then departed the house, leaving the rear door unlocked, as was his custom. He wanted everything to look and feel natural. Nothing out of the ordinary.

He drove the Buick east toward town and turned off 17th street onto Mission Road. It would lead past the Presbyterian church and past the Methodist church and ended at a cul de sac in front of St. Elizabeth's. That week, the entire street had been overflowing with news vans and their satellite dishes along with tables under temporary tents – canopies for the press. This morning it was empty and lonely feeling.

To the right and slightly behind the church was a single-story red, brick house. The rectory for Father Mise. He could see a light on in the manse. He didn't wait. Eduardo got out, locked his car and walked to the front door of the St. Els's, as it was called by the locals. He knew it would be unlocked and waiting for his entry. He crossed the marbled narthex and entered the nave. Stretching in front of him between rows of oak pews, was a wine red carpet leading to the sacristy. To the right and to the left of the center aisle, were two double-door closets with lattice worked wood across their fronts. On either side of the closets were shelves full of candles for prayer and remembrance. He entered one of the doors on the right-hand side of the church. He soon heard footsteps, and Father Mise spoke, "Eduardo?"

"Here," he answered in a hushed and reverent tone.

The door to the closet next to his opened and closed; then the red drapery separating the two units was pulled back and through more teak lattice work, he could make out Father Mise's tired face.

"Good morning, Eduardo."

"Padre."

"What brings us together at such an early hour?"

"I am usually up at this hour feeding my herd and tending to my ranch," explained Eduardo.

"And I too, am up this early, usually praying for my flock and reading the Holy Scriptures for divine guidance."

"I suppose, Padre, that is what I have come for. Divine guidance."

"I see, well, I'm not sure I can give divine guidance, but we will give it our best shot."

"Bless me, Father for I have sinned."

"Lord, you know all things and you know I love you, please hear the words of your servant Eduardo and find in your most holy heart room for forgiveness of his sins."

"Lord God, Lamb of God, you know all things, Please hear my confession."

"In the name of the Father and the Son and the Holy Spirit… Amen."

"Amen. Padre, can a man be forgiven for a sin he has yet to commit?"

Father Mise paused, before answering, choosing his response carefully. "Do you mean like harboring an ill thought or hatred toward someone?"

"Yes. I suppose."

"And you have not acted on this notion...right?'

"No, Padre. It is just that. A notion."

"I believe the Holy Mother Church teaches that hate is a sin. It is in your heart, therefore it needs to be cleansed. It needs to be removed, before it can, like a cancer, grow into something even more vile."

"And can I be forgiven if I harbor this hatred?"

"Certainly, Eduardo. God the Father sent his Son to us for just that mission. To offer us forgiveness and atonement for our sins."

"Even if I haven't done anything yet?"

"Even if you carry the thought within you, you carry the sin."

"I see."

"Eduardo, you have been under a lot of stress recently... what with the events of this past week. You have no doubt found anger deep inside you. I know I would have. In fact, I did. I had to ask the Holy Father to forgive my anger before I delivered that scathing homily at your loved one's funeral. I got on my knees and asked God to grant me the peace to know what I was saying was the truth and was spoken for healing not for division."

"And did God talk to you?"

"He gave me peace, Eduardo. A deep abiding peace. That's why later today when I stand before the bishop, if there is to be retribution about what I said, I will know that God is on my side. Truth was on my side."

"Yes, but have you actually heard God's voice. You know, has he actually talked to you? Spoken to you?"

"You mean like we are speaking now...here?"

"Yes."

Father Mise paused again. Thinking back though his years of

ministry, he had never been asked this question, not this directly. "When we grieve, we long for answers. It is part of the process. You may be angry at God just now. I could understand that. You might be looking for a way to express that. To talk it over with him. Sure. I would want to, as well. I often want to in times such as these. But the important thing to understand is that we need to listen as much as talk."

"To what?"

"To his message for us. It is not always a voice … or words, as we know them. True, the bible and the liturgy can give us guidance and it is his words. The Church teaches us that it is God's Word. But God speaks to us in many ways. Ways that aren't encrypted in a written language or a spoken tongue."

"Like what?" Eduardo asked.

"In your heart there will come a feeling of right and wrong. It is a gift of God. He is giving you direction.

"If you have hatred in your hart, he will give you a path away from that feeling and into peace. But you have to look for his directions."

"You yourself said at the mass the other day you didn't know why God allowed this to happen…"

"You're right. And I still don't and I still seek an answer from him. But in the big picture, God's will has a plan. In the hurt and anguish you are feeling just now, there is a path God has laid out for you. To make this world better. To heal yourself and perhaps others. I do not know what it is just like I do not know why all of this happened. Especially to someone as precious as Cynthia and as wise as Rosa. But God knew what he was doing. There is a plan. And we have to trust him in this."

"Trust God who has taken my family from me?"

"Yes. I know it sounds…it sounds harsh and hard…and it is. But that is exactly what God wants us to do. Trust in him. Place our faith in his hands and let him live through us."

"And how am I supposed to do this?"

"Again. Wait on him. Listen for him. Believe in him. He will be there. You just have to seek him out. The mystery of our faith is that God is more grand than our minds can understand. And he controls history and the future in his hands everyday."

"Was he at the mall the other day?"

"I am sure he was. I am sure he immediately welcomed your daughter and your wife into the Kingdom. As soon as they left this body, he was there…with his Son, our Savior Jesus Christ to accept them into the Kingdom. To wrap them in his loving arms and reassure them that everything was okay. And that he is looking down now on their father and their husband to help him move through this trying time. To grow in the faith because of it."

"But you have never heard him? Not his actual voice?"

"No, my Eduardo. I have not heard the actual voice of God. But many a time, I have been in his presence. Not just when we offer the sacraments of Holy Communion – the Eucharist – I am in the presence of the Holy Spirit then…but at other times, as well. The other day at that homily during the funeral mass… God was there. He was speaking to all of us. He was using me as an instrument."

"You think God was wanting you to say all of that?"

"Not just wanting to…he was saying it through me. He was saying the truth. For justice. For peace… for a revival of a nation."

"Thank you, father. You have been most helpful to me."

"Eduardo, say ten Hail Marys and follow each of them with Our Fathers and pray constantly to hear God in your life. In the name of the Father and the Son and the Holy Spirit. Amen"

"Amen." Eduardo crossed himself and exited the small confessional booth.

God had a job for him to do. It was time to get going.

37

the office of the National Gun Association

Raymond Gilstrap ran the NGA with an iron fist. He had since the mid 1980's, when he turned the fledgling association of gun clubs and hunting organizations into a massive money-making juggernaut. Thanks in part to the generous contribution of numerous gun manufacturers and ammunition suppliers, the NGA became the largest single lobby in Washington D.C. and perhaps in every state capital, as well.

The growth spurt came about when Raymond, new in his role as head of development for the organization, discovered through a research study conducted by a major ammunition company, that people didn't like the U.S. Constitution to be toyed with. Wave the flag. Wave the red, white and blue. "Our freedoms are precious to us. And the Second Amendment is key to protecting and nurturing our most sacred freedom: freedom from tyranny." And he found a way to turn that message into a call to arms – no pun intended– call to money: a call to influence peddling at a level that no one in the halls of Congress had ever witnessed.

Oh the country, coming out of the hippie, radical days of the 60's and 70's and the racial unrest days of the 80's, loved this new song being sung. This was America. We had a God-given right to own guns. All kinds of guns. And Raymond Gilstrap was placed on Earth to protect that right.

He and his NGA were there for one thing. To protect your right to own a gun. Period. The founding fathers all but wrote his job description. The NGA wasn't about shooting clinics under Gilstrap's leadership. It wasn't about summer camps where young people would learn the sport of shooting or the craft of reloading a shell or the historic examination of a musket. No, that was for others to do. Let the scouting organizations do that. Or the Rotary club. The NGA was placed on Earth to collect money from gun-loving, gun-ravenous men and women who believed that it was their God-given right to own any gun their heart desired – the government be damned; and then to dole that money out to the powers that be to ensure the security of the sacred Second Amendment.

And by God, he had done it. The NGA was the most powerful force on Capitol Hill. Trade unions, teachers' groups, tax reformers, school lunch program advocates, higher education activists, even the Catholic Church all paled in comparison to the might and power of the NGA.

But Raymond Gilstrap was nervous. He called a special meeting of his executive council together at their Washington D.C. headquarters on K Street. Seventeen executives from around the nation had flown in. Represented were gun owners (one – and that was just for P.R. show) gun makers, ammunition manufacturers, and a few troublemakers –known as the press police – inside the organization. The talk around the giant table before Gilstrap strode in was that membership was down again. The tenth year that the number of NGA members had fallen.

"Not to worry," said, one of the gun makers' reps. "We'll just pour more dough in. We've got plenty. We don't need members to get our work done. We need dollars. And we got 'em. Plenty of 'em."

Everyone in the room smiled. They knew that to be the truth. The NGA ran off of gun manufacturer donations. That and the boys who make the bullets.

Gilstrap entered the room and stood at the end of the table as he was in the habit of doing. Every eye was cast his way. "We've got a real problem. A real big problem." Raymond Gilstrap never started a meeting with a negative note. He was the most positive man one could ever meet. So for him to launch a meeting with the recognition that there was a problem facing them, then there must be a huge problem.

"Did anyone see the funeral services from that mall shooting the other day?"

A couple of hands were raised.

And did you two notice anything unusual about it?" They shook their heads no.

"The networks caught it. They put it on the air live. Even our buddies at FOX broadcast it live. Hell, they couldn't cut away, it was too powerful and it would have looked like chicken shit to leave a funeral of this sort in mid sentence."

"What happened?' asked one of the gun lobbyists sitting in the group.

"I'll tell you want happened. Father Richard Mise is what happened. That sonofabitch laid out the best plan to destroy us there has ever been proclaimed on live TV. And it ran and ran and ran over and over on social media and all over the country. Early news. Mid-day news. Evening news. Late night news. National networks and local TV stations. And again the next day and the next."

"We've always had a crack pot or two taking pot shots at us," said the Executive VP for funding.

"Not like this. This was inspired."

"Wasn't Wadsworth down there running cover for us. Interference?"

"Wadsworth gets cornered by that NBC ass, Rawlings and has nothing to counter what's being said. He high-tails it and shags out of there with his tail stuck up his ass. And we are left looking like clowns. No wonder our membership is leaving us.

"But wait, there's more and it's a lot worse. Last night Parsons ran a poll with Rice University. Now to be fair there had just been another active shooter on a campus in Southern California, but still the poll goes out and it comes back 80 -20. That's eighty percent of the population wanting major gun control."

"We should wait a few days and run it again further away from these shootings." Said Jessie Becom, head of legislative liaisons.

"Jessie, do you have any idea how many heads we'd have to turn to make a dent in numbers like these. We've never scored this low. Hell, even after Stoneman Douglas, we still pulled a 48.9. And that's with those kids crying all over TV and that town hall bullshit meeting. I'm telling you, we are at a twenty. Actually to make it even worse, it's not really twenty… it's nineteen point eight. Think about that for a moment."

The seriousness of the numbers was taking hold of the people gathered around the conference room table.

"You let this get started and get going sideways, the President is going to see his chance and then we've got gun control coming out of our asses. The Democrats and liberals have been just waiting for this moment. It is their tipping point. It is here now. It is powerful. America is turning its backs on us. In huge numbers."

"Yeah, but they will never give up their guns," said one of the gun makers.

"You think. Yesterday in Norman, Oklahoma…gun country… a crowd of two thousand gathered at a police station and turned in their guns."

"University town. Doesn't count." Again it was Becom.

"Jessie, the handwriting is on the wall. It won't take much effort to push this administration back to the gun control issue. And that fuckin' priest's speech the other day set a fire under activists all over the country. Rick Cross of Texas said he received over a thousand calls for gun control. Pro gun control. And that's even trying to filter out the leftist callers. It was moms and dads. In Texas for God's sake. Fuckin' Texas."

"What should we do?" Asked one of the bullet boys.

"We need a plan. Something to turn this thing back our way," said Gilstrap.

At the side of the room Randolph Gates slowly stood. His six foot five frame was an imposing figure. Gates was a long time Washington insider who had helped steer the NGA to its prominence and helped get Gilstrap planted at the head of the organization. But somewhere deep inside the catacombs of the group, Randolph Gates' opine still reverberated a lot of power as his deep baritone voice spoke.

"Do nothing." He paused waiting for the assembled to calm.

"Do nothing." Again he waited.

"Do nothing. Wait them out. They will forget. They always do. The numbers will come back in our favor. Wait them out. Get our people in Congress to stall any movement. Get committees to close ranks and wait them out. America will forget."

"Randolph, with due respect…nineteen point…"

"I don't give a damn. Just hunker down, get invisible and wait them out. It will go away. We own Congress. The President can't pass gas on the Hill without our people helping him. We can get past this. Wait them out."

"That's your plan?" Asked Gilstrap. "At nineteen point eight…you want us to withdraw – to shrink inward and just wait."

Gates nodded. "Just wait them out. Tell your contacts in the halls of government to wait them out. Let them know it will blow over. National elections are far enough away we've got time on our side. One or two Representatives will get bruised in mind-terms, can't help that. Collateral damage. But we'll hold both chambers. America will forget. Wait them out."

And the NGA had a plan.

It had always worked before. No reason it wouldn't work again.

America has a very short memory.

38

the stall

The phone had been ringing all afternoon and into the evening. At dinner, Senator Rip Torrance of Florida had taken three calls from Rick Cross of Texas and another from Representative Alan Hall, from Kansas. They were trying to make sure Rip had enough leverage to delay the hearings that were to take part in his subcommittee on the ban of assault rifles in the United States.

"The NGA is depending on us, Rip. We don't want this mall thing to throw a wrench in the works."

"Not to worry," said Torrance to Cross. The Florida Republican was seated across from NGA lead council, David Hopewell. "I've got NGA here now, and we're going over our strategy. Gale Rivers, from Georgia is going to join us soon, to sew up her part in the House.

"All we need is a few weeks," said Cross, the right-wing leader of the Senate's Republican strike force. He and Torrance had worked closely together for three terms fending off gun control activists, although both had faced stiff competition in their latest elections. The common belief was that NGA money had bailed both of them out in the closing days up to election; buying huge TV ad schedules to push them over the top against their lesser-funded Democratic challengers.

"You'll get your weeks. This bill won't see daylight before Valentine's Day…and then the whole hoopla will have died down."

"Good."

"But Rick, we're going to have to give something. Some ground. We're going to have to throw the President a bone. It's not just in the Senate. Rivers has said so in the House, too."

The NGA lawyer at the table with the Senator from Florida frowned and shook his head. The NGA policy was never give an inch.

Cross could almost see the NGA attorney shaking his head, when he said over the phone, "No, the NGA will not approve even a slight shift in our stance. No compromise. No giving in…not even an inch."

"But Rick, the latest polls have us way, way down. It is no longer a popular issue."

"We control the House and the Senate and now we control the United States Supreme Court. We don't need the American people. We will keep our Second Amendment and we will not give in…not an inch."

"But the President doesn't have the same cover to hide behind. He will need to save face with the American people."

"No way. I'll talk with him. No backing down."

"Not even on assault rifles?"

"Not even on the boxes they come in." Cross paused. "Get a grip, Rip. No steps backwards. Not now. There is no reason to. We own the country."

The call ended and Hopewell, the NGA lawyer repeated the party lines. Don't give in an inch. Torrance understood the words, but disagreed with the politics. "I've been at this a long time. If that tide turns like the polls say it is turning, we will erode any leverage we have. If we give assault rifles up as sacrificial lambs, we will come out smelling like heroes."

"Who is a hero?" asked a tall blonde woman in a lovely gray suit. She was Gale Rivers, Republican Representative from Georgia, arriving fashionably late for dinner. Her suburban Atlanta district wasn't as solid Republican in her last election as she had hoped it would be and Rivers was doing everything to shore up support from lobbies and their money as she could. She knew the next election would be a slugfest.

"I was saying we could look like the white knights on our steeds coming to the country's rescue if we gave in on assault rifles and let the President paint a picture of moderation in gun control."

"It'll never happen," said Rivers. "I've just gotten off the phone with Dr. Tim Crawley of Rice University. Tim used to be at Georgia Tech, I've known him for years. Smart, smart man. Knows his numbers and how to apply them. He says he's never seen any landslide like this. The avalanche has already started. We have crossed the tipping point. You're going to have to offer more than assault rifles."

"Preposterous," said Hopewell full of bluster and venom. No one ever talked about the NGA like this. This was treason. He had to stop it. "If you two want to be re-elected, then you will need our money to see that it happens, so I suggest you'd better devise a plan where giving in anything never occurs."

"Says who?" Asked the defiant Rivers.

"Says Raymond Gilstrap. And others. People who think we need to ride this out. To lay low and let this whole thing blow over."

"Oh, the old ostrich ploy," Rivers said, as she ordered a gin and tonic from a white jacketed waiter.

"I don't care what name you give it, our plan is to lay low. Be out of the line of fire. Let the President take the heat if he wants to. But we will be silent and let the talk subside. And it will. America has a way of forgetting how mad she is. Americans never hold a grudge."

"Unless they are from the South," joked Torrance.

"Whatever," said the lawyer. "You know what I am saying. We don't back up on assault rifles or large volume magazines or anything. We plant our feet firmly on the Second Amendment and stand there in the face of any onslaught."

"That priest over in Texas has named it the Death Amendment and that is really taking off...like naming the Affordable Care Act, Obamacare...great, great P.R....it is tainting our product," said Rivers, herself a former advertising agency chief executive, who understood marketing and branding as well as anyone in Washington.

"The product you refer to is the Constitution of the United States…"

"Yes, but his words have turned that against us. And it is working. Again professor Crawley says that the numbers will slide even more before the end of the year. I don't know about you, but I'm not sure I can overcome an opponent that wraps herself or himself in that banner. It will make me look like a blood sucker."

"Elections are still a year or more off," said Torrance.

"Easy for a Senator to say, Rip. I've got to raise money and votes every two years. That means work all the time at re-election. And this whole thing could turn the House upside down. Then, where is your mandate? Where is your majority? Where is your power base? Huh? You lose the House… the Senate is next."

"It will be…"she cut the lawyer off.

"It will be gone. Starting from scratch and the Second Amendment will be tattered and torn and shredded and piece-by-piece will be dismantled. I tell you, this hide and wait is the wrong strategy.

"This isn't like abortion where we nibbled away at the edges until we had our way. Bit-by-bit ripping the heart out of the pro-choice movement. These gun control activists are coming at us with power saws and chain saws and bulldozers ready to cut us down and bury us."

"Then what do you suggest, Gale?" Asked Torrance.

"Take it head-on. Make this guy look and sound like an un-American activist. A scary, irrational zealot who is out after our freedoms. Paint him as a traitor to the American Way."

"I dunno. K Street is pretty adamant that we hunker down and not fight this. Let it blow its own wind out and wait." Hopewell was delivering the NGA line, but even he could see the valid merit of River's suggestion.

"Tell you what," said Torrance reaching a compromise. "We'll stall. We'll get things all mired in subcommittees – both in the House and in the Senate – if you'll take Gale's plan back to K Street and run it up the flagpole there. But we'll have to get the White House on board with this plan. The President has to back our play."

"Can you make that happen?" asked Hopewell, knowing he had an equally tough sell at NGA headquarters.

"Maybe. Just maybe." Said Rivers.

39

Thou shalt not shout.

The bishop in Tyler was pissed off. Royally angry. Theologically angry. So angry that he made Father Mise wait over an hour outside his diocesan office just to show his displeasure with the national broadcast in which the priest had taken part – hell – the sensational spectacle he had led; not to mention the on-going press the local parish priest was receiving from every corner of the nation.

His name was Monsignor Gronklin. He would never be remembered as particularly bright or loving or kind or even a good leader. He was more like a real estate developer. His job was to build buildings. In this case, that would mean building a network of parish churches across East Texas and to see that they flourished and raised money. And that– that Gronklin was good at. He would have been successful in the fast-food franchise business. After all that is what he was doing. Come dine with us on the Eucharist and give your money and we'll bless you. Only thing missing were girls in tight service uniforms and catchy jingles.

But what really set the Monsignor off was that Rome loved the televised event. LOVED IT. The Papal dispatch was full of news about the small church in Lincoln. The power of the homily. The truth in the message. The power of a voice led by God.

Jesus Christ, no mention of Gronklin! He was furious. He should have been invited and allowed to lead the services. To be sure, he would have never gone off against guns the way Father Mise had, but who would? That was foolish. Stupid really. All those grieving people and here the man of God – a man of the most holy cloth – was up there pronouncing the evil in our world as guns. No business of the Catholic Church. The Church's business was soothing troubled souls and collecting alms in the progress. Had been for several thousand years.

Guns and gun ownership was the purview of the government. Souls belonged to the church. Let us not confuse the two. That would be his message to Father Mise. You got the wrong message. We should have been there trying to ease pain and comfort souls, not disarm a nation. Not our job.

"It was my job to deliver the truth."

"Your job is to preach the gospel."

"My job…"

"Your job is not to preach about gun control."

"My job is to preach the truth. Scriptures tell me that. God told me that," Father Mise already knew that Gronklin was angry. He also knew that Rome was in love with him. He was a folk hero in the halls of the Vatican. So fuck this fat pious prick who, along with his red face and thick, wine-swilling lips, had been yelling at him for over an hour.

"Your job was to soothe the masses – to ease their hurt."

"Their hurt was being eased by the mystery within the Mass and by the music and by each other and by God. My job was to point out the root of their suffering. The gun."

Gronklin exploded and put Father Mise on a six week sabbatical for rest.

"I am not tired."

"But I am tired of you," said Gronklin.

"You just don't want to rock the boat with your rich friends. You don't want to disturb the politicians with whom you dine, with whom you play golf. You don't want the church to have to take a stand.

"For what? Guns? What if the sin of the day had been slavery or prostitution, or heaven forbid – abortion? You would have been buying billboards to fight these things. And you have. But guns, which are destroying American homes and families… you turn your back on because it doesn't sit well with your brand of social justice or politics."

"Shut up."

"No. God told me to speak the truth. Your ears do not want you to hear the truth."

"Eight weeks of sabbatical."

"What is this, a sentence or are you giving me rest and comfort?"

"Get out. Go away. I want you to report to St. Alban's in San Antonio. It is a home for priest, like yourself, who need some time away from the pressures of the local parish."

"I don't need time…"

"You will take time."

"Or…"

"Or I will have to tell Rome of your infidelities and drug abuse. They would hate to know their current favorite son is such a sinner…"

"What? I have none. That is a bold-face lie…"

"Then go. Go to see Father O'Brien at Saint Albans. He is expecting you. Rest and come home relaxed and ready to help your parish. And while you are away I want you to think and re-think about this silly nonsense of guns being talked about from the sacred pulpit."

Father Mise drove back from Tyler as angry as the Monsignor had been before their meeting. He switched on the speaker in the car for his cell phone and called a number he had been given years earlier by a priest at his seminary in South Bend.

"Pronto," said a very Italian sounding voice.

"Father Groppa?"

"Si. And this is?"

"My name is Father Mise. I need some advice from the Vatican."

"Very well my son. It is late in the day here, let me get your number and I will have the Pontif's secretary give you a call tomorrow. I assume it is about your sermon the other day...the one broadcast live?"

"Yes."

"And your local bishop is disturbed with you about its contents...no?"

"Right again."

"Very well. A word to the wise. Press on. God is on your side. Truth is on your side. The Holy Father is on your side. I will have his secretary, Cardinal Lorenzo call you. And have faith my good father. Have faith that all will work out. Preach the truth and God will smile."

Father Mize was packing later that evening in the Rectory, when his phone rang.

"Father Mise?"

"Yes. Who am I speaking with?'

"My name is Eve Kholemann with NBC News. We would love to have you as a visitor on our Sunday news show: Point/Counterpoint. Bob McAdoo, whom I believe you know, will be the moderator."

"When?"

"As soon as possible. Your message is truly resonating with the American public and we'd like to talk with you about it."

"I am supposed to go to San Antonio for a sabbatical..."

"We'll send a jet. You'll be gone for a day... maybe two. We can even then fly you to San Antonio."

"A day or two?"

"Yes."

"Send your plane to Shreveport. I will meet them there."

The bishop wasn't going to like this.

40

The President would like to see you.

Walk into the White House and a wave of history washes over you. Stand there during a crisis and that wave turns into a tsunami of sheer power. The tide of energy, conquest and action would sweep even a stone monument away in its path. That day was such a day. A command was given and it was to be followed immediately. America might well depend on it.

Will Holt got such a command at the end of the day. It was to be followed up on as soon as possible, which in White House terms meant why hasn't it already happened?

Like many of the President's employees in and around the Oval Office, Will was a lawyer. And while he had never practiced a day in his life in a courtroom, he was quite knowledgeable in the ways of the law, especially when it came to the Constitution itself. After having clerked for Justice Sam Pete of the U.S. Court of Appeals in D.C., the three years following his graduation from Harvard, he began to write numerous articles for his former employer, the think tank – The American Foundation, a rather centrist-leaning organization whose said goal was to see that the country kept to a steady coarse of conservative management with a slight dose of quasi-liberal visions for the nation's future. Unlike the more staunch think tanks who usually leaned toward one aisle or the other, The American Foundation saw the need in a balanced formula and that had married very well with the current administration's idea of running a country. To that end, Will was summoned one day to 1600 Pennsylvania Avenue and offered a job as a legislative liaison for the White House. He took the job almost immediately. His old boss at The American Foundation was pleased to have Will Holt buried in the upper echelon of the President's thought leaders: The men who really run the country.

Will's day began with a phone call from the President's Chief of Staff requesting he attend a briefing in the Oval Office concerning the recent spat of gun violence. It was a subject about which Will had penned numerous legal opinions for Justice Pete, as well as having written a major paper about guns and specifically the rights to own them for a New York Times Op Ed piece, which had originally caught the eye of the NGA. But after an interview with the gun lobby, it was decided that Will was too wishy-washy on guns to be entrusted with a spokesperson role for the organization. They passed on him. It was then he ventured to The American Foundation and made a name for himself in trying to revamp the Brady Bill in Congress. Twice he almost had enough votes, but alas, the NGA thumbed their noses at the American voters and prevailed with their bought and paid-for legislators. And that made Will Holt work even harder to return the country to the people, who, in his eyes, actually own the Constitution. On that, he and the President agreed eye-to-eye.

"There's a fellow in Texas...a Catholic Priest, who has lit a fire under the voters...Geno, want to share your numbers with us?" said the Chief of Staff.

Gene Lowery, a tall, balding Californian who had advanced degrees in math and logistics, stood and began reciting sets of numbers that to most lay people would have caused their eyeballs to roll back in their sockets. Sleep was easily achieved listening to Geno, unless, you knew where he was heading and what the numbers meant. Will Holt understood clearly what the data meant. The American people overwhelmingly now wanted gun reform. And they wanted it so much that slight nods to it, in the way the President had been thinking of going, were not going to work.

"For gun control at the highest level – complete lock down of all guns –thirty-one percent…pro…but take that down just one notch, gun control with an outlawing of automatic and semi automatic weapons and a limit of magazine capacity, and the number jumps to eighty-five percent in favor." He paused to let the numbers sink in. "Gentlemen…and ladies, the numbers do not lie. America is fed up with gun violence and they want something done about it. Not lip service. And not a total repeal of the second amendment."

"You mean the Death Amendment," joked the Secretary of Energy, a man Will Holt found to be obsessively ignorant of most worldviews except those espoused in the skyscrapers of Houston. If it wasn't about the oil patch, it had nothing to do with energy…that was his idea of running the department. Will had no idea how the President had picked such an obtuse individual to fill such a vital role. But, the secretary did come from a wealthy Texas family who had sway over a lot of dollars and voters in the Lone Star State.

"Laugh all you guys want to at the priest who came up with that phrase, but he has captured a real voice in America," said Geno as he brought up another slide in his PowerPoint presentation. "Over ninety five percent of the people could identify the phrase and where it had come from and what it meant. That's in less than a week. Ninety-five percent. I bet sixty-five percent of the people in this country don't know both of their Senators…or the Vice President for that matter. But we're talking about ninety-five percent. The guy is a folk hero."

"Yeah, but how is that translating with people giving up their guns?" The question came from the Attorney General.

"It isn't. Not yet anyway. Not in a huge way. But it is starting…and what else is happening," a new slide came up, "the number of people willing to turn in their assault guns is up over thirty percent. It is still a minority of gun owners, but with a growth like that, even the staunch gun owners are starting to see that we need real gun ownership laws and checks. And certain arms need to be outlawed. Or else…"

"Or else what?' Asked the President.

"Or else there will be a constitutional crisis…an uprising and we'll lose the Second Amendment…sorry the Death Amendment… all together."

"Holt, any thoughts on these numbers and the constitutionality of such an uprising?"

"Sure, one word. Prohibition. The numbers behind it were far less than these. These numbers should scare some folks to death. Look what happened to alcohol with a smaller voice than the anti-gun movement has right now," said Will.

"Like who, who should it scare?" asked the President.

"Like the NGA," said Will. "You can't turn their ship around in numbers this shallow. No support. They've run aground."

"They sure are keeping a low profile after this mall shooting," offered the Vice President, a member of the NGA and at one time ardent spokesman for the organization, but had fallen out of favor with the K Street lobby when Raymond Gilstrap took the reins of power.

"A low profile is their tried and true strategy in these times. Big shooting, hunker down." It was Geno again, and again he had numbers to show how each time a shooting occurred, gun sales went up, but membership in the NGA went down. "But there are two anomalies in these numbers. Uvalde and Lincoln. For some reason the American public have finally said, that's it …we're through with this shit. Sorry Mr. President" The Chief of Staff nodded at Geno to continue. The President himself seldom swore, only then when unfiltered ears could not hear him.

"We need to adjust our strategy," said the Chief of Staff. The President nodded his agreement.

"Might I suggest we get the priest up here. And get him on our side. Maybe we could look like we're on the side of the angels." It was the Attorney General.

"Do it," said the President. "Get him here and let's get this thing under control. Let's get a rein on this movement."

"It is not as organized as that, Mr. President," said Geno.

"I realize that Gene. That's why I want the good Padre here on our soil. We'll get him to organize this movement for us." The President stood, as did everyone else in the room. He started to walk out, then suddenly stopped. "Holt, get me Father Mise."

The order had been given. The most powerful man in the free world wanted the small town Catholic priest from Texas in the White House and it was Will Holt's job now, to make that happen. ASAP.

"Why isn't he here already, Will?"

41

Everybody has something to hide. Find his closet.

FOX News was slipping in the numbers game. The big three networks along with CNN were starting to move past the right-wing voice of the Republican Party. And that bothered some special interest groups, none more than the National Gun Association. So they called a meeting with the network.

It was a hush-hush conference in a small West Virginia mountain lodge where senior FOX News executives and members of the NGA steering committee came together to discuss a plan to reverse the tide of support rolling away from them and toward the anti-gun movement.

First to speak after a scrumptious breakfast had been served, was NGA leader, Raymond Gilstrap. He didn't mince words about the current situation.

"Since the mall shooting in Lincoln, Texas we have been playing defense. Backing up on our heels. That will not do. I have watched as you, the network folks, have evaded the tough topics. They need to be addressed up front and forcefully."

"But wait, Raymond," said the head of network news. "...you guys are the ones who have been hunkered down in your 'do nothing, say nothing' approach to another mass shooting. Don't go laying the blame at our feet. Your spokespeople will not come on the air and defend guns. Will not stand up for the Second Amendment. You have gone dark, so we have nothing to work with."

Gilstrap paused and considered his next thought carefully. "Very well, we will send you spokespeople to take our point of view. But there is a bigger problem out there."

"You mean the preacher from Texas," said one of the FOX executive producers.

"He's a priest and yes. That is exactly what and who I am talking about."

"He's had his day in the spotlight. Let him go," said the executive producer.

'That's where I disagree with you. I think he is picking up steam. He is the face of a new movement in America." Gilstrap was standing his ground.

"Well, if it is a new movement, it isn't very well defined and not at all organized. Ask the other side what they want out of gun reform and you'll get a dozen different answers. They can't even decide among themselves." The FOX executives all nodded in agreement with their head of research, who continued. "Our numbers show this guy's very popular. Not sure that is actually translating into a movement to halt the Second Amendment. Maybe to pinch assault rifles, but even his popularity can't go that far. Not yet. Besides, he doesn't have any organization behind him. And it was just one televised sermon. Had we known what he was going to say, we would have never put it on the air."

"But you did," said the NGA attorney Hopewell.

"Sure we did. If we had pulled the plug in the middle of his talk, we would have truly played into the hands of those who accuse us of being hypocrites," said the head of FOX News.

"It may have started as just one sermon, but this guy is starting to congeal a big portion of America, and there is a group of thinkers who see this as an opportunity to take the feelings of America and exploit it – to turn it against us. Just look at social media. The guy is everywhere. His homily is played and replayed daily by thousands. Perhaps millions. With that kind of momentum, gun reform could become a repeal of the Second Amendment or at least a major revision to it. We cannot let that happen. We will not let that happen." Gilstrap was almost shouting.

All the heads nodded in agreement.

"So we will do our part at the network, but what are you going to do?" Asked the head of broadcast news.

"I think we are going to have to give ground. Some." Gilstrap hated the words coming from his own mouth.

There was an audible groan in the room.

"I know you don't like that and believe me, neither do I, but to get the White House back in line, we may have to support their ban on assault rifles and high capacity magazines. The President ran on that, and even though we have backed him off of it recently, this Lincoln Mall shooting has him revamping his campaign ideas. But, if we give in now, we'll treat it like the Brady Bill…Once they roll out the assault rifle ban and the limits on magazine capacity, we'll start nipping at it in courts around the country where we have jurists who favor us. A lawsuit here and a lawsuit there and soon it won't be the law of the land. We'll treat it just like the anti-abortion guys did. It will make it to the Supreme Court, and we own those fuckers. And that will give us time to shore up the Second Amendment support."

"Are you sure you can stop it there?" Asked the evening anchor for FOX News.

"Yes. I believe we can…if…and this is a huge if…if we can get to the priest and quiet him."

"How do you plan on doing that?" Asked a FOX executive.

"Everyone has a skeleton or two hidden in their darkest closet. We need to find his and expose it. We need some digging into his past. Into his associates. His friends. His seminary days. There has to be something we can color him with."

"Like maybe he liked alter boys or something?" asked the anchor again.

"Or something. I don't want this to be us against the Catholic Church…I mean for Christ's sake the Pope is talking this guy up. He is a most popular item. So I want to go after him. Just him. Limit the exposure to Father Mise."

"You want us to put investigators onto him?" asked the FOX executive producers.

"Sure. We've already got some in the field digging, but any help we can get from the network the better. And it has to stay very, very private. I do not want to tip him off. I do not want the Democrats to know or even the White House until we are ready to make our move. Do we understand?"

They all were in agreement.

"Let's get to work quickly on this guy and we may not even have to sacrifice assault rifles."

They broke into smaller groups to organize how they would go after Father Mise. By lunch, they had their plans mapped out and assignments made.

Father Mise was going down. And who better to assist them than Texas Senator Rick Cross.

42

Remember to close the gates.

Eduardo pulled into the driveway of a small hotel outside of Bristol, Tennessee. He was more than halfway to his destination. He checked in and went to his room. He had purchased a suitcase at a Target in Little Rock and disassembled the AR 15 so that it would rest comfortably inside the luggage: the magazines and boxes of bullets, too.

He took a shower and changed shirts. He put his work boots back on along with the jeans he had worn from Lincoln. He laid down on the bed and napped. At two in the morning he turned on the television. With the volume quite low, he watched as a tape of Senator Rick Cross from Texas was replayed from an earlier news show. He was being interviewed by a FOX reporter.

"I am sure that the young man who created such a tragedy in Lincoln had many problems he was dealing with – parents divorced – a split home life – bullied at school, a social outcast...the perfect breeding ground for a crazed shooter to brew his hatred and vile contempt for our society.

"This was no gun show nut case, as some have painted him to be. No way. In fact, each and every one of those guns he used had been bought legally by his father. Or was bought by a friend and given to the family as a gift. Perfectly legal. No, this young man was on the edge and he snapped and he happened to choose a gun – an assault rifle – and a pistol – to carry out his vengeful, sadistic feelings on our fellow citizens. It is this kind of illness we need to stop. We must stop.

"Just yesterday the Governor of Texas issued a proclamation saying that our state was backing more research into mental illness and crime. Trying to understand how people can come undone and wreck such havoc on their fellow citizens. We will do all we can, as a state, to see that mental health professionals are versed in spotting the signs of those with acute problems – those who could conduct violent acts.

"And I call on the President and his party to show a bi-partisan support to my mental illness bill that would appropriate sixteen million dollars into the study of mental instability and violence on a national level."

"Senator Cross, do you really think sixteen million is enough?" Asked the FOX reporter.

"Mercy no. But I am waiting on more funding to come from the House of Representatives. In fact, Georgia Republican Representative, Gale Rivers, is going to work on a plan with her appropriations subcommittee to wrestle away close to a quarter of a billion dollars that was earmarked for alternative energy and put it to work in this study. Her funds and mine, when meshed together, will make a real nail we can drive into the problem facing America today."

"Why not just eliminate assault rifles all together?"

Cross had not expected that question. Neither had Hopewell, who was standing off in the wings as the staged interview was transpiring. Even the director of the Fox News program was caught off-guard with the young reporter's sudden break from the approved script.

"Well…" Cross stumbled…" Well… it would violate the Second Amendment…"

"The Second Amendment doesn't specify what type of arms people can bare, nor does it seem to limit the government's ability to make certain mass-killing weapons off limits to ordinary citizens."

"Will not be abridged." Cross regained his footing. "It says that the government cannot take away the rights of the citizens of the United States from owning and carrying firearms. Our freedom to own...to bare arms shall not be abridged."

"But they were writing about muskets. Single shot rifles at the time. And for an organized militia..."

Cross cut him off. "It is an old argument of the Left. Limit the guns and crime will go down. Nonsense. Not until you address mental illness."

"But the Brady Bill proved otherwise, Senator. When assault weapons were banned, gun crimes, especially mass shootings fell. The numbers are there in black and white. What do you say to those statistics?"

"Not according to a Duke University study..."

"A study funded by the NGA..."

Rick Cross smiled and excused himself, as he departed he reminded those watching that the people of Lincoln need their thoughts and prayers. Thoughts and prayers. He had another pressing appointment he had to keep, but as he walked away he frowned at the FOX producer who stood next to NGA lawyer Hopewell. That had definitely not gone the way it was supposed to. Someone got to the young reporter. Now someone needed to reprimand him.

But FOX did not. Instead they kept him on the story. His interview nudged their news numbers. People sat up and took notice. After all, FOX was in the eyeball business. And the young reporter and his feisty manner – right or left – got people's attention and that would mean ad revenue, whether the NGA liked it or not.

Eduardo turned the television off. They were always arguing. Guns or no guns. Guns killed my daughter and my wife, he thought to himself. Guns did. And the NGA ran the gun business. They needed a dose of their own medicine.

That night as he slept, Eduardo dreamed he was seeing his cattle and his horses slowly wandering out of an open gate and vacate his ranch. He had forgotten to close the gate. Faster and faster the herd moved toward freedom. He could not budge. Something was holding him down. Eduardo struggled. He was trapped as he watched the animals leave his property. Oh, to be able to close the gate to stop them, but he could not. He was chained in place. Slowly the last one left, a small horse, and on it rode his younger daughter, Cynthia. She looked back at him as she passed through the open portal and waved farewell.

Eduardo slept deeply into the morning. Sun crept into his room, awakened him from his dream and he arose. He took his suitcase and moved into the parking lot of the hotel; loaded his car and drove away.

He had work to do.

43

Judith and Hal Davenport

The couple who had met at Baylor and had been married in a chapel there on campus, was laid to rest in a family cemetery seven miles outside of Waco, Texas. A few hundred people stood in a cold north wind as they watched the two caskets being lowered into the rock-hard, Central Texas caliche dirt. Dusty remnants of the pile of white soil swirled around them and then away, as if lifting the Davenports from their place of final rest and into the blue Texas sky. Men grabbed for their hats and women held their wraps closely around them to ward off the harsh breeze.

A string quartet from Baylor University played several hymns and the assistant pastor of the First Baptist Church in Lincoln read a scripture then said a few words. These were not the firebrand words that Father Mise uttered, but they still had a bite – a sting– to them.

"Into The Lord's hands we place Judith and Hal today. Into his care we leave them." The Davenports' children were in tears, sitting a few feet from the combined gravesite. Several members of the Patriot Farms executive committee were in attendance. It was their second service in as many days, having buried Perry Reynolds outside of his family home in Altoona, Pennsylvania the morning before. "Our Lord and Savior Jesus Christ has met them at heaven's door and ushered them into the kingdom. They are at home.

"I know Judith and Hal. I know their devotion to the word of God and to the ministry of Christ here on earth. I know of their devotion to each other and to their children. And I weep with you at their passing. But I also rejoice in knowing that they are safe and sound in the bosom of Christ. He has accepted them into the land of Milk and Honey and they shall be there waiting on each of us, to join them in paradise.

"I also know that they would look down on us here today and ask, how did we let such a thing happen? How did it come about that such a horrific attack could have snuffed out their lives, as well as those other nineteen people – especially the young lives in their care that tragic afternoon. How?

"It is a question we each must ask ourselves.

"How did it happen and when is it going to stop?

"I do not always agree with my neighbor, Father Mise on things of theology. We have our own sheet music from which we play. But his sermon the other day at the funeral of Rosa and Cynthia Parker gave me pause. Made me take a moment to stop and ponder the disease in our land.

"We need reform in our hearts. But we also need it in our laws. Reform for the mentally ill. Reform for our police. Reform for those who sell and buy guns. And most of all, reform of our laws for those who use guns in such violent means.

"Thou shalt not kill says the Ten Commandments. It is a sin. A mortal sin. And when it is carried out with such weapons of mass destruction against such innocent victims, I feel that it is our time as Christians to rise and say, 'Enough is enough.' That is what we owe Judith and Hal. And all the others who we've laid to rest in our soil these last few days. The knowledge we will not forget them, but rather we will work to make our nation whole again.

"One law at a time.

"My prayer for you today is to love each other. Hold each other. Remember those we have lost. And do not let their deaths – their lives– be in vain. Speak out. Let's end this gun violence. Amen."

The crowd was mostly Baptist and that meant mostly conservative southerners; yet, it was surprising how many people approached the young pastor after the ceremony and thanked him for the words of respect and the challenge of power he had given them.

On his drive back to Lincoln, the young Baptist minister made it a point to seek out Father Mise and offer him any support he might need during his time of "self examination" as the Diocese in Tyler had called his sudden sabbatical. Everyone in Lincoln – everyone in the world – knew what had happened.

And in Rome, they were extremely angry with Bishop Gronklin. But the powers that be in Vatican City knew to let time play out its hand. That is how God works his miracles.

Time. He invented it. He would use it. Amen.

44

Welcome to
the network.

Father Mise was way out of his league. Way out of his comfort zone. He was in a huge city with millions of people, all seemingly talking at once, all moving about with a rapid pace as if where they were headed was the most important matter on Earth.

Life and death.

They were in a rush to make the matter their own and to solve what troubled the world. Right now. Right then.

As he entered the NBC Network Operations building, he was greeted by Eve Kholemann. "Welcome to the Network Center, Rev Mise."

"Father Mise. We save the title Reverend for those further up the food chain than myself. For some reason. Makes Rome nervous."

She laughed. "Father then…welcome. Follow me, I have some people who would love to meet you." They walked to a bank of elevators and she placed her hand on the black screen to the right of the cab. It read her palm and the door opened. Inside the cab she repeated the process, then pressed 44. They waited while the elevator lifted them from the ground floor up forty-four flights of steel and concrete until they arrived at The News Center. He knew it was because the giant sign on the wall said so. Stepping out there was even more hustle and bustle about, as interns and P.A.s ran around fetching copy, sodas, coffee and answering phones for on-air personalities who were busy doing on-air personality sort of things.

They walked down a long hall, the exterior of which were glass windows looking out and onto Manhattan and through the forest of high rise buildings, one could just make out the Hudson River to the west and a corner of Central Park to their north. The din of the city had faded from them, the chaos of sound and drama far below their lofty perch above the city. To the inside, were rows of glass cubicles with men and women busy watching monitors or typing stories or editing text that was about to go out to educate a world on what was happening on the seven continents today.

There was an air of authority on the floor. An air of purpose. A feeling that what was going on here truly mattered...perhaps more so than those places the people in a hurry down 44 stories on the streets of the city thought mattered so much. Here it was life and death. It was taxes and earnings and power and truth and justice.

Welcome to the News Center, Father Mise.

His eyes were wide.

From what he saw on monitors of a war zone, it was about life and death. And suddenly he flashed back to the mall. And that was why he was here. The killings.

They rounded a corner and into a conference room and to a long table filled with a half dozen people. Beyond its glass walls he could see the evening news studio and beyond that, the control room, where decisions were made in split second increments, decisions that kept that truth and justice and the flow of information moving.

A man stood and extended his hand. Lewis Rice. Head of NBC News. And next to him sat Bob McAdoo, his old fish-eating buddy. It was good to see a familiar face.

"Bob," he said informally.

"Father Mise. Good you could join us. Welcome." Bob nodded to a chair across from him and Mise sat down. He was dressed in his black clothes and a black coat with a white priestly collar. He might be officially on sabbatical, but for this trip, he wanted to be thought of as a man of God.

"Ever been on TV before?" asked a director, whose name was also Mise.

Father Mise laughed. "Yeah. Thanks to Bob here, I've been on screens all over the world apparently."

Everyone in the room enjoyed a laugh. The guy was a natural.

"I mean have you ever been on a formal, in-studio show?"

Mise shook his head. "No. But cameras do not bother me. Crowds do not bother me. Just guns."

And there... he had said it. Something they had all been wondering about. Would the Catholic priest from Texas take up the fight, after he had said so much and so strongly at the funeral mass the other day in his local parish church. And there it was. No guns. Just what they wanted to hear.

"Don't care for guns, do you, Father?" It was Bob McAdoo.

"Guns themselves I don't have any feeling for one way or the other. What we allow guns to do and how we allow it to happen concern me gravely."

"All types of guns?" Asked the director also named Mise.

The priest shifted toward the director in his chair and leaned in a bit. The camera was going to love this guy. "Guns kill people. Let's get that argument out and in front of us now. That is my belief. But there is more to the problem than just guns. There is mental illness. Poverty. A no-way out mindset of some who feel trapped in our country. Add to that high-powered, automatic weapons and virtually unlimited magazine capacity and you have armed conflict in our schools, our churches, our shopping malls and on our own streets. I can guarantee you the founding fathers did not have this in mind when they wrote the constitution."

"You speak of the Second Amendment, am I correct?"

"You want me to call it the Death Amendment? It made a lot of headlines, no?…So, I will call it that. The Death Amendment. I don't want to take peoples' rights away. I just want those rights to be logical and fair….and available to everyone. Life. Liberty and the pursuit of happiness. Those are the rights Americans should be sharing. Should be owning. And you can't have that if you have a country soaking wet in the blood of gun violence."

The room was very quiet.

"I wish we had taped that," said Mize, the director.

Everyone nodded.

Father Mise said, "That is just the beginning. I am just getting warmed up."

He was going to do great on the Sunday Morning news talk show. Now they needed to find a counter-part to Father Mise to try and stay up with this free-wheeling priest.

"We'll tape the Sunday segment on Friday afternoon. Day-after-tomorrow. There will be a guest on first who will be a spokesperson. A talking head for the gun lobby. We'll ask him or her some very tough questions and we expect to get the same old thoughts and prayers and guns don't kill people, people kill people argument. Then we will run your segment where you can rebut everything they say.

"We will not be the in the studio together?' asked Father Mise.

"No," explained Eve, we do it separately to give the responding side more time to organize their thoughts for countering the NGA."

"Do you do it this way each Sunday. I afraid I am usually at work during your segments…"

"I understand, Father, Yes. Our segments are always divided. A point of view – usually one rather radical, followed by a counterpoint. We leave it up to the viewer as to who is right and who is wrong."

"Will my words be edited?"

"No…only if you do not yell obscenities on the air."

He laughed. "I'll try and refrain."

"You'll do fine, Father. I know you will. Mrs. Samples … that's her over there talking with Bob McAdoo…she will be your make up artist, so on Friday afternoon, she will powder you and apply the appropriate makeup to let you look like you truly do…you see under the heavy lights on the set, you'd wash out and look like a ghost without her careful touch ups…and we don't want that, now do we? I tell you this because some people who have never been in the studio are taken back with the makeup and lipstick and etcetera that accompany appearing before camera. Plus, we have an assistant producer who will drive you to and from your hotel. And if you prefer, we can also provide you with a personal bodyguard while you are with us."

"Why would I need that?" asked the priest.

"As soon as promotions started on the network about your appearance, we have received hate mail aimed at you. Nothing to really concern yourself with…Mostly Kooks. But, Kooks…"

"…Kooks have guns. Yes I know. But I do not think I will need a bodyguard. But thank you just the same," said Mise.

"Very well. Let me show you the set from where we will record your segment."

As they walked deeper into the bowels of the network operation, Father Mise suddenly felt quite small and all alone. His was a singular voice going against an entire national machine, well oiled and funded with deep pockets. What could a local parish priest do to sway a country, to change the discourse of a land? How could he affect the argument? He felt defeated even before he started.

As they opened the door to the set, Bob McAdoo stepped up and asked Eve if he could have a word or two alone with Father Mise. She promptly left the two men alone. The set was dark, except for two dim lights overhead. Bob motioned for the priest to follow him onto the small stage and take a chair behind the massive desk on which was emblazoned the word…counterpoint. The sign would be flipped for the first guest and it would read: point.

"You are starting to have doubts…second thoughts about the mission here, aren't you?" Bob asked.

Mise nodded. His throat suddenly felt quite dry.

"It is expected. Many guests who come to this point get that feeling. It is a bit like stage freight. Only I think it is deeper. More profound."

"I actually feel a bit overwhelmed," confessed Mise. "Like, what have I gotten myself into?"

"Reasonable. Reasonable. I can understand that feeling. But allow me to remind you why you are here.

"Before you sit in that chair, I will have another guest there. And the sign below you will read 'point'. That person will be trying to sell America on the notion that what happened at Lincoln Mall and all the other locales of mass shootings was the work of mentally disturbed people and that the majority of Americans who own firearms are in no way responsible for these actions. He…or she…depending on who is sitting there…they will tell us that the gun is not the issue. That the true issue is the mental health of those who would inflict the kind of pain and suffering the young man from Lincoln inflicted upon his neighbors. The kind you saw and ministered to.

"And that is why you are here. You saw it. First hand. You were there in an instant of the last bullet being fired and you rendered first aid…along with prayers and thoughts…but you were actively there trying to save lives, as well as souls that had been taken by gun violence.

"No one else can say that.

"No one else delivered that sermon at the funerals of the mother and daughter as you did.

"America heard you…the world heard you. Your voice is their voice at this moment in history. You can either use it…or lose it. Your time is now. Six weeks from now, this time next year… I don't know when…they won't remember you. Not unless you speak now. Then, just maybe you will start a real movement in America. Can't promise it. But it is a good chance your testimony here will begin something.

"I can't say why it didn't happen after Sandy Hook. Or Sutherland Springs or Uvalde or Nashville or Stoneman Douglas or all the other places where masses of people fell dead under the power of assault weapons…but it didn't. It happened at Lincoln Mall on the thirteenth of November. And it happened at Saint Elizabeth's Church under your leadership. During the homily you spoke over those two precious souls… and it will be repeated from pulpit and classroom and political stump speeches across this land…if…and only if you are willing to keep pushing America for reform. It is on your shoulders, Father. God has placed it there.

"Remember Cynthia. And Rosa. Allow their stories to be told. It is for them you do this."

Father Mise nodded then asked, "Do you prod the opposition's speaker the same way you just inspired me?"

"I don't have to. The almighty dollar prods them. They are paid to be the shills for death in America. It's the way the system works."

On Father Mise's return to his hotel, he asked his escort to allow him to visit Saint Patrick's Cathedral. He wanted a few minutes of prayer and devotion there. Upon entering the famed shrine of Catholic faith, he found a pew and brought down the kneeler and knelt. He began to pray, his hand moving along the Rosary beads he grasped, suddenly next to him was the production assistant assigned to be his transportation coordinator.

"What are you praying for, my dear?' he asked her.

"The end of all if this shit in our country." She blushed. "I'm sorry for that kind of language in a church."

"Not to worry. God has heard far worse and I think he probably agrees with your sentiment. Where is your local parish?"

"I'm not Catholic. I'm Jewish. It's just that you seem to have such a peace about you and such a power, I wanted to pray to the same God to give you even more strength and to get the word out that this…" she pause searching for a less offensive word than she had used before…"that this shit stops."

"Amen." He said with a smile on his lips. "Peace be with you."

"And with you, Father Mise."

She bowed her head, as did he. Somewhere in the far reaches of space, time, history and the vast universe, he envisioned God whoever he was or she was, wherever they were…listening to him, a lowly parish priest and her…a young Jewish girl… asking for the same thing. Peace. No guns, Just peace.

45

Be on your best behavior, Senator Cross.

The junior Texas Senator and a delegation of others from Capitol Hill sat around a giant table in the White House. They stood as the President entered, with his troops of assistants and lawyers filling the seats behind those seated at the conference room table.

This was a negotiation meeting: all about we will give you this if you give us something of value in return. Lawyers call it quid pro quo. What it really amounted to was a form of extortion. A rendition of pirates taking over the ship. Senator Cross knew he had the President by the soft hairs. And he was willing to squeeze. The President could not get his legislation through the labyrinth of committees on the Hill, without Cross's assistance. And without that legislation passing, the President was a lame duck – plain and simple. And that, while very well understood by the participants in the room, went unspoken. Cross and a Senator from Kentucky and a Representative from Georgia were there to confirm and assure the

White House that it had their support on the tax bill and the farm bill...if...and here was the big if...if the President would back away from gun control. Back away once and for all.

The meeting started as one might expect. Cross made reference to the farm and tax bills in the Ways and Means committee, under the scrutiny of Georgia's Gale Rivers. He suggested that Gale and her colleagues might be persuaded to see their way to approve the majority of the new laws if certain conditions could be met by the White House.

"What kind of conditions?" Asked the President, knowing full well what was coming. He had not risen to the highest seat in American government by not understanding politics and who was holding what card at any given time.

"We need your assurance that the re-issue of the Brady Bill will not be supported. And that no new legislation come from or be supported by the White House on gun control. That simple."

"No gun laws. And I get my tax bill and my farm bill?"

"Bingo. That easy. Pretty short meeting, no?'" With that Cross began to rise assuming he had won the day. The President remained seated. It was an embarrassing moment for Rick Cross.

"Sit down, Senator. You need to hear what I have to say." The President rose as Senator Cross took his chair again. "I ran on a simple pledge to the American people. Send me to Washington and I'll clean up the mess facing this country. I will fix the tax code. I will build industry and create jobs. I will strengthen our defenses both here in our own streets with qualified, well-funded police backed by judges who will be tough on crime and with an armed forces that would be seen as a deterrent to any nation who would try and challenge us. I promised a new farm bill that would give family farmers a chance to make a living– a real living off the land. And I would revamp the banking laws, giving the little guy a fighting chance against the powers of Wall Street. And you know what, Senator Cross?... I won. I beat your party's candidate hands down. And one of the other things I promised the American people I would do while here in this honored house, is that I would rein in the gun violence that has swept across this land.

"To be sure, I have taken a step or two back and away from that promise. But no more. Today; and you can go to your buddies at the NGA and tell them this: today the gloves come off. No more guns. No more free rein with the Second Amendment. Your party packed the courts with anti-abortion rights judges, so I am going to pack every judgeship I can find with men and women who will take a far less lenient look at the Second Amendment than the current fad in conservative legal circles. I am going to make it harder and harder to buy a firearm without registering it… getting a license for it …and having training using it. And I want it to contain a chip that tells law enforcement where it is at all times. And I am going to suggest that our laws become stiffer and stiffer against those who use guns in crimes and to those who illegally sell them guns.

"It is going to be a new day in America before I am finished. I want guns off our city streets. Period." Cross started to interrupt him but the President pressed on, "If I don't get tax reform or a farm bill or a banking code, so be it. If I face a backlash from lobbyists trying to unseat me, so be that, as well. But until I am defeated at the polls, I am going to get out the biggest broom I can find and I am going to sweep away the guns, Senator Cross. And if that means I don't get re-elected, so be it. I didn't come here to get re-elected, I came here with a promise to the American people to clean up the mess that people like you created.

"Your party says liberals like me, are soft on crime. Well, we are about to show you a crime bill that will have gun owners racing to burn their guns. No one is going to slither under this law.

"Tell Gilstrap and the others at the NGA, they've got a war on their hands. Now, the negotiations are over. And yes, they were quick. You may leave now, Senator."

It took less than ten minutes for the details of the meeting to get back to the NGA offices, and half that time for them to get to all the major news organizations.

America was at war.

46

The same old song and dance now has a new tune

The call came to the NGA while Senator Cross and the others who had just been at the White House were still in their K Street offices. Gilstrap looked up from the call and announced. "NBC wants Cross on the Sunday talk show to take up our cause for gun rights. You up for it?"

The Texas Senator, known for his outlandish swagger, simply grinned. "You bet I am. Who am I up against?"

Gilstrap also had a huge grin on his face. "Father Richard Mise."

The NGA had their boy fired up. Thanks in no small part to the President of the United States who had made him mad. He was going on TV and tell the nation what a horrible leader they had and one who wanted to rob them of their rights while taking away their guns. Oh yes...he was ready.

Briefings began and talking points sharpened. Cross was being prepared for a Friday afternoon showdown. Bob McAdoo would be the host. He was a fair journalist who would give Cross plenty of room to make his arguments. And those arguments would bury the backwoods pastor so deep that he wouldn't be able to dig his way out with a steam shovel. Cross actually began to laugh. "This isn't going to be a fair fight. He'll go down in flames."

In New York City, Father Mise exited Saint Patrick's and got back into the limo and under the direction of the young NBC production assistant. He was driven back to his hotel in midtown. He went to his room and removed his shoes – still the old crappy ones he had gone to the mall to replace less than ten days ago. He still had not gotten around to replacing them for his tired feet. They were no longer a source of embarrassment for him, instead they reminded him of the day – and the day reminded him of his cause – his calling.

He jotted a few notes down in a small pocketsize notebook and placed it on his folded coat. He closed his eyes as he laid his head on a soft pillow. He slept comfortably and soundly until dinnertime. He went to the restaurant in the hotel, had a salad and some fruit and then returned to his room for nightly prayers and scripture reading.

He was ready.

The lights in the studio were far harsher than he had expected. He was washed in their bright glow. It felt as if NBC was trying to bake him alive, rather than serve him up as a speaker for their show. The make-up lady said this was why he needed the powder and the rouge and the lip-gloss. "It is all there to make you handsome."

"There's not enough makeup in New York City to do that," said Mise.

She laughed. "Nonsense. You are a good-looking man. I can't help it that you are off the market. That's your dealings with the good Lord. But for me, I see a handsome face that America will be watching and listening to."

She led him to his chair behind the desk, as he watched another woman dressed in a similar smock as the one his make-up artist wore, touch up the edges of Bob McAdoo's face.

"Looking good, Mr. MacAdoo."

"And right back at you, Padre. Are you ready?"

"If I say no, will you cancel the show?"

"No way. Once the lights are on, the show, too, must go on."

"I pity those not in church who will be stuck with my ugly mug in their faces on the Sabbath, trying to explain the mysteries of American jurisprudence."

"Just stick to the gun issue and the rest of America's law and order will take care of itself." Both men laughed.

"Did you get to see Senator Cross's segment?"

"No. I was in prayer and in make up."

"He missed a great show." It was the Senator himself who had strolled back out onto the set. Father Mise rose and extended his hand to the short Texas Republican. He founded it sweaty and somewhat flaccid. "I am sure that these cameras and these lights will not at all dilute your power of oratory. Too bad it will fall on deaf ears. America has already made up her mind. Gun control legislation ended when the country did nothing after Sandy Hook. You kill twenty little darling elementary school children and do nothing...that's the kind of commitment America has for change. Good luck Father. You'll need it."

With that the Texas Senator swaggered off and into the darkness of the shadows on the other side of the cameras.

"Don't worry. He has had his say. Plus he's a bit of a wind bag."

"Might I see his segment, to know what I am up against?"

"For sure." McAdoo yelled to someone off the set and the next thing Mise knew, a TV monitor was in front of him, as were a pair of headphones. He noticed his makeup artist frowned knowing she was going to have to re- vamp his hair after placing the headset on.

Bob McAdoo introduced the Senator, who really needed no introductions. He was constantly in front of news cameras at every opportunity he got. "Tell us Senator, what do the gun rights folk say to a community like Lincoln, Texas…in a county that voted heavily in favor of you in the last election?"

"Yes they did. And I am most grateful for their support. Then and continuing today. I would tell my constituents there that the horrible tragedy that has come to their community is just a part of the sad state of affairs that the current administration has allowed America to endure. We are drowning in lawlessness. Our police have no backing. Our courts are overflowing from activist judges who allow backlogs of trials while releasing dangerous criminals onto our streets…liberal judges who turn their back on the very laws they have taken oaths to uphold…and our own government tries to take away what rights we still have left, tries to take them away. Take away our guns. That is not the answer. As bad as the crime in our streets has gotten, I think every American home should have a gun. If for no other reason than to ward off potential trouble."

"So arm everyone? Is that your goal?"

"No…but to have access to protection from the lawlessness in our society, yes. Own a gun. Own it the proper way…"

"And what is the proper way? You and the NGA have turned your back on gun show loop holes and you and your fellow Texas Senator even sponsored a bill to repeal the gun show law."

"Guns are not the problem, Bob, lawlessness is. Mental illness is. Poverty is. The lack of a moral compass for our country is at the root of the problem. And this administration has turned a blind eye to those things."

And so the argument was set.

Father Mise removed the headset. The makeup artist quickly stepped in and combed his hair and then backed away to admire her craft.

Bob McAdoo introduced Father Mise with a short clip from the sermon he delivered during the funeral mass in Lincoln, now more than ten days ago. After the fiery clip finished, McAdoo turned to Father Mise and asked, "Still believe it is the Death Amendment?"

"Yes. The way we interpret it today in our courts and in our society, it is a license to kill."

"And what would you do, Father? What would you have America do?"

"Well you just heard the words of my United States Senator. A man who is supposed to represent me. Yet, I have received thousands of letters from people who agreed with my words at the Parker's mass. People from every state in the Union. People who believe it is time to take back our country from radicals like Rick Cross. Men who try and paint reasonably minded folk like myself as dangers to democracy. He'll tell his followers that I, and others like me, want to take away their rights. Where are the rights for Cynthia Parker and her mother Rosa Where are the rights for the eighteen other victims in the mall massacre in Lincoln, Texas?

"The rights of life, liberty and the pursuit of happiness can not be achieved here in America if we have to constantly look over our shoulder and wonder where the next round of bullets are going to come from… or always have to preplan our escape in case of shooting when we go to the grocery store, or to the theater or to school…or shopping for a birthday gift in the mall.

"America is tired of the gun lobby holding America hostage. It is time America fights back. I say repeal the Death Amendment. And replace it with a sane set of rules for gun ownership. But more than anything, I want to see laws that make it a very severe crime to sell or use illegal guns.

"My Church teaches me that it is wrong to take a life, but I believe to stem the tide of violence of a gun crazed America, if a life is taken in the commission of a crime, and a gun is involved…then the shooter should face capital punishment."

There was a silence. Bob McAdoo had not expected such a strong statement from the priest. "You would give somebody the death penalty for using a gun in a crime? Is that what you are saying?"

"If they shoot and kill someone during the commission of that crime. Yes. Then…maybe then…they will stop and think before wielding a firearm. And another thing I would do, is totally get rid of – make illegal – assault-style firearms and large capacity magazines. I believe no gun should hold more than three to five shots. Period."

"I also do not believe the rhetoric being heaped on this administration. I have not always agreed with their policies, but I think it is a sideshow to whitewash the facts that the gun lobby owns and controls Congress. Our congressmen are bought and paid for by the gun manufacturers through their lobby. This isn't an organization concerned with hunting safety or youth clinics in how to safely handle and shoot a firearm. It is about channeling more and more money to Capitol Hill to protect their little realm...their fiefdom...the Death Amendment."

"Some would call you a radical, father."

"Yes. And they called Jesus a radical. And Martin Luther King, Jr. And others who fought for social justice. I fight for the rights of people to live their lives in peace. Away from gun violence. If that is radical, then I am a radical. And I am proud to wear that badge." He touched the silver cross, which hung around his neck. "My sister gave me this cross when I entered the priesthood. When she did, she told me, 'wear this and let it remind you of the truth and the truth shall set you free.' Today that cross reminds me that we have a mission to bring peace back to America. And we can't have peace, with guns."

On Sunday, Senator Cross and Gilstrap and Hopewell of the NGA all sat watching the replay of the sessions on Point/Counterpoint. "You've got to hand it to him. He is on message and he is tearing away at our cover," said Hopewell.

"The problem with him," said Gilstrap, "is that our research folks and the ones from FOX have found nothing on him. He even washes out his plastic before he recycles. We've got to find a way to shut him up. To discredit him. Rick, you know his bishop. Go to Texas and do some arm twisting."

47

A recording is worth a thousand pictures.

Photographer Julian Meadow had been sent to Shreveport, Louisiana to record the milestone of the 150,000th flight in and out of the municipal airport by Delta Airlines. The mayor was on hand and other dignitaries both state and local were on hand to grin broadly for Julian's camera. After the festivities a plane landed and taxied toward the far end of the terminal where private flights boarded and deplaned.

He wandered down the hallway until he saw who was coming off the flight. U.S. Senator Rick Cross, NGA chairman Raymond Gilstrap and his top legal aide David Hopewell. And there in the crowd of assistants and luggage carriers was Patty Hale.

She was as lovely as that freshman year at Grambling when Julian had dated her. Then she broke his heart by leaving the Louisiana school and moving to George Washington University, where she earned her B.A. and her law degree. She was recently employed by David Hopewell to assist him in tracking gun litigation for the NGA. She didn't like the job, but she did like the paycheck. So she put aside her personal feelings about guns and worked the dockets with precision and haste…her hurry was to make enough money to buy her own house and then to fund her own practice. Maybe right back in Shreveport, her hometown. The South needed a good black female attorney. She was almost sure of it.

She saw Julian and immediately recognized him. Excusing herself from the entourage surrounding the senator and the NGA chairman, she made her way to Julian and gave him a huge hug. "I can't believe I'd run into you here. You look great." She said. It sounded sincere. At least he hoped that tone in her voice was sincere.

"And you, as well. Where are you? What are you doing here? What are you doing period. And how have you been?" I think that's all my questions," he said as she laughed and kissed him on the cheek.

"I'm here working with the National Gun Association. I'm a lawyer for them. I travel America watching and recording litigation over guns. Not my most favorite subject, but God, Julian, they pay me like I'm a queen."

"I always said you were my queen."

"Yes you did."

Someone from the group yelled at her that they were going to the coffee shop. 'Join them soon,' they shouted. She nodded back.

"Pretty distinguished company you're keeping there."

She waved her hand. "Cross. He's a bag of hot air. We're down here to get in front of some bishop from Tyler about that priest who is going around stirring up trouble over guns. My boss and the head of NGA, Gilstrap, they think the Bishop might have some strings to pull to rein the guy in. I think they're nuts."

"How are they supposed to rein Father Mise in?"

"You know him?'

"Well, sure. Everybody in this part of the country knows him. He's something of a folk hero."

"I told them that."

"So what's the play?"

She shrugged. "Pressure the bishop into pressuring the priest into laying low. Shutting his mouth over guns."

"That bishop...his name Gronklin?"

"Yeah. He's from Tyler. But we're meeting him at a restaurant out on Cross Lake. Ironic, no? Cross on Cross Lake?"

"Sounds like you have a good lunch ahead of you."

"Oh no," she said, "its over drinks and supper tonight. I don't think we'll even see the bishop until after eight."

"Well, have a good dinner. How long are you in town?"

"In and out. Got a trial to go watch over in Oregon right after this."

"Say, Patty, I'd love to get together again. For old time's sake."

"Let me get off the road and I'll drop you a message. Maybe you can come to D.C. and see me."

"I'd love that," he said.

"I assume you're not married..."

He laughed holding up his empty ring finger. "Still loose. Still looking. And what I'm looking at right now, has me wanting to settle down."

She kissed him again on the cheek and hurried off to the coffee shop, but over her shoulder she yelled, "You keep that finger free... you hear me?" He waved to her as she disappeared around a corner. He smiled and then immediately called in a favor from a friend at the restaurant on Cross Lake.

He was given access to the security camera room at the restaurant. He had access to several private rooms and even had audio. The man who had given him access was paid in cash and told not to mention it to anyone else. He was also slipped two very good Jamaican weed joints. Then Julian went to the bar, had a drink and ate a fish sandwich. He returned to the room, locking the door behind him, he waited.

At seven thirty the parties arrived. He turned on the listening device so he could hear the conversations and monitor the levels. Then he started his own recording that he had tapped to the restaurant's system. This felt like cloak and dagger work. Not the run -of -the —mill, chamber of commerce hurry —to- Shreveport- and -take -a -picture -of -dignitaries -at the —airport kind of day. This felt like the CIA and the NSA all rolled into one.

As he watched his monitor, he couldn't take his eyes off of Patty. He was definitely going to call on her in D.C. She still scratched that itch deep inside of him.

The conversation started off fairly innocently. But before long Senator Cross got impatient with the small talk and launched into why they were there with Bishop Gronklin. "We need your help, Sir. We need to silence this Priest…Father Mise. He is making a lot of trouble for us. A whole lot of trouble."

"I am afraid I don't have as much control over him as you might expect. There are those above me…those in Rome, for example, who love his message and his courage for preaching it to the country. And I am not totally sure I don't agree with some aspects of his homily."

"But he has been on TV and on other outlets spouting off…"

"Spouting off? Is that what you would call it?' asked Gronklin as he interrupted the Senator.

"I thought he was supposed to be on sabbatical. Resting. Away from the action, if you will." Said Hopewell.

"Yes. I instructed him to seek some solace and quiet time to replenish his mind, his spirit and to give him some reflection on his calling. He needs to have some space – distance himself from that horrible incident at the mall."

"Yet here he is traveling about the country making speeches and raising his voice against…'

"Again Senator, he is free to speak his mind. It is in the Constitution. I believe it is the First Amendment. Not the second one, you are so careful to protect. But rather, the first one."

Julian could not believe his ears. The bishop was putting these guys from Washington in their place. Holding his own, as it were.

Gilstrap spoke. "We do not wish to silence anyone from their constitutional right to free speech, my good Father. We ourselves enjoy it greatly. As does the church. But there is a radical element at loose in our country, who might just be using the words of Father Mise to stage a bit of insurrection and I would not want that to be splashed back onto the church, to sully your excellent record in building this wonderful diocese.

"One man should not plunge this great country of ours into chaos."

The bishop could feel the leverage about to be applied. Julian too, in his lair, turned the microphone volume up, just to make sure he caught everything being promised.

"We might find it in our best mutual interest, if Father Mise might be moved away. Say off premises for a while. He has been known to minister in Mexico. Perhaps a revisit to the land to our south would do him and us and you...yes you...some good."

"You want me to send Father Mise to Mexico?"

"Perhaps. Or even further. Say Central or South America..."

"You are not a Catholic are you, Mr. Gilstrap."

"No why?"

"If you were, you would know that a bishop from a small, fairly inconsequential diocese doesn't have the power to move people around in their ministry between countries. That would take the work of Rome or at least the presiding Bishop in New York to have some say, not to mention the bishop of the receiving country. It's not like the NGA, where you can snap your fingers and people are hired and fired at a moments notice."

"And you don't think Rome wouldn't want to get a trouble maker away from such a hot topic in America..."

"Rome doesn't see him as a trouble maker, my dear man. Rome sees him as a hero."

"How else could we keep him quiet, or at least out of the way for a while. To let all of this cool down. Why enflame the radical fires now, just after such a horrible event in your own backyard? It is a time for America to cool off. To slow down. To think."

"I might have some sway over him to let things settle. Perhaps at risk of losing his parish. He loves his parish so. And they love him."

"And might we offer a tidy sum to the work of the Lord if that were to transpire. Perhaps several million dollars to build a clinic or a hospital or a school or two?"

The bishop sat upright and smiled. "Donations to God's work are never discouraged under my watchful eye. The Lord's ministry must be funded."

"Then do we have a deal?"

The bishop paused and thought. "I will get the tongue of Father Mise quelled and you will find a way to get the diocese's coffers filled with three million dollars ...then I think we can say that this meal together was a successful breaking of the bread."

Julain stopped the recording as the parties left the restaurant. He then, using his laptop, made two backup copies ... one for himself and one for a friend. He called that friend some time after the ten o'clock news had finished in Houston.

"Channel 2 news...how can we help you?"

"Is Bruce Tunney around?"

"One minute, please."

Soon a voice came on the phone and Julian recognized it as the producer from Channel 2 for whom he did a lot of work and whom he trusted very much. "Hound Dog, I've got a gift for you. For you and your buddy, Bob McAdoo. You'll get it by special delivery tomorrow afternoon. Use it as you see fit."

The next afternoon the entire nation knew of the deceit being played out under the table by the NGA and by United States Senator Rick Cross. Even the Catholic Church had some egg on its face. But that was, according to Hound Dog, collateral damage.

The NBC Evening News led with the story of corruption and bribes, playing four long segments of the tape. Soon ABC, CBS,

CNN, FOX and even the BBC were running the stories. The Wall Street Journal, the New York Times and the Washington Post, along with the Los Angeles Times all sent reporters to East Texas to interview the bishop, who was so caught off guard from the melee of reporters and TV crews at his door, that he checked himself into a mental health care clinic outside of Austin.

The Vatican in Rome sent out a message, which hailed the Monsignor as "a fine man who needed to regain his balance after the terrible acts in his diocese." They also again wrote of their "support and prayers for Father Mise as he attempts to turn America from her gun-induced evil."

Six weeks after the dinner, Julian Meadow got a call from a long ago, former girlfriend. She had lost her job at the NGA, but was about to put her shingle out in Marshall, Texas with a personal injury law firm. They thought a gorgeous and very bright black face addressing juries across the South would be good for business. "I like the money, Julian. They pay me well."

And he showed her his finger was still free of any gold band.

48

An eye for
an eye

Eduardo Parker, from the darkness of his motel room, watched the news conference. Rick Cross was standing in front of the Lincoln Monument, its Georgian White marble surface reflecting and glistening like alabaster under the lights that shown through the slight drizzle blanketing Washington. The Senator was all but swearing at the 'main-stream media' who were out to crucify him and others of his belief over this 'foolish gun issue'.

"They'll stop at nothing to bring this country down. You take away our guns and America will start to fail. We will become a second-rate power and others ...alien nations... will soon be on our shores taking advantage of us. Foreign powers will no longer see us as a threat, but rather as a weakened country of people too afraid to carry our own weapons." The Senator had taken on the timbre of an evangelical preacher, his voice quivering as he ranted.

"America can't stoop to believe the slanderous video clips edited together to make it look like we would try an silence a man of God from his anointed mission. You can't trust the media. You can't believe their lies.

"This issue is tearing us apart. My thoughts and prayers go out to the victims, the families and to the community as a whole. It was a terrible act…"

Eduardo turned the TV off and loaded the two extra magazines that don Carlos had provided him. Now he had four sets of 30 bullets…he had the firepower of 120 rounds. He was ready.

That night he drove away from the motel. He didn't plan on returning. On a phone he had purchased at a drug store, he called the office of Senator Cross and was told by staff there, that after the Senator was finished speaking at the Lincoln Monument, he was due to address a group of fundraisers at the Matador Club, then after leaving the popular Republican enclave, he was hosting a private dinner for friends. He would be glad to call the party back tomorrow or the party could leave a message. The office reminded him that… "the Senator was always seeking donations from those who believed in the causes he stood for." Eduardo hung up.

He drove into the heart of the city, its wet streets glowing from the reflection of lights in the neighboring office buildings. The Capitol, with its dome lit under the illumination of a million watts of bright candlepower stood in the distance as a sentinel of democracy and might. He found the street where the Matador Club was located and after several attempts, located a parking spot among the Mercedes, Cadillacs and the limos and SUVs all waiting to retrieve their special guests.

Eduardo waited patiently. Before nine, the doors opened and onto the sidewalk spilled a large throng of well-dressed people. These were the movers and shakers of the city. Soon Senator Cross and Representative Rivers emerged from the doorway and stood together, their photographs being taken with the incessant explosion of flashes from the ubiquitous crowd of paparazzi and their digital cameras. Eduardo stepped closer, his overcoat drawn around the rifle underneath. His hands felt clammy. The gun was heavy. Suddenly he raised it and released several rounds. The explosions of the bullets leaving the chamber shattered the festive night air and the crowd began to flee in multiple directions simultaneously. Another Senator, this one from Kentucky, stood over Cross and looked right at Eduardo. The rancher from Texas squeezed the trigger again and again. A couple, in fine evening wear, standing behind the Senators went down in the next barrage of gun fire, along with two photographers. And two others, dressed in formal attire, who had been crossing in front of Eduardo fell dead. He was an associate justice of the Supreme Court and his wife was a lobbyist for the oil industry.

A security guard from the Matador Club rounded the corner and drew a gun and shot Eduardo. It ended his life on a wet sidewalk among those he had just gunned down. Three United States Congressmen, one Congresswoman and two U.S. senators. A Supreme Court Justice and two other bystanders: all dead, their blood starting to flow along the wet contours of the sidewalk and mingle together in a crimson river.

Eduardo's mission was complete.

His message was clear. Guns kill people. It was a note penned to the inside of his coat.

49

It has to end here. And now.

It was just before eleven o'clock in Washington. The evening news casts had yet to commence, although there was much chaos in every news organization, each trying to find out what had transpired on the sidewalk outside of the posh Matador Club. Details were sketchy.

The President was seated behind the huge oak executive desk in the Oval Office. An American flag was on his right hand side and a flag of the presidency on his left. There was only one camera in the room. It was focused on the President in his dark, blue suit, white shirt and deep burgundy tie. He looked very somber. He began to speak.

"My fellow Americans, I come to you tonight with a most heavy heart.

"Our nation has seen yet another mass shooting. This time on the streets of our nation's capital.

"Two prominent United States Senators and four members of Congress along with a United States Supreme Court Justice and his wife were gunned down outside of Washington's Matador Club. Others were injured and I am told members of the press may well have died in the spray of gunfire. Police are still investigating the crime scene and more details will come out.

"But tonight as I deliver this tragic news to you, I do so not as a reporter of the day's events, they will come on your televisions, following me, but tonight I come to you as a sad, sad leader of a nation that is gravely ill.

"We are infected with a gun violence that has now reached the hallowed halls of Congress. Senators and Congressmen and women are dead. The thought leaders of our country, slain in our streets. Lives lost to bullets.

"It has to end. It has to come to a complete end. It has to end here. And it has to end now.

"Tomorrow morning I am going to ask the leadership of both parties to come to the White House and to sit with me and draft new legislation that changes the way we handle the gun issue in America. I don't care if it requires us to toss out the Second Amendment, that's fine. Let's start over if we need to. Draft common sense, clear-language laws that protect our citizens and gives us all a chance to breathe easier. To live in peace.

"I do not want your guns. Do not listen to those who say the government is coming after your guns. We are not. But I am damn sure going to make it tougher for those who own guns to have them and to carry them and to arm themselves. It is going to be as hard to own a gun as it is to get a driver's license and to register your car and license an automobile and to insure that vehicle. That's what gun ownership is going to look like in America. Every gun. A license and a chip to let us know where it is at all times. And the removal of that chip would be a federal felony.

"I've had enough killing. I've had enough death on our streets and in our schools and in our places of worship. We can't even go to the grocery store or to the shopping mall without gunfire. Without the fear of being a casualty of guns.

"Enough is enough.

"If you don't like it, tough. Vote me out of office in two and a half years. But if you agree with me that we have had too many deaths, that there is too much killing going on in our land, then I want you to rise up and write, text, call, email, or drive and see your representatives here in Washington. Let them know where you stand. Do it tonight. Not tomorrow. Tonight. Let them know you are watching. Let them know you know they have, in the past, been bought and paid for by the gun lobby. You know it. And I know it.

"We have given the gun lobby every chance to sit down and work with us to draft legislation that would bring peace to our shattered world, but they have refused us at every turn. And not just my administration. Going back to Ronald Reagan's administration…a President, who himself was gunned down on the streets of this city, the gun lobby has worked diligently to block gun reform legislation. Each and every administration since then has faced their blockade on logical, safe gun reform. And when we did get it, they worked in the courts and in the halls of state legislatures to weaken the Brady Bill, which would have put an end to the sale and ownership of assault rifles and their high capacity magazines.

"Well listen to me, and hear me…we are getting rid of those guns. Once and for all. If you own one, get ready to get rid of it. It's going to be illegal in this country. Mark my word it is. I know I said I wasn't coming for your guns, but with assault guns and high capacity magazines, I draw the line."

"You want to hunt deer or shoot skeet or have a sporting clay outing, fine. But you don't need an assault rifle to do that.

"I never want to have to come back to this office, before that camera and have to announce another mass shooting in our country. I don't want another family to suffer what those who have felt the sting and sorrow of death from gun violence have been through. No more. No more. No more.

It is time for guns to be gone from the American way of life.

"May God Bless America…and God bless you."

At NBC, Bob McAdoo who had been on the air with the network's news bulletin of the night's shooting, was amazed at the President's speech. Eve was busy getting reporters assigned to members of Congress and to the state's capitals and deep inside to the infrastructure of both parties in the American political system. She even called for one of the most experienced journalists, Royce Hursh, to go to the NGA and ask for a sit down interview with Harold Gilstrap. "And don't leave their fucking building until you get one." She looked at Bob, "Hell, I'd swear the White House had that speech in the can and waiting."

"Eve, you ..." He waved her away. McAdoo then picked up a phone and dialed a number only he knew. Father Mise answered. He was still in New York, having now appeared on three other network shows. "Father."

"Bob, how are you?"

"Tired. Did you see the President's speech tonight?"

"Yes. Horrible tragedy. More violence. But remember, Bob, live by the sword, die by the sword. That's what happened to Senator Cross and others...I am not justifying it. Just saying."

"We have just learned the name of the shooter," said McAdoo carefully.

"Yes?"

"Eduardo Parker."

There was a long pause. McAdoo decided not to say a word until Father Mise spoke.

In tears, Richard Mise told Bob McAdoo he was going to have to call him back. "Before you go, father, do you want to come in and address the nation? This is kind of your horse now. Where will you ride it?"

"I've got to get back to Texas. There are those in my flock who are going to need me after this evening."

The phone went dead and Father Mise left for the airport two hours later.

50

All Alone

Ella Parker had been planning a wonderful spring – her senior year of high school; senior parties, graduation, a prom and everything one could think of for moving on – for matriculating into adulthood. College was just ahead. She would try for a degree in accounting. Maybe law after that. She had her eyes on the future.

Then came the 13th of November.

Her life began to swirl out of control. Her kid sister. Dead. Her mother. Slain. And now the news of the night, twelve days after the massacre, her father is dead in the streets of Washington, having shot and killed eleven strangers and wounded half that many in the same spree. Over what? Over his anger of them not doing anything about silly guns.

Now she was an orphan.

She sat on the bed in the guest room at Jose and Anna's house. It felt a bit lumpy. Not at all like her own bed. But what was her's? She didn't know anymore. Her life was upside down. She didn't have a home. She didn't have a family.

She was on the video call earlier with her brother, Roberto, who had returned to Lubbock for school, when the news came across the computer screen. Eleven more shot and killed in Washington. And then there was her father's name. Eduardo Parker of Lincoln, Texas. She gasp at the same time Roberto began to shout and scream. She hung up in tears.

She was an orphan.

No home.

No future.

Adrift in a hostile world.

By nine o'clock the police were at the house and wanted to talk with her, but Tio Jose had made them leave. "She is too upset to talk at this time. Tomorrow, possibly tomorrow. But call first." And they left in respect for the young lady who had lost her family.

She sat on the edge of the lumpy bed and stared at the walls, the flowered paper fading and cracking with age and peeling at the corners. But she didn't notice. There could have been buffalos on the paper or dragons; she wouldn't have known. Or cared. She simply stared, not seeing anything. Not feeling anything. Afloat in a fog of sheer misery. Slowly she began to drown. The pity and the grieving process had begun.

For some, grief takes on the form of anger. Others start with fear. Some have an empty feeling, a nomadic sensation that nothing is real. Nothing matters. It is into that category Ella drifted. She was moving through a world of emptiness.

She knew she was alive because she had her feelings – her senses. She could taste the salt of her tears and feel the prick of her fingernails as she dug into her own soft flesh. She could see and hear and smell; yet, with all her faculty present, she was away from the reality of being at any particular place. She was afloat. Adrift.

Nothing was holding her down.

There were no laws of nature.

Nothing made sense.

The only thing that felt good was to cry. So she lay down and closed her eyes and let the tears flow.

She was an orphan.

51

The President needs a word with you

Father Mise had stepped outside of the hanger's door at Westchester County Airport and was on the damp tarmac walking to the private jet that had been offered to him by the Archbishop of the New York diocese.

He had not asked for it, but rather Bob McAdoo had called in a favor. And knowing the archbishop was good friends with a wealthy Wall Street hedge fund manager with multiple jets at his disposal, he made arrangements to be sure that the priest had a quick and undisturbed flight home. "He doesn't need a hoard of people harassing him in an airport," said McAdoo to the archbishop, who agreed immediately and made two quick calls to secure the flight.

Two men dressed in tailored business suits approached the priest a few steps from the plane's stairs.

"Father Mise?" Yelled one of the men.

He nodded. The whirl of the spooling jet engines made shouting mandatory for carrying on a conversation.

"Come with us. The President of the United States wants to have a word with you." They flashed credentials of the Secret Service.

"But I'm on my way to…"

"Doesn't matter. The President has requested to see you. We'll arrange for your transportation home later." With that the lead agent took him by the elbow and gently, but firmly guided him away from the jet and toward a waiting SUV. The other Secret Service agent boarded the plane and explained the situation with the pilots and they quickly extinguished the jet's engines and called it a night.

You don't argue with a call from the White House.

The SUV drove to the far side of the airfield where another jet, this one with Air Force markings on it, stood ready to taxi. The Secret Service agent and Father Mise boarded and in no time were airborne and heading for Washington.

At the entrance to 1600 Pennsylvania, the black SUV stopped and an armed guard looked inside. He flashed a light into Father Mise's face and then checked the Secret Service officer's credentials. He nodded and a gate was opened and the SUV continued up a slight incline and then under a portico and out of the rain, now pouring quite heavily. A damp set of stairs led to the doors of the executive wing of the White House: the West Wing.

Father Mise exited the SUV as he had been instructed to do and waited at the side of the vehicle until the agent was next to him. Again the slightest of nudges at the elbow signaled him to proceed into the doors of the White House and along a carpet that led to the Oval Office. There, a young staff member in a finely pressed suit and a bright crimson tie, carrying a notebook computer stopped him and said, "You are about to enter the office of the President of the United States. The conversation you have therein may or may not be recorded and anything you say will be considered to be the property of the White House and this Presidency. Do you understand?"

Mise nodded. He felt like throwing up. This was far worse than being on network TV with millions of unseen eyeballs staring at him. Suddenly he became acutely aware of his scruffy shoes. He felt a momentary embarrassment about his footwear, hoping no one would pay them any mind.

"I need your response verbally. To be recorded."

"Yes I understand. And yes I agree,"

"Relax. He's a nice guy," said the young man.

The doors of the Oval Office opened and the Secretary of State marched out in a seeming huff and had a look of utter anger on his face. It was one of those faces that said 'I have either ordered the death of my best friend, or I have just divorced my loving wife because she was cheating on me'. He was as grim looking as any individual Father Mise had ever seen, and he had certainly seen his share in his forty-five years of life. With the door open, Mise took a step, but was grabbed from behind by the Secret Service agent. "Not yet," was whispered in his ear.

The young man in the neat suit with the lap top entered first and announced to the President that the "Catholic priest you requested, Father Richard Mise, is here, sir"

"Send him in Dave," said the President.

Again the gentle nudge at the elbow and Father Mise slowly entered the most powerful office in the free world. Wars had been launched from here. Battles planned. Crises managed. And foreign dignitaries read the riot act that if they didn't get in line with the United States their countries would be in real peril. Kings and Queens, Prime Ministers, and Dictators had all been ushered into the rarefied air of this important office.

And now he was inside it as well. The office seemed much smaller than he imagined – much more intimate.

A photographer in a dark suit circled the room quietly taking quick pictures as the President approached the priest and extended him a welcoming handshake.

"Father Mise. Good to finally have a chance to meet you. Sorry to interrupt your travels on such a heavy night. I am told that the shooter – the man who killed Cross and the others at The Matador Club – was one of your parishioners. Am I right about this?"

"Yes. I had just heard his confession…of sorts…just the other day."

"I see… sad, sad business… Well, anyway… I have heard so much about you." The President was taller than Mise had imagined him to be. The Commander in Chief's face had a tired, weathered look to it. The wrinkles in his skin appeared to be exaggerated that evening. His jaws sagged.

"I hope that is a good thing," said Father Mise.

"To be sure. Your reputation precedes you. And it is a totally good thing. Please. Sit. Would you care for something to drink? Water?"

Mise declined.

They sat on a sofa in front of the giant desk from where the President had just addressed the nation three hours earlier. "I'll get straight to the point. We grabbed you before you could get on that plane and fly away and brought you here because we think America needs you."

The President paused to let that remark sink in.

"You have stirred the emotions of a lot of people in the land. You have raised the bar of argument over guns to a level …well to a level we have never experienced. Our polls are going off the charts when we ask about you. In both directions. Those who love you…they really love you and those who hate you…well, I would try as best I could to avoid them." He grinned. It was a grin from the man who had at his disposal a button to destroy half the world if he so chose.

"What do the numbers mean?" Asked Father Mise.

"They mean that over eighty percent of the people in the United States believe in you. In what you are selling and they are buying it."

"I sell only one thing. The love and peace of our blessed Lord and Savor, Jesus Christ."

"Yeah, well we both know that's not totally true. You've got a really good pitch about getting rid of guns in our land and it has struck a nerve. A very deep nerve. A nerve that has been buried for a long time is now tingling with your words and message. Jesus or no

Jesus… Catholics, Baptists, Jews, and even Atheists are buying what you are selling. Even some Republicans."

"I don't think of it as selling…"

"My words. Not yours. Semantics aside, you are the mouthpiece for a strong and vibrant movement the likes of which we have not seen, not since Carrie Nation and the prohibition movement."

"I don't feel like the leader of a movement…"

"I don't care what *you* feel like." Interrupted the President. "The nation feels like it for you. They are sensing you leading this movement. From the grassroots upwards. You, my good Father, are the mouthpiece that is speaking their outrage for them.

"Speak and they will follow. You don't even have to speak loudly. They are listening very carefully. And are ready to act. That is what our research has shown. You have become something of a cult hero."

"Cult kind of scares me. It is not a thing a good Catholic likes to be associated with…"

"Again my words. And whether you like the words or not, the actions of the people are what we are interested in. The White House… Me…I am interested in tapping your power to help us turn enough heads out there and we'll start to sway the pig heads on Capitol Hill.

"I called on the American people to arise and call their leaders tonight concerning gun control. And they did. But not in the numbers we think you could elicit."

The President turned to a man who was standing silently behind Father Mise. The priest had not even noticed his presence in the room. "Greg, get B.J. or Geno in here with their numbers. Tell him to bring them on a computer…not a projection show. Small audience." The man left and in no time a plump, hunched back man in a rumpled suit that was a couple of sizes too small for him came shuffling into the office. He sat between the President and Father Mise and opened his notebook computer.

"B.J., please share with the good padre here the latest numbers on recognition, recall and results. Don't be bashful, tell him the good, the bad and the ugly." And B.J. did.

Fifty minutes later, Father Richard Mise agreed to make three televised appearances with the President to the nation about gun control. And he agreed to a speaking engagement in at least ten U.S. cities at the direction of the President's P.R. machine. But there was a caveat. He would do it, but only if and when the White House flew him home to Lincoln so he could minister to the Parker family first.

It was agreed and before two in the morning, he was on board a private jet with absolutely no markings on it, headed for East Texas Regional airport. There, a car was awaiting him to drive him to the church rectory in Lincoln.

At nine the next morning he approached the Parker household of Jose and Anna and was met by two uniformed police officers waiting outside on their front porch.

"Morning, Father."

"Good day, officers."

"We were waiting to have a word with the young girl. We believe she was the last to see Eduardo before he left for Washington."

"Well, gentlemen, I do not know of any of that. I came on a purely spiritual mission. Give me a few minutes with her and the family and I will return and address your concerns."

With that Father Mise entered the house of his good friends José and Anna. It felt good to get back to the business of being a parish priest.

52

Sometimes words are not enough

Jose came to the door and let Father Mise in. He asked the two policemen if they cared for more coffee. Anna had been filling their cups during the early morning hours. They said they were fine.

Father Mise turned and addressed the two patrolmen. "I believe I was actually the last person to see Eduardo before he left town. He came to me for a spiritual discussion. I will be more than happy to come and talk with you at your headquarters, as soon as I have had a chance to minister to Ella."

Both officers, upon hearing that piece of news, agreed and left the small ranch style house and drove off.

Anna escorted a very fragile-looking Ella into the living room and she sat on the sofa across from Father Mise's chair. He nodded to her aunt and uncle to let them have some privacy and the couple stepped away and into their kitchen. Ella wore a plain blue pleated skirt and a white cotton button down shirt, the uniform of the high school girls under the new school dress code. He doubted she had changed clothes in a day.

Her eyes were puffy and red. Her cheeks were bare of any makeup and her nose was running as she dabbed a tissue at it. Her hair had not seen a brush in some time.

"Ella I know you are hurting. I know I would be. And I know it is a very confusing time. A very trying moment in your young life. So, if you wish to talk or to just sit and be together…whatever you need, I am here for you."

For several long minutes Ella looked away. She turned her head away from the priest and looked off into the far distance. Her eyes were fixed on something or someone that only she could see. Finally, after what felt to Father Mise like an eternity, she looked back at him and calmly said, "I no longer believe in God."

He nodded. "I understand. But I bet he still believes in you."

She shrugged. "Maybe."

Father Mise decided to shift his approach. "Ella, there are a lot of people out there who care for you. Your aunt and uncle. Friends. Your brother. Me. The people of Saint Elizabeth's. You may feel alone and isolated just now, but we care for you. We love you and we don't want you to hurt.

"But I know you are going to hurt. It is a natural thing for humans who have suffered losses like you have just endured, to hurt. It is part of life. The pain, my dear Ella, will subside. It will slowly ebb away and you will then be left with recovery. You see, the grieving process comes in many steps. And it may last for years. But just waking up every morning to face it, just realizing you are in the midst of it, is a sign that you are okay. You will press on. Each breath you take is a step in recovery."

He paused.

"As I said at Cynthia's and Rosa's mass, I do not know why God allowed any of this to happen. He has shown me something recently that I am starting to make some sense out of, but only because I allowed him the time to open my eyes and see his plan.

"And that is what I wish for you. Whether or not you believe in God, at least be still and wait for him to show you his plan. It is there. And I assure you, you will find it if you seek it."

"I don't feel like seeking anything. I don't feel like doing anything. I don't want to be around anyone. I just want to go back into that room and be alone."

Father Mise nodded. "But hiding away in that room isn't going to bring back your parents or your sister. And it will not help you forget the hurt and pain you have right now. But getting out into the world and facing its challenges, will help wash away the scar of these terrible incidents. Helping others. Sharing with people who are also hurting. Giving of yourself and your gifts; Ella you have so much to offer this world. Don't give up. Cry for a while. Hurt for a while, but pick yourself up and march on. Have courage. Have faith. Restore your drive. Find a cause."

She had tears in her eyes, and he realized that the words were empty to her just then. He moved next to her on the sofa and placed his arm gently around her thin shoulders. She leaned into his chest and began to shake. She wept for fifteen minutes until she was cried out.

Suddenly she stood as if nothing had happened and reached for his hand. "Let's get some breakfast."

He nodded. It was a small – a very small step. A breakthrough some counselors would call it. But he saw it as a tiny step in a long march back to reality. But at least she had taken the first step. She was trying.

Ella and her Aunt scrambled some eggs and made toast and poured the priest some black coffee. They sat and after a prayer, "Bless us oh Lord for these thy gifts…" they broke bread together and once or twice during the meal Ella would remember something and just start to softly cry. Once her aunt started to her, but Father Mise caught her eye and motioned her to take her seat again and to let Ella have the space to let her emotions flow. And each time Ella stopped crying and continued with the meal. By the time dishes were washed and dried, with Farther Mise leading the way at the sink, Ella was laughing and telling stories about how jealous she had been of Cynthia's intellect, especially in math and her audacity to take on the boy's math club from Longview.

"I guess they'll win uncontested now," said Ella, without so much as a tear in remembrance of the recent tragedy.

"I bet that girl would have eaten their lunch," said Father Mise.

"You know it," said Ella, as she placed her dishtowel down and took the Father's hand. "Thank you for coming today. I'm going to be okay."

"Ella if you need me, you know where to find me."

He turned to leave and she stopped him with her words, "I wish you'd take that homily you delivered for us… I wish you'd take it to all of America. They need to hear it over and over again."

He turned and put both hands on her shoulders and looked her squarely in the eye. "I am going to do just that. And I'm going to do it in the memory of your sister."

"No more guns, father. No more guns."

He left for the police station to be interviewed about his discussion with Eduardo before he left for Washington.

53

I have a favor to ask

Bob McAdoo called the rectory. It was a few minutes past ten pm. Richard Mise answered. "I was hoping you were there," said the newsman. "I have a favor to ask."

"A favor?" asked Mise. "And good evening to you by the way."

"Yes…well hello, Father."

"Call me Richard."

"Okay, Richard. We are on first name basis now, so I suppose we are friends?'

"You are in my Rolodex."

"I feel special."

"Don't. My dentist is in there too and I do not like her."

McAdoo laughed. "I need a favor."

"Everybody seems to want a favor from me. You, the White House, my congregation. My bishop. Rome…"

McAdoo cut him off…"Yes. I am drafting an essay…an open letter of sorts…to America. About gun violence. I could use your assistance."

"Mine?"

"Father, your words ignited an entire national movement. Yes, your words. I could use a good dose of them right about now."

Mise was astonished at the request. "First the President of the United States wants me to address the nation and make speeches with him all across the country and now the anchorman of one of the mightiest news organizations wants my words for his open letter…"

"Easy Tonto. This is just a look-see project. I've written it. I just would like your view of it. Your edit. Your…"

"My seal of approval?"

"Yeah. Of sorts. But also a twist or two of a phrase here and there. I am a newshound. I see a fact…I report a fact. A equals A and B equals B. But you see an A and it becomes a rainbow. You see a fact and you paint a picture. I am looking for that artistry in this letter."

"A rainbow?" Father Mise was lost in that analogy.

"You have a way with words that touches peoples' souls. I guess it is a seminary thing?"

"I don't remember taking a course in seminary in how to touch souls. Save them…yes. Touch them…not too sure," said Mise.

"Okay. But admit that you have a way to turn a phrase that is literary in scope. Not just black and white journalism. I need a spark. I need a hook. I need something to take my words and elevate them with the fervor your homily had."

"That takes a lot of knee time."

"Knee time?" asked McAdoo.

"You know. Getting down on your knees and seeking the words God wants you to say."

"Is that the secret to the special sauce?"

Mise laughed. "Never thought of it quite like that. But yes. I suppose it is. Remember back to when you were going to ask your wife to marry you. Did you just give her the facts or did you woo her a bit?"

"I was big on wooing in those days," confessed McAdoo.

"There you are."

"Where?" asked McAdoo, somewhat lost.

"You need to woo America. You need to get real quiet. Real still. If you believe in God, go to Him or Her for some encouragement. But be still and listen…find a way to woo America into seeing the truth your way."

"I have. I called you."

Mise laughed. "Okay, send me a draft and me and God will pour over it. But no promises. I hear he's a CBS guy."

McAdoo laughed and said he was pushing the send button on his laptop right then. In an hour, Father Mise and God knows who else was pouring over the manuscript and soon a painting emerged.

America has a problem.

America has amnesia.

We forget the pain and suffering caused by mass shootings; the ripple effect through our society of the loss of loved ones and friends, and neighbors. The loss of life at the hands of guns.

Every time we come face-to-face with another mass shooting in this country, it flows across the fabric of what is just and right about America and pulls it apart at the seams.

America does indeed have a gun problem.

It is a disease crippling our rights of freedom and liberty.

But there is a cure.

You.

You are the cure.

The lawyers hated this passage above all others. McAdoo fought four times on four drafts to keep it in, but alas, it failed. He later confided in his good friend, Father Mise, on the road giving speeches with the President of the United States, "They were scared to death of those words, Richard. That was exactly the kind of power I was looking for from you. And I thank you, for those words inspired the ones which followed."

54

The following is an editorial comment

The network's lawyers had poured over the script for hours. They had made numerous edits. The first two drafts looked like a battlefield with the red ink covering the pages like trails of drying blood.

By the fourth draft, they were getting into the flow of the words. Bob McAdoo kept at them; forcing them to back away from their position of not wanting to offend anyone.

"I want to offend the entire goddamn nation," he said at one edit meeting, as he slammed his fist down on the conference room table. "I want America to feel like shit when I get through. We've let this go on far too long. It is time to do something. Something concrete."

Eve Kholemann walked in and signaled it was time to record his segment.

One of the lawyers reminded everyone in the room that it had been almost fifty years since the network had run an editorial on the nightly news. That was in 1974 at the resignation of Richard Nixon. "And before that, you had to go back to 1963 at the death of John Kennedy when the next-to-last editorial was spoken on the news. That had been spoken by Chet Huntley. This is a very rare occasion. Let's be very careful out there."

This was to be entitled an Open Letter to the American People from Bob McAdoo. He had even asked that the network not endorse his words. In fact, they could run a disclaimer before and after his comments saying, "…the words in the Open Letter you are about to hear are the words of Bob McAdoo. Who takes full responsibility for them and are not meant to convey the opinion of this network nor its affiliates in any way. Ladies and gentlemen, Bob McAdoo…"

The lights came up on him with the title Open Letter superimposed electronically in silver type behind him. He was dressed in a dark, navy blue suit, with a pale blue dress shirt and blue and red striped silk tie that Elaine had picked out for him. She would, for the first time in many years, be standing in the wings of the studio for this broadcast. It was that important to him: to all of the network. The director in the booth, realizing the significance of the moment, had sweaty palms as he gave the countdown, three, two, one, camera one roll." He followed that with a whispered, "Knock 'em dead, Bob," into the earpiece of the network's lead anchor.

"Good evening from New York, I'm Bob McAdoo." He began to read from the teleprompter in front of him:

I would like to speak to each and every one of you tonight
about a matter of most importance to our country right now.
More than the economy.
More than jobs.
More than tax reform or foreign wars.
This is about a war raging in America.
On our streets.
In our schools, across our neighborhoods, into our stores…
and even into our homes.
It is a war being waged with guns.

Guns are killing massive numbers of our citizens every day.
Your friends. Your family members...
and many may be, to you... total strangers...
but not to someone.
As my good friend, Father Richard Mise of Texas reminds me...
To someone, those statistics are people.
Real people.
Relatives.
Fathers.
Mothers.
Daughters.
Sons.
Not just numbers in some spreadsheet upon which we keep score.
But once were living, breathing people,
Now gone.
At the hands of killers using guns.
Every time we come face-to-face with another mass shooting in this country, it ripples across the fabric of what is just and right about America and pulls it apart at the seams.
America does indeed have a gun problem.
It is a disease crippling our rights of freedom and liberty.
There is a sickness spreading through America,
It comes from ignoring certain truths...truths, which we seem to conveniently forget.
It is time America quit fooling itself that there is not a gun problem...
There is. And it is growing out of control.
In the last two weeks we have had a mass shooting in a mall in Texas, a college in California and now...even on the streets of our nation's capital...killing elected officials and by-standers...
...all killed with powerful assault rifles and their life-destroying bullets.
This week alone fifty people have lost their lives in mass shootings. We are told that the statistic say more than 150 deaths have occurred

because of gun violence this month alone. And we are only partially through the month.

It is a terrible tragedy.

But it can be stopped.

There is a cure for this disease.

You have the power to stop it.

The President, last night from the Oval Office asked you to call your elected officials in Washington and demand that they do something.

Tonight I am asking America to do more than that...

To march on Washington...

march in mass...

make it the largest gathering of mothers and fathers and teachers and clergy and students and business leaders and thought leaders of the American society that the Capital has ever seen.

March and ask for concrete change.

Here are some things we can ask for...

Things we must demand.

Outlaw ownership all weapons of armed mass assault rifles and their high-capacity magazines.

Outlaw the ownership of all weapons earmarked for armed forces.

A list will be created of those specific arms.

But no more owning of bazooka and grenade launchers by civilians.

Outlaw the sale and ownership of any gun that is not registered to a licensed owner.

No gun show loop holes.

Demand that all guns, be registered and contain a chip that signals law enforcement of their locale at any given time.

Before you become worried about big brother, this is already in force on your automobiles.

And speaking of that, every gun owner will have to have insurance for each gun he or she owns…and to get that coverage must first pass an FBI-created training session for each gun registered to them.

…and those underwriting the insurance will have to demand that guns be kept unloaded, in locked safes, or else the individual will forfeit the right to those arms.

But we need deterrents to the use of these firearms, as well.

So let us demand that:

If an individual uses a firearm in the commission of a crime, whether a gun involved in the crime, shoots someone or not, then the penalty for that crime shall be life in prison without the possibility of parole.

And should that individual kill a person during such a commission of an armed crime, the death penalty shall be enforced as the punishment for such an act.

I hate the death penalty.

Always have.

But at a time when my fellow citizens are being mowed down with machine guns and weapons of war, it is time we take the drastic measure to make it a capital offense to kill using a gun.

Make a potential assailant think twice before he grabs a gun to settle a score. Thinks twice before walking into a church or temple and destroys lives.

The deterrents must be as powerful as the acts they try to stop.

There are going to be those who stand up and say it is going too far…

but for far too long we have done nothing because of the gun lobby owning our legislators.

It is time we take back our country and let those in the halls of the Capitol know that they cannot be bought any longer.

If we can't get the Congress to work with us, then vote them out and elect officials who can and will stand with the American people.

We will arise as a nation and free ourselves from the horrible specter of gun violence.

And if the cry comes from those who advocate strict legal interpretation of the Second Amendment, then let us abolish it, as well.

We've changed the constitution before, we can do it again…

to protect communities…

our children…

our schools…

our homes…

and our lives…

Join me, the first Saturday in December to march on Washington and demand change in our country.

It is time to say no to guns.

It is time to make sweeping changes to free our country from their threat.

May you find the will and the way to arise and stop this epidemic in America.

It begins the first Saturday in December.

Let us show the world, America is serious about becoming a safe society once again.

Together, we can do it.

Thank you and good evening."

The lights lowered and the camera was turned off. The recording was finished. It would air in less than an hour. Network brass had decided that affiliates would not be advised of the special Open Letter ahead of time.

For some reason, Bob McAdoo felt like the power of his original words and those of Father Richard Mise had been stripped away with all the legal editing. But his wife assured him it sounded strong and to the point.

Eve came up and gave him a big squeeze, as did the director. A production assistant handed him a phone and Hound Dog was on the line. "Did you do it, yet?"

"Yeah."

"How did it go?"

"You tell me in an hour."

"Will do. Bob, thank you for doing this. From all of us. Thank you."

An hour later Bruce Tunney called back. All he said was, "Holy shit, you nailed it, man. You nailed it."

Bob and Elaine took their daughter out to eat that night and from tables around them, they could hear chatter about the news and the Open Letter. And typical of New Yorkers, the tables next to theirs said nothing directly to the McAdoos about the evenings' event.

In Lincoln, Texas Father Mise watched the evening news as Bob McAdoo delivered his editorial. It sounded polished and yet, sincere. It was the right tone and the right message. Just what the country needed to hear. He would call his friend in New York tomorrow, he promised himself, and get a copy of the transcript. There were portions he wished to work into the speeches for the tour that lay ahead of him with the President. He planned to be in Washington, D.C. in the streets on the first Saturday of December. He would lead the march on Washington.

He felt uncomfortable with the role he had agreed to play. He was, after all, just a local parish priest. But some power greater than himself had called him to take the lead. Called him to see that lives were saved and gun violence eradicated in America.

He was the priest, after all, who had witnessed and lived through a horrible shooting. He had to keep reminding himself of that, because somewhere in some part of his brain, some mechanism was trying to bury the scenes of that horror.

The more he thought about it, the more he realized that is exactly what America was constantly doing.

Just keep forgetting the killings.

55

Hunker down. The worst is yet to come.

The National Gun Association was constantly running polls. Trying to find out what the American temperament over gun ownership was at any given moment in time. That night – two nights after Bob McAdoo's Open Letter the numbers looked dismal.

The research guy said that approval ratings for the NGA were at a historic low. Less than five percent. Way beyond the tipping point he said, rather mathematically.

Americans were responding in huge numbers to both the President's speech and to the Open Letter aired by Bob McAdoo on his network. Obviously other networks had not run it, and that meant the eyeballs they owned had not seen it. But the other news outlets had begun to report about it with the massive shift in numbers that their research departments were reporting, as well. And on social media the President and McAdoo were everywhere. You couldn't find a site that didn't have at least some portion of either speech on it. Every talk show in America was plugged into the movement.

The research guru at NGA addressed the elephant in the room. "Ducking and hiding is not working. We are falling so far behind and there is going to be so much pressure on Congress to act, that we will not be able to stem the tide."

"Yes and there's going to be that march in December. The one McAdoo called for," Hopewell reminded the room.

"That could be gargantuan numbers. Families coming together to march. Mothers and fathers bringing their kids to let them see democracy in the streets," continued the statistical master of research numbers. "We could see more than a million people in D.C. that weekend. It could make the Vietnam protest and the Civil Rights marches pale in comparison."

"The tide is turning and we can't continue to ignore it."

"We had a plan to discredit the priest, but that blew up in our face. Now we need something huge. Something that will have repercussions so deep it will stop this country in its tracks." Gilstrap was ranting as much as thinking.

From the side of the table the lone, tall figure of Randolph Gates stood. That evening he was dressed in all black and looked to some in the room, as they would recall later, like Father Death. "You people are fools. You run around trying this or that. I told you what to do.

"Do nothing.

"It will blow over. America will not remember this.

"And I am damn sure America will not get off her ass and come to Washington to march to get rid of guns. Do nothing... all of this will go away and we can get back to business as usual. Trust me.

"Doing nothing will work."

The room looked at Gates and there was a silent, but collective sigh of relief. It was like a father figure telling you everything was going to be all right. Just let the storm blow over and we'd come out of the storm shelter into bright clear skies with birds singing and flowers blooming.

Just don't do a damn thing.

America won't do anything to stop the flow of guns.

Wait her out.

56

Karen Ray

Karen loved hot dogs. But she hated mustard and David Perez had just squirted mustard on her hot dog from a small finger packet. She made a face at him and he stuck his tongue out at her. She returned the favor.

"You are yucky." She said.

"So are you." He retorted as only a schoolboy of age five can do.

The preschoolers were ganged together at a long table in the food court and the chaperones sat at either end. Karen picked up a packet of catsup and squirted David's hot dog, giggling the entire time. She loved catsup on her dog, but mustard was yucky. She bit into her hot dog and got a big mouthful of bun, warm meat and yellow tangy juice. Hum…that wasn't as terrible as she had remembered.

"Good ain't it?'

"We're not 'spose to say ain't." she corrected her friend and current adversary.

"Mustard's good, no?" He asked with a smirk on his face.

"Yes. It's okay. Here, have some more catsup." This time she sprayed a packet onto David shirt. He immediately shouted and returned the favor getting the red sauce all over Karen's white blouse.

Before long there was a full-scale catsup and French fry war going on around them. It had escalated to several children on either side of David and Karen. Mrs. Davenport moved in quickly to secure a truce. A catsup détente was reached. And the kids went back to eating, although snickering still continued across the table at the warring sides.

Someone in the food court, near the front, popped a balloon. Karen wanted a balloon and wondered if she still had enough money to buy one. Her daddy had given her five dollars that morning as she left for school. She had never had so much money. But her older brother, Rick, who was in high school and who did the driving chores for the Ray children had talked her out of three dollars. "I need to buy my lunch. The school's going to buy yours."

So she relented and gave him some money. Three dollars.

She loved Rick so much. He was always driving her to and from school and to get ice cream or snow cones. Rick was in high school and the girls thought he was so cute. She did too, even though he was her brother. He would take her to do all kinds of things. The mall, once a week was a treasured time with him. (The reality was, it was a time Mrs. Ray could have some peace and quiet at home and do her writing at the kitchen table. She had a novel started and was trying to finish it. It had only taken nine years so far.) Rick would also take his sister after their trip to the mall, to soccer practice. She wasn't very good at soccer, but she got to see Betsy there and she and Betsy were best pals. Betsy was sick that day and didn't get to go on the pre-school outing at the Lincoln Mall. Rick took Karen and her friends to see all the Disney movies in the theater in Longview. Lincoln did not have a cinema. Betsy was so jealous of Karen and Rick's relationship. She too had an older brother in high school, but he had nothing to do with her. "He thinks I am a brat," she confided to Karen one day as they swam in the Ray's backyard pool.

"Rick loves me. Someday I'm going to marry a boy just like Rick and have a bunch of babies."

"I thought you were going to be a vet?" asked Betsy.

"Yeah. And that, too."

David kicked her under the table. She kicked back but couldn't find his legs. She peeked under the table and found him sitting on his legs – now curled up under his lap. He smirked as she came up from below. Another pop. And someone screamed.

Karen looked up and saw the boy from The Burger House trip and fall, ice cream cartons tumbling along with him. Someone was spraying his white uniform with bright red catsup, too. Then she saw a young man dressed in all black. The young man came and pointed a gun at Mrs. Davenport. Pop. Pop. Pop. Her friends around Mrs. Davenport were suddenly screaming and trying to get under the table. More explosions.

Karen had told Mrs. Davenport she wanted to be a veterinarian when she grew up. She loved animals. Loved taking care of them She had a dog and a cat and she would get a plastic, toy stethoscope and listen to their hearts then pretend to treat them for ailments. The animals were fairly obliging to these youthful medical games, especially the puppy. The cat, less so. But still she wanted to take care of cats and dogs when she grew up.

She looked up right into the eyes of the young man holding the gun, facing her.

He reminded her of Rick. About the same height. Maybe the same age. She wondered if Rick knew him. Rick liked to dress in black, too. This boy's eyes were wide and wild-looking, like he had seen something that scared him. He was breathing hard– panting – as if he had run a long, hard race. He stared right at Karen. Something inside her told her this young man wasn't like Rick at all. That he was scary and should be avoided and she tried to slide away, to get under the table but he pointed the smoking rifle right at her and then he squeezed the trigger.

The End

This wasn't a very happy book. Not to write. And I suppose, not to read.

But it wasn't meant to be. It was meant to make you mad as hell and to get off your duff and do something about the madness gripping our country.

We can't continue to watch as people are slaughtered day-after-day and then do nothing about it. We can't just continue to sit there and offer our thoughts and prayers.

We have to do something about it.

I recommend we go to Congress – you, to your Congressperson and deliver the list that Bob McAdoo suggested.

It is time for change in America.

Ten Things To End Gun Violence Now.

1. Outlaw ownership of all weapons of armed mass destruction. That includes assault rifles and their high-capacity magazines.
2. Outlaw the ownership of weapons earmarked for armed forces.
   A list will be created of those specific arms.
   But for starters, no more owning of bazooka and grenades by civilians.
3. Outlaw the sale and ownership of any gun that is not registered to a licensed owner.
4. No gun show loop holes.
5. Demand that all guns, be registered and contain a chip that signals law enforcement of their locale at any given time.
   Before you become worried about big brother, this is already in force on your automobiles.
6. Every gun owner must have insurance for each gun he or she owns…and for each gun, must pass a mandatory training course that is established by the FBI.
7. And those underwriting the insurance will have to demand that guns be kept unloaded in locked safes, or else the individual will forfeit the right to those arms.

But we need deterrents to the use of these firearms, as well. So let us demand that:

8. If an individual uses a firearm in the commission of a crime, whether the gun involved, shoots someone or not, then the penalty for that crime shall be life in prison without the possibility of parole.
9. And should that individual kill a person during such a commission of an armed crime, the death penalty shall be enforced as the punishment for such an act.
10. And if necessary, abolish the Second Amendment, as well. We've changed the constitution before, we can do it again... to protect our towns and cities, our children... our schools... and our homes... not to mention...our lives...

In conclusion: Nothing changes unless you raise your voice for change.

John Crawley

About the Author

John Crawley is a graduate of the University of Texas at Austin.
In addition to penning his numerous novels, he built a thirty-year
career in advertising, specializing in TV and Radio and helped
build dozens of national brands. He has taught creative writing and
advertising at East Texas State University (now Texas A&M
Commerce), TCU, as well as guest lectured
at The University of Texas at Austin,
North Texas University, SMU
and LaVerne University in California.

John is an award-winning photographer, an avid cook, a
devoted husband, as well as a guitar and mandolin picker.
He occasionally finds time to fly-fish and to ride his
bicycles. John is married with three grown children,

Find all of John's books at www.johncrawleybooks.com

Printed in the United States
by Baker & Taylor Publisher Services